I0704102

Published by: Cinnabar Moth Publishing LLC
Santa Fe, New Mexico

Cover Design by: Ira Geneve

ISBN-13: 978-1-962308-36-6

Library of Congress Control Number: 2025934533

The Path of Redemption

TOM HAWARD

For Autumn. Always follow your dreams.

Prologue

Southwark
London
2030

Soldier Marcus was used to crucifixions. Hell, most soldiers were used to crucifixions, because most soldiers had performed crucifixions. Even on his days off, Marcus enjoyed watching the odd high-profile execution when it was streamed on the Roman News Network. There was a catharsis to watching a nail gun blasting a six-inch steel rod through the wrists of a rebel or (more satisfyingly) a politician who didn't realise he was being recorded whilst slagging off the emperor.

This one, though, this was different. In so many ways. Marcus was finding it hard to believe that Maximus Nero, the son of Caesar, was performing a crucifixion in London, in such a public way. Looking through his helmet eyepiece and zooming in on Maximus, Marcus also couldn't believe the madman was going to drive the nails in by hand. It was slow and primitive. It was also pointlessly hard work. Maximus appeared unperturbed by any of this as he was happily laying out all his tools in front of the cross he was going to use. The cross was empty and whomever Maximus was going to crucify was secret, as Marcus and the rest of his legion weren't allowed to know anything apart from the clear instruction they had to guard the southern approach to London Bridge and kill anyone who tried to disrupt what Maximus was doing.

Marcus flipped his eyepiece up and walked away from the vantage point he'd found for spying on what Maximus was doing. There were other crosses lining London Bridge, but in the cold January night, the bodies nailed to those crosses were quiet. If any were still alive, they were conserving energy, swapping between trying to breathe and trying to push themselves up on their nailed feet so their lungs were able to intake some life-saving oxygen. The orange glow of street lights showed the odd misty puff of breath feebly forming and then dispersing, like death swatting away the attempt at clinging on to life.

Indeed, the early morning, just before the arrival of dawn, was quiet. Quiet didn't mean calm and he was feeling the pulse of adrenaline rushing through him. All the soldiers around him were because if they were guarding the son of Caesar then there was a good chance rebels would be appearing. It wasn't guaranteed, but Maximus wanted to make a show of crucifying someone and he believed twenty-five soldiers as his protection was a necessary element to that.

When Marcus and his comrades were called up to be ready to go immediately, a few soldiers pulled out their phones and texted their loved ones saying they were going on a dangerous shift and to be prepared. Marcus scoffed at their fear and told them so. The response was that Marcus was new to this city and he should prepare himself for encountering Boatman King or The Beast, because that encounter would likely be his last on this earth.

Marcus wasn't worried, though, because the only reason he fought to be transferred to London was in the hope he would meet The Beast face-to-face. It would be then that he would watch the life in The Beast's eyes extinguish.

Marcus had lived in Rome. His mother had died when he was very young, so it was a life of being brought up by his funny and caring father. Marcus was only a young teen when his father had surprised him with tickets to his first gladiator match at Rome's colosseum. It was a spectacle like no other and they were blessed with watching Maverick 'The Beast' Kirabo fight. The Beast was headlined to fight against a champion gladiator from every continent, at the same time. It was an incredible show and Marcus watched re-run after re-run for weeks after, reliving the excitement of Maverick being the victor.

That wasn't the only surprise, as when the fight ended there was an announcement of a lottery draw where members of the public submitted their names for a chance to fight The Beast. The winning ticket was Marcus's father. Father and son squealed with excitement at the thought. Marcus's father was paired with a top trainer who would teach him, over six months, how to fight like a champion gladiator and if he won, then a prize of one million gold coins would be his.

Marcus's father took to the training like nothing else in the world mattered. He even fought some warm-up matches before the main even. And showed a natural aptitude for entertainment combat. He dispatched fighters easily and skillfully, showing his fighting instinct primed and ready. So when it came to fighting The Beast, there was a lot of confidence floating around the Team Marcus camp (obviously the Team had to be named after Marcus, the lucky mascot). Xander, the trainer, even commented that Francesco was one of the most naturally gifted fighters he had ever seen.

News of Francesco's stunning rise to elite fighter was plastered over news channels and talk of an upset and possibly a new contender to take the gladiator throne was quickly circulating. *Monster Vs Mortal* was the headline. Tickets sold out. Merchandise flew off shelves. Marcus even bought an action figure of his dad. Fight fever gripped Rome and their colonies.

Of course, all it was was fluff and pomp to sell tickets and distract people from whatever hardship they were experiencing. Emperor Augustus II knew that most of the population wanted distraction rather than to face up to the banality of their own lives. Francesco helped with that distraction because he was 'one of them.' A regular guy who showed it was possible to become more than man. Maverick Kirabo wasn't seen to be a man. He was viewed as an abnormality. An abomination. The masses loved him because of who he easily he killed. And oh, how easily he did kill. His gladiatorial skills were legend and some believed he was a god incarnate. Francesco became a figure that might either prove Maverick was not a god or prove man was able to dethrone a god. Either way, the public rooted for Francesco because, really, it showed the masses didn't love Maverick, they were simply afraid of Maverick.

Marcus wasn't interested in any of that, all he was interested in was cheering on his hero, his dad. His father had become an icon and Marcus grinned with pride. Marcus was a celebrity at school and everyone wanted to be his friend. Marcus felt like a star. When it came to fight night, Marcus thought he would burst with excitement and anticipation. Everyone was saying how amazing Francesco was and how skilled he was. Marcus was shocked at his dad's fighting abilities, but his dad was his hero so he guessed his dad would be an amazing gladiator too.

Maverick was told that the fight was a global spectacle, so to ensure it stayed that way and to go easy on Francesco, to prolong the fight and therefore the coverage, Maverick was also reminded that the man he was fighting was an amateur and under no circumstances was he to kill him. Maverick thought about how he had been dragged from his family home to become a gladiator, tortured by one of the most deprived men in existence in the hellscape of Aestii and then paraded around the world like an object. He decided the powers that be could go fuck themselves and he would fight as he wanted to. For poor Francesco, that was a mixed outcome. The negative was that within thirty seconds of trying to show off his newly acquired sword skills he was skewered with Maverick's, but the positive was that he died so quickly he didn't feel any disappointment in his debut gladiator performance.

Marcus had watched in horror as his dad was butchered, and he nurtured that horror for years and years so that it became pure hatred for the man that murdered his father.

So, on the night he was guarding Maximus Nero, he was praying Maverick would turn up. Even in that hope to see the man who killed his dad, he was still shocked when he saw The Beast in person. So shocked that he forgot to even draw his sword but stared a moment whilst Maverick put his sword through Victor, Marcus's roommate. Seeing his friend die ignited the rage he felt about his dad's death, and he ran toward Maverick shouting, "You killed my father!"

This actually stopped Maverick in his tracks. "You what?"

"You killed my father!" Marcus was almost hysterical.

"Who the fuck was your father?"

"Francesco. He won the opportunity to fight you."

"You might want to check the terms and conditions of the competition because it doesn't sound like your dad won much," said Tobias, Maverick's fiancé, who was standing close behind, wiping the blood of another soldier from his sword.

"Shut your mouth."

"Be careful how you speak to my fiancé, son of Francesco."

"I will speak however I want. Especially to an inferior race like you," said Marcus.

Now, Maverick was six feet five and born in a town in Jinja, Uganda. He had experienced racism physically and verbally. He was born and raised on the racist arrogance of colonialism and most of the time he shrugged his shoulders because sometimes being angry all the time about it only infected yourself. It didn't change culture. There was something about standing in front of a racist man on a cold evening in London, though, that made Maverick's blood boil. It was so intimate in its arrogance. The man's arrogance. That Maverick lost it. "How about you stop talking yourself," he said and lurched at Marcus.

When Faust, a Centurion at the time of the incident, examined Marcus's dead body, he was amazed that a human being had the strength to be able to almost tear a man's jaw off. He found the ghastly spectacle of it hypnotic, seeing blood pool in the destroyed remains of Marcus's head.

Tobias had been shocked at the primal rage of Maverick and had said as much to his boyfriend. Maverick had shrugged though, and said that there was nothing primal about punishing someone for their abhorrent and backward views. Tobias didn't disagree.

When Marcus was finally identified and a search for next of kin showed his parents had died, Marcus's anger was for nothing, because Francesco's fight against Maverick was so insignificant that the Empire felt no need to even record it. The only record of Marcus's dad being a gladiator was in Marcus's head.

Chapter 1: Memory Palace

The Kingdom of Aska
London
2032

Augustus Faust thought about the shock and awe of seeing one of his soldiers with his jaw torn off. He thought about not only the brutality but also the almost superhuman ability to do such a thing. Even as a Roman centurion, trained in inflicting suffering, he had been humbled by such an act. He remembered seeing the dead man and for a moment struggling to piece together what he was looking at. The human brain takes for granted what it will process when information is passed through the eyes, such as the basic structure of a human head. When looking at a human being who doesn't have a jaw where it should be, it can cause the mind to stutter as it tries to process what's being seen. And Faust's mind at the time certainly did stutter.

He had met the man who had performed such ferocity and, now, after all he had seen and experienced, Maverick 'the Beast' Kirabo's actions seemed to fade into the background of depravity compared to what he had seen in recent months.

Faust floated over the images of the dead soldier for a little longer, and then placed the memories in a box and slid that box into a cupboard inside his memory palace. He didn't need any more blood-soaked corpses wandering his palace. There was enough blood in his presence in the present. With that in mind, he looked over to the corner of the room he was in and saw former Legatus Titus fitfully sleeping on the floor, curled up in a ball as if trying to escape the reality of where he was. Faust grimaced at the sight of Titus because the former Commander of Britannia was most certainly able to curl up into a very tight ball, as he was missing hands and feet. He was missing hands and feet because they had been eaten. Not by Faust, that was for sure. No, they had been eaten by a man whose actions made Maverick Kirabo's jaw tearing seem like child's play.

Chapter 2: Imprisoned

Boatman King stretched and then he winced at the pain down his right side. He knew his ribs weren't broken but they were, at the very least, bruised. He tried to put it out of his mind that he might have to fight again today as that would mean his bruised ribs would very likely be broken by sunset. And broken ribs were a bitch to deal with. He climbed out of bed and swore as pain jolted up his side. He was no stranger to pain but what was it about ribs that felt worse? He padded into the lounge area and saw Faust sitting at the dining table, drinking a coffee. The curled-up abomination that was once the most powerful man in Britannia was shaking in the corner of the room. Boatman felt nausea dance around his belly at the sight of the wretched creature. Evil had consumed that poor soul and vomited up the personification of terror. It had been months (two, three? Boatman wasn't sure) since Faust and Boatman had been imprisoned, so the sight of Titus, although revolting, was also sanitised to a degree, and Faust and Boatman were able to sit at the dining table in the morning and have their coffee like everything around them was normal.

Normal was a distant memory though.

The obscene and the surreal were the new normal, and Boatman was struggling to remember life being any other way. Boatman poured himself a coffee and sat opposite Faust. "How did you sleep?"

"Same as always," the Roman said. "You?"

"Same as always."

"Not good then," said Faust. They didn't have anything else to say out loud and Faust drank his coffee whilst drumming his fingers on the table. Boatman just stared into space whilst slowly sipping his drink. Every day, Faust and Boatman exchanged the same mundane words and appeared to sit at the table, absent-mindedly, whilst they savoured their first (and only) coffee of the day.

When they were first abducted, they were locked inside the small house they were in, but apart from the thick steel door and bars across the windows, there wasn't much else to indicate being imprisoned. Both men knew this rather relaxed way of being held hostage was most likely a ploy to keep the men off guard but they struggled to know how in the first couple of days. They were able to eat two meals a day and walk freely around the small building. Even though the men knew it was a false reality, human nature can't help itself and after a couple of days with no clocks and no interaction with the outside world, the men's tongues relaxed and they started sharing ideas about how to escape based on previous experiences. Unbeknownst to the prisoners, their every word was being recorded. Faust and Boatman had made an escape plan, through whispered conversation, but the minute after they had worked their plan guards entered the building. The armed guards made Faust and Boatman get to their knees and then their captor, Bjorn Aska entered the house.

Bjorn Aska was a terrifying presence, standing at seven feet in height and shoulders as broad as the crosses the Romans used to crucify traitors. He grinned when he laid his eyes on his prisoners, "Hello to you both. How has your stay been so far?" The question was rhetorical as he didn't wait for a response. "I've been listening to your rather fanciful plans for breaking out of my rather generous accommodation and I admire your optimism of managing to get even a few steps from the front door before being torn apart by gunfire. Even so, I made it very clear to you both when you first joined us here that your co-operation is key. That your co-operation will ensure no-one is hurt and that we can build a fruitful relationship."

"Relationship?" Boatman didn't hide his patronising tone.

"Well, of course, dear Boatman King." Aska over-enunciated Boatman's surname as if to mock it. "I very much thought about eating you both, but gluttony doesn't win wars. You will be much more useful to me as comrades helping to overthrow the tiresome Roman Empire." Aska eyed his prisoners, "For now."

"You seem to be forgetting something," said Faust.

Aska arched an eyebrow.

"You're asking the Grand Protector of Rome to help you overthrow the Empire. I'm the leader of the Empire."

"*Were* the leader of the Empire, Herr Faust. You obviously seem to be forgetting something."

"Which would be?"

"You have gone missing. Presumed dead or abducted. If dead, well, the Senate has already enacted powers to take control of Rome. If presumed abducted, they will have done the same thing but also restricted your access to all databases and assumed you have been tortured and therefore given up sensitive information about the Empire. You are officially an outcast, Herr Faust, and therefore no longer that rather clumsy title of Grand Protector."

Faust had nothing to say. He knew Aska was right and was annoyed at his own naivety for thinking Aska didn't know about the procedures and safeguards in place at the higher echelons of power in Rome. "So, what do you want?"

"What do I want. Well, to begin with, I want loyalty."

"You'll be waiting a long time," Boatman said.

Aska smirked and squinted at Boatman, "Will I?" He turned his head and looked over his shoulder, "Titus, here boy!" Aska clicked his fingers and Titus came scuttling over on all fours and sat by Aska the way an obedient dog would. Aska stroked the top of Titus's head and Boatman felt this strange dissonance: for years he'd enjoyed the thought of seeing Titus's blood spilled, but now he felt anger at the inhumanity of Titus's treatment. He felt pity for the man. Aska looked at Boatman and said, "Titus here shows me utter obedience and he was a man who boasted of ruling Britannia." He clicked twice and Titus lowered himself into complete subservience. "Of course, I know you would be much harder to break than this pathetic excuse for a man. Which is why I'll gain your loyalty in a different way."

"And how would that be?" Boatman asked.

"You might think me a brute and primitive, but I read people. I read them very well. And I could see your pity for the thing next to me, which is why it will be the receiver of punishment for your insolence. And every time you defy me, Titus here will know my wrath."

Faust started to speak up, "Hold on a second…"

"No!" Aska was red-faced. He grabbed Titus by the hair and with strength even Boatman was impressed by, lifted Titus off the ground. Titus whimpered at the pain, but it was barely audible. He knew not to make a fuss for fear of greater punishment if he complained. Aská then dropped Titus and kicked him in his side. The force of the kick cracked a rib and Titus yelped. Boatman was known for his almost superhuman speed and went from being on his knees to holding one of the guard's guns in his hand and pointing it at Aská. The guard on Faust pointed his gun at Boatman, but Aská waved his hand and the guard focused it back on Faust.

Aská laughed. "Really? We're going to keep doing this dick-measuring nonsense? What are you going to do?" Aská kicked Titus again. Boatman stepped forward with his gun. "Seriously, what are you going to do? Shoot me. You die. Faust dies. Titus dies. You don't see your wife again. You die having achieved nothing."

"But you'll be dead."

"And? What does that even achieve? The Empire still reigns. You just killed a rebel leader in the back end of beyond. I mean, do you even know where you are? You're stranded and all you've worked for means nothing."

Boatman's wife, Olivia, had always pointed out to her husband that one of his biggest weaknesses was that his ego struggled to give him a sense of clarity in certain situations. His sense of superiority meant his decisions were based on an omnipotent worldview. Boatman always denied this, but now, in this situation, he knew his wife was right; he wanted to pull the trigger and be done with this abomination of a man, but the satisfaction would be fleeting and inconsequential. Boatman lowered his gun.

"Thank you," Aská said. "Even so, loyalty has to be earned. Give the gun back to the guard and go sit down." Boatman did as he was told. Aská thanked Boatman again. "Now, like I said, loyalty needs to be earned and a lack of loyalty comes with a price. Titus, here boy!"

The guards kept their guns trained on Faust and Boatman whilst

Aské left the building with Titus scuttling behind. Neither Boatman nor Faust truly understood what Aské meant about earned loyalty and transferred punishment until later that evening when Titus was returned to his house but having to be carried because he was now missing a foot.

Chapter 3: Spiro

The Republic of Indigenous America
2032

Olivia King was sitting on a bench, in a park, in the capital city of the Republic of Indigenous America, Spiro. Spiro was on the east coast approximately three hours from the thriving port of Accomack. From this port the Americans sent ships up and down the coast trading their rich resources. The ships carried an abundance of silver, nickel and oil which was exchanged for gold, a primary source of income in the Roman Empire and therefore a great tool for buying allies in the Empire, such as Bjorn Askå. Askå as an ally was a delicate but very beneficial source of information for the RIA and also a level of protection against the Empire because he kept the Empire distracted. He also fed the RIA secrets which gave the RIA ammunition against the Empire if they ever needed it. Things were changing, though, and Askå as an ally was appearing to unravel, which is why the 35 (the council which ruled the country) decided to provide shelter to Olivia King and her comrades.

Olivia watched the world go by as people ambled around the

park enjoying the warmth of the sun and sitting by the large lake in the centre of the park. She had forgotten what it was like to relax. She was so used to running and looking over her shoulder she had forgotten what it was like to simply *be*. As she tried to not feel uncomfortable by sitting on a bench like any normal person would, a shadow loomed over her. She looked up and a man was standing over her. He said, "Money for your thoughts?"

"You will need a lot of money."

The man smiled and held out his hand, "I'm Newen." Olivia shook his hand. "May I?" He held his hand out.

"Of course," Olivia said. She shuffled over a little on the bench and Newen took a seat.

"How are you finding Spiro?"

"It's beautiful. I was thinking how I'd forgotten what it was like to just sit down and watch the world go by."

"You can't watch the world go by when you're always running from it."

"I've forgotten what it's like to not be running."

"I'm sure you're exhausted."

"I can't remember not being tired."

"Rest assured, you can sleep as much as you like here."

Olivia shook her head. "I'm not sure I can. My husband is missing, presumed dead. My adopted daughter is missing, presumed dead. My brain won't switch off from that."

"If Askå took them, I'm afraid I know what's happened to them."

Olivia inhaled sharply. "So much for the comforting chat from the welcoming stranger."

"Comfort only goes so far. I'm sure being the wife of Boatman King means you're very used to direct and honest conversation."

Olivia shrugged. "You'd be surprised how indirect my husband could be at times."

Newen raised an eyebrow. "I guess the person portrayed can be very different to the person known."

"Very different." Olivia paused and then said, "I know people enough to know that they don't merely stop by for a chat. What is it you want?"

"Thank you for your directness, so it's important that I'm direct. I work for the 35 and we would appreciate any information you can give us about your experiences and encounters with those in the highest positions of power in Rome."

"I'm not sure I want to rehash my experiences of those from Rome. And besides, the ones I was unfortunate enough to meet are dead."

"But anything about them, no matter how insignificant, could help us stay protected from a potential attack."

Olivia laughed, but it didn't hold much humour. "A potential attack? Of what I know of men in power, information is never about defence and being protected."

Newen looked hurt. "You think I want to use the information for nefarious reasons?"

Olivia stood up. "You didn't bring us to your country out of charity." Olivia started to walk away, "It was nice to meet you."

Newen thought about calling after her but knew he had lost her. If he wanted her trust and confidence he needed to use a different approach.

Chapter 4: Safehouse

Olivia walked the perimeter of the park and then through a gate which put her on a pathway that snaked through to her accommodation a matter of minutes away. The house itself was a two storey, narrow townhouse but was beautifully cladded in redwood. It was part of a row of six houses and Olivia's comrades were staying in the others. As she faced the house, Tobias and Maverick were to her left, Bella and Alypia to her right.

How they came to be in Spiro was still a mystery to Olivia. Ten weeks ago Olivia had been in the tunnel system of London. The Romans had discovered their new HQ as well as Bjorn Askå and what followed was hell. Olivia had escaped Rome's clutches and her husband's loyal soldiers had managed to lead her out of the city unscathed. Maverick, Tobias and Bella had shown their skills and got free, taking Olivia and an injured Alypia Faust to a safehouse away from Britannia's capital city. The safehouse, though, was a temporary solution and no-one could agree the next steps.

Maverick believed the only course of action should be to follow Askå back to his kingdom to retrieve Boatman. Tobias had been reluctant of such a plan, saying, "Have you ever thought about doing something which doesn't involve almost certain death?"

Maverick growled, "Tobias, we need to go after him."

"I'm not questioning that, Mav, but we're currently holed up in a safehouse which makes the word 'safe' seem ironic, and have barely any resources to try and charge into the kingdom of a complete lunatic."

"Aska won't expect us to follow. We'll catch him by surprise."

"That giant nearly took my head off with a battle axe, I don't think he gets surprised easily."

Maverick grunted. "You can stay here, and be scared but we need to bring Boatman back."

"And die in the process?" Olivia said, confused by Maverick's urgency. "We've barely escaped London with our lives and now you want us to walk into another version of hell."

"Hell is all we have dealt with, Olivia."

"Thanks, I love you too." Tobias said.

Maverick ignored his fiancé. "Look, your husband needs us. We can save him."

"You barely saved me in the city you controlled, so I don't hold your opinion with much credence, to be honest, Maverick."

"She is right, Mav," said Tobias. Maverick usually would have kept fighting his corner but, instead, stormed off to bed.

Bella had put her hand on Tobias's shoulder and reassured him that he and Olivia were right, and going after Aska in their current state as a team was, indeed, a suicide mission. Tobias had gone to find his partner and Maverick was in bed, lying on his side. Tobias got undressed and climbed in bed, curling up behind Maverick, putting his arms around his broad chest. Maverick, although in a foul mood, didn't resist. "What's the real reason you're determined to go after Boatman right now?"

Maverick didn't say anything for a few beats and then said, "He needs our help."

"I know he does. We all know he does. That's not what I'm asking."

"I couldn't save him."

"Who? Boatman? We were under attack, there was no way of getting Boatman out of that situation."

"No, not Boatman."

"Mav, I don't understand. Who are you talking about?"

Tobias felt Maverick's chest heave, trying to fight back tears. Tobias was taken aback as he couldn't recall the last time he had seen Maverick cry, if ever. He didn't stop hugging him, though. Maverick took some time to compose himself and said, "Damba."

Tobias then understood completely. Maverick had travelled to Rome, after the death of Emperor Nero, to find his brother, Damba, and finish what he had started what seemed like an eternity ago by killing the son of Nero, Maximus. What unfolded was, in Maverick's eyes, complete failure, as Damba betrayed Maverick and declared allegiance to Maximus and Rome. Maverick's last sight of Damba was one of Damba choosing to give Maverick to the whims of Maximus. Tobias then understood why Maverick was determined to save Boatman, because maybe this time he could succeed where he failed before and maybe this time he could do what he believed himself to be the best of the best at: killing.

Tobias didn't know what to say, but he let his words come out nonetheless, "You might still find Damba again."

Maverick's chest heaved once again. His words came out slowly, as if saying them might somehow make them come true. "But he might reject me again."

"He didn't reject you, he was forced to give you up. Mav, he was a prisoner of the emperor, what else was he supposed to do?"

"He said he enjoyed being in Rome. He felt noticed."

Tobias had never heard Maverick talk like this before. To be vulnerable and unsure. "He would have said anything to stay alive," said Tobias.

"Well I have no idea if he is still alive."

"We'll find him."

"I don't think he wants to be found or saved," Maverick said. The Beast pulled his fiancé in closer and almost whispered, "Do you think I can be saved, with all I have done?"

Tobias was struggling to know who the man lying next to him was. He had never known Maverick show any signs of remorse or contrition. "Have you banged your head or something?"

"I must have, because I'm still with you."

"You didn't bang it hard enough then, because we're still not married," Tobias said.

Maverick simply huffed and didn't say anything else. And after that brief confession, lying in the dark, in a safehouse in Britannia, Maverick Kirabo didn't utter any more words questioning his redemption.

After a week hunkered down in the safehouse, trying to regain some energy and also give Alypia more time to recover, the futility of what they would do next became apparent as they were short of options on how to get out of Britannia. And if they got out of Britannia, they weren't sure where they would go. They knew they still had time to figure something out as, from the outside looking in, Boatman and his followers had been killed in a huge explosion in the tunnel network. Faust and, unbeknownst to him, Askå, had followed Boatman underground to Boatman's secondary HQ. Askå had abducted Boatman and Faust and set a trap to obliterate the HQ and the surrounding tunnels. And as Askå looked on at the entrance to the tunnels, it appeared his trap had worked as a gargantuan explosion rocked almost the entirety of London, presumably killing anyone still in the tunnel network.

In fact, Bella and Maverick discovered the trap and manufactured the blast so it appeared they had all perished. Askå assumed Boatman's followers were dead. Rome assumed the same, but also Boatman was included in the deceased. With these beliefs in place, it gave the rebels time to assess their situation and try to find a way to safety. The problem they faced was that they weren't sure where that safety would be. Rebelling against Rome left few places to hide.

"We're ghosts," said Bella. "No-one is looking for us."

"Even so, I bet our faces are plastered on most screens around the major towns and cities," Tobias said.

"Your face, maybe, but that's probably just a deterrent for kids at curfew," said Maverick.

Bella carried on talking, Maverick and Tobias's jibes like white noise to her, "If we don't exist anymore, surely there's somewhere we can go or someone we still have connections with who can get us out of Britannia?"

"What about Caledonia?" Maverick asked.

"We've wasted that route," said Olivia. "We barely got out of there alive."

"Surely Boatman had more than one route out for you though?" Bella said.

"Why would you think that?"

"Because you're his wife."

Olivia's mouth faltered when she went to answer, the sadness that had overwhelmed her for so long when it came to her marriage bubbling over, "I feel for you all. You all look at Boatman as some infallible being. He's just a man. Sorry, no. He *was* just a man." Olivia felt her eyes sting and she left the room, unable to look at or interact with the people who saw Boatman as a man without a flaw. One of the flaws Olivia saw, which only she could really comprehend, was that for all of Boatman's fearless leadership, she knew he had sacrificed her life for a chance to get closer to the emperor. He may not have consciously done it, but she knew Boatman analysed and overthought everything; and therefore he had allowed his mind to omit the thoughts which related to how much danger he had put his wife in.

Olivia's life had been traded with like she was cattle, and she felt like cattle when Maximus tortured her and crucified her. And as she sat in her room, she looked at her wrist and felt the scar from the nail was her own branding. It was at that moment she decided to be as reckless as her husband.

Chapter 5: Hospital Visit

Eight weeks before Olivia had found herself standing in front of a beautiful house in the capital city of America, she decided that she would regain a sense of control. Olivia had realised that her friends and comrades only saw the world through the lens of Boatman. They believed he would always provide a solution and if he didn't then maybe there wasn't a solution to be had. With that in mind, they also believed Boatman was far more important than reality showed. Bella, Maverick and Tobias had been stressing about how they would leave the safehouse they were in without being recognised. In Olivia's experience, most of the general public barely knew the faces of anyone outside of their own family, let alone inconsequential rebels. And inconsequential was more than appropriate because it enabled Olivia to do what none of her friends thought possible: walk through the streets of London without being recognised.

Hospital Tiberius was a hub of activity when Olivia arrived. She had wandered from the safehouse to a nearby train station and hired a taxi into London's city centre. If the taxi driver recognised her, he was very good at pretending he couldn't care less about who he was transporting. Olivia had disembarked approximately a mile from the hospital and ambled to the hospital so as to not raise any suspicions about her. Although, as she approached the hospital she realised she could have run there as no-one even cared about her. It hadn't occurred to Olivia why the name of the hospital sounded so familiar, but it was where victims of crucifixion were taken.

The Romans knew how to kill and even with the rebellion apparently obliterated, that didn't stop them hunting for any information about the rebellion's origins and crucifying sympathisers in the process. Although for centuries the crucifixion was the final nail in a person's coffin, so to speak, whilst a person was crucified, they still had the opportunity for redemption in modern day Roman rule. The Romans had perfected the execution method to achieve maximum misery and maximum prolonging of pain. When a person was crucified they would be nailed to a wooden beam which was bolted into a steel upright. The upright was attached to a hydraulic system which raised and lowered the cross with ease. It saved a lot of time and manpower as the nails were also driven through people's wrists with a nail gun. It was all about efficiency.

Once the victims were in place, a saline drip was fed into them so that they stayed hydrated for longer, a macabre way of giving life whilst it slowly ebbed away. Interestingly, emperor Augustine, the father of Nero II, introduced the saline drips. He was considered to be an emperor more associated with mercy, but absolute power always yielded absolute sadism. On the top of all the crosses were cameras so that authorities could monitor if someone had died, and also the images were lived streamed around the country. Any of the general public could watch the crucifixions via the dedicated streaming channel, The Crucifixion Channel. The amount of viewers the streaming channel had each day was consistently, morbidly high.

Quite often, victims hanging from the crosses would beg for

mercy and claim they had vital information about the rebellion or about other clandestine plans to defy the Empire. If the information appeared to be genuine, they would be taken down from the cross and rushed to Hospital Tiberius. Olivia knew of this because whilst she was a therapist for Roman officers she regularly listened to accounts of when victims were taken down and the agony they endured. Over months of therapy she often saw the horror in some of the officers' eyes and the toll constant torture took. That horror, though, was mixed with a deadness that was never regained. Some officers spoke of quietly visiting those who had been taken down from the cross, watching from afar as they were plugged with tubes and stitched and prodded whilst interrogators tried to get information from them. Yes, Olivia knew this hospital by reputation, so was not surprised at all how no-one even noticed her walk in, let alone recognised her as the wife of Boatman King.

Olivia had walked into the hospital wearing a small rucksack and strolled up to the reception. She said to the lady at the desk, "I'm sorry to bother you, but I'm here to cover a shift from another hospital and no-one emailed me with any information about where I go to get my uniform."

The lady smiled and titled her head as if this was a common complaint and said, "Communication isn't this hospital's strong point. Where are you meant to be?"

"I'm covering a nurse's shift in Crucifixion Aftercare."

"You poor thing. No wonder they didn't email you; they probably ran out of the hospital as soon as their shift ended. The nurse's changing room for that department is on the third floor and it's the fourth floor where you'll find those poor sods." She tapped a few keys and then passed Olivia a card. "You'll need this for locker access."

Olivia thanked the receptionist and then made her way to the third floor. She was amazed at how easy it was to walk into the hospital, pretending to be a nurse, without anyone checking her genuineness, but hospitals were a place of trust and healing. And they were swarming with soldiers, making rebels not even consider them as place to attack Rome. After all, why would you put yourself in such close proximity to Roman soldiers and why would you attack the injured and dying?

After Olivia found her way to the changing room and dressed herself as a nurse, she made her way, not to the Crucifixion Aftercare floor but to the ground floor, and went to where major trauma patients were being cared for. She entered the department and soldiers were everywhere, milling around, looking bored. She quickly scanned the whiteboard by the entrance and beelined for the room she needed. There was a solider guarding the door. "I need to check his saline," said Olivia.

"I'll have to come in with you," the soldier said.

"And I need to change his diaper. The last one caused a mess."

The soldier wrinkled his nose, "Just be quick. And don't say who is on guard. He lost it last time a nurse woke him."

"Why don't you grab us a coffee and then he won't see you."

The solider smiled at the suggestion and scuttled off.

Olivia entered the room and could smell the rotting nature of Maximus Nero. She went to the closet and heard Maximus stir and fumble for his phone. She went over to his bed as he was about to type a message to tell the nurse to go away, but as soon as she spoke he froze and realised who was in front of him. The woman he'd failed to kill. The woman who was saved and in her saving put him in the state he was. Before had the chance to press an alarm, Olivia placed a pillow over his face and held it until he stopped breathing. She turned the heart monitor off. When she left the room the soldier was waiting with a coffee and she told him not to go in the room for a while as the emperor had shit himself again and the smell needed time to clear. The soldier didn't argue and Olivia walked away feeling relief that her tormentor was dead.

But when she had got back to the safehouse and locked herself away in her room, she sobbed. She sobbed and sobbed. She felt disgust at her actions for taking a life, no matter how grotesque that life was. She felt anger at feeling that guilt. She felt anger that she had ever been driven to such an action and cried at the continuing resentment she had towards Boatman, even though it was possible she might never see him again.

And so, now, Olivia stood in front of the guest house she had been kindly given and didn't know what to feel. She felt a sense of loss that she wasn't looking over her shoulder. She knew that was strange and, as a therapist, knew it was her brain processing a lot of trauma, but she still couldn't deny that she felt empty not hiding underground and listening to Boatman devise his next ambush on a legion of soldiers. She walked into the house and tried to compartmentalise some of the darker thoughts she was having. One particular thought was a sort of relief that maybe Boatman had died. And she also tried to process that she, too, had taken a life and that she had done it so efficiently. Maybe she was closer to the darkness she saw in her husband than she realised. And maybe that's why she struggled so much with who Boatman was. Because, as a therapist, she knew a lot of people's problems simply came from the fact that everyone projected. The people we hated most were usually the people we were most similar to. And that chilled Olivia.

Chapter 6: Dog Walk

A knock at the door jerked Olivia awake from a nap on the sofa. By the gods, she was tired and knew some of that tiredness was more than a lack of sleep. She opened the door and Newen was standing there. He wasn't alone, but had a fairly large Carolina dog sitting patiently next to him. It had big ears and a golden coat and tilted its head when Newen spoke, "I wanted to apologise for my behaviour earlier."

Olivia waved her hand, "It's fine."

"It's not. You're a guest here in Spiro, not someone just to be tapped for information. It was rude of me," Newen said.

"But you still want that information."

"If and when you're ready but, honestly, your comfort and settling in comes first." Newen rested his hand on the head of the dog beside him and scratched its ear, "Which is why I brought Wicker with me. He's part of the welcoming committee." Upon hearing his name, Wicker started panting.

"He's very handsome," Olivia said. "How old is he?"

"He's four and a very good judge of character." Newen looked at Wicker and commanded him to say hello. With that, Wicker looked at Olivia, barked once and then raised his left paw.

"Nice trick."

"My dog doesn't perform tricks, he either welcomes or savages. You passed the test."

Olivia rolled her eyes, "Yes, I'm sure I did. I appreciate the apology and the introduction to Wicker, but it really wasn't necessary."

"Actually, the apology was secondary. I came over to see if you would like to take a walk with me and Wicker."

"It's kind of you to ask, but I'm not particularly in the mood."

Wicker barked again and raised his paw. "Look, you're turning down a dog," Newen said. "It's not just a random walk. I'd like to show you a bit more of Spiro and assure you that myself and the 35 are focused on making you all feel as at home as possible."

Olivia found it alien to be considering something so pedestrian as taking a dog for a walk and thought that, in itself, was a good reason to go. "Give me five minutes," she said and closed the door on Newen.

Less than five minutes later, Olivia was dressed in jeans and a jumper and walking beside Newen whilst Wicker trotted ahead, nose to the ground and tail wagging as he savoured the smells. They took a path away from the park, Wicker clearly knowing the way, and headed towards the forest which skirted the edge of residential buildings, including where Olivia was staying. There was a wood-chipped path which took them into the forest and soon the canopy of trees meant sunlight pierced through like spears of light breaking the canopy. Wicker eyed something rustling in the greenery ahead and bounded off.

"Will he be okay?"

Newen smiled, "He'll be fine. He'll come back when he realises whatever it was was faster than him. He likes the chase but doesn't ever catch anything."

Olivia looked up and around and marvelled at the height and beauty of the trees. She was also stunned at the cacophony of noise from the birds in the forest. It was true music to her ears. "I've never heard so many birds at once."

"That's the sound of happiness. We would never take their habitat away."

"Help clear something up for me that doesn't add up."

"Happy to," Newen said.

"I've literally only seen Spiro and it's idyllic. The people appear content and everything is creepily peaceful."

"Creepily?"

"Definitely. I've lived in chaos for years, hiding underground or hiding in some remote settlement. Always looking over my shoulder and wondering when I would be taken away and crucified. Then I come here and it's as if violence and the Romans never existed."

Newen was confused, "But surely that's a good thing?"

"I'm sure it is." Olivia shook her head, "I know it is! It's just hard to accept goodness when your world is built on badness."

"So the goodness doesn't add up in your mind?"

"Not really, no. It's just confusing. If you have built something that exudes contentment, why do you fund a monster like Aska? Surely you're better off isolating yourselves from the world?"

"The world's too small to be isolated," Newen said.

"But by engaging with a lunatic, you draw attention to yourselves."

"We have always found that ignorance doesn't stop lunatics paying you attention," Newen said. "And keeping Aska close to us is likely a much better approach than alienating him."

Olivia shook her head, "The world is just men scheming against each other."

"And without the scheming we probably wouldn't have a world."

They continued walking through the forest, Newen giving a potted history of the RIA and also what made them quite unique in having resisted Roman invasion for two millennia. "It's a long way to go to leave with your tail in-between your legs," said Newen. The RIA had invested a lot of money in their coastal defences, making potential invaders reluctant about the size of losses they would suffer to even mange to reach the RIA's shores. After emperor Augustus managed to take control of Britannia in the 1960s, after Churchill surrendered, he sent spies to the RIA to try and infiltrate them and determine potential weaknesses. They never returned, and it was never concluded whether they died or betrayed Rome. Frustrated by this, Augustus agreed to work with some mercenaries from the Aquitana region. They were led by a man named Columbus who wanted to plunder the RIA. Columbus's intentions were to establish himself in the RIA and break away from the influence of the Empire. Augustus agreed in principle to help Columbus, in spite of his rather vocal plans, because, like so many others who believed they could defy and Empire, their naivety was short-lived. Ultimately, Columbus was a talented seaman which Rome was lacking in and the Empire had the funds to give Columbus the best ships he needed to make his mission successful.

Rome had, for a small time in the early stages of their domination, built a powerful navy, but soon realised the expense wasn't viable. Also, the Empire was elite at ground warfare, but it wasn't so proficient at battle at sea. The Empire advanced in speed and ferocity through its land conquests and emperor after emperor focused their time on how to conquer through land. The RIA, though, needed proficiency at attacking from the sea or sky and that's where subcontracting elements of the Empire's work came into being. Columbus was seen to be a man who would give the Empire value for money.

Augustus had been warned by his closest advisor, Jonas, that the reliance on Columbus was naive and to never trust a man who viewed other peoples as subspecies. Usually the emperor would have listened to his advisor's reticence, but he had become so focused on reaching his ultimate goal of the RIA, he was desperate to believe Columbus was his way in.

The ships Columbus had under his command were equipped to bombard ports with ferocity and relentless firepower. It was believed those in charge of the RIA would seek to broker a deal to stop such attacks in order to protect innocents. The RIA though, were different. They tended to jump ahead, unafraid of consequences, because they were underestimated as the information had about them was limited.

When Columbus and his two other ships had sailed within ten miles of the east coast of the RIA, close to the port of Accomack, he sent a message out to Spiro, warning the leadership that unless they allowed unhindered entry into port, they would be fired upon. Columbus made a point of highlighting the extent of damage his three ships would be able to inflict. Columbus was confident safe passage was inevitable because Roman intel could not ascertain any major coastal weapon defences in operation. No silos for missiles. No huge artillery guns. It appeared the RIA used their ports for trade and leisure without fear of invasion. Columbus was going to change all that, he thought. What Columbus had thought and what actually transpired were completely different.

The RIA did, indeed, only use their port of Accomack for trade and leisure and made no apologies for that. They never wanted their guests or trade partners to ever feel like they were entering a place of unrest. The 35 who ruled the RIA, though, they knew unrest was always inevitable and sought people who might help them keep their country safe. One particular man was Nikola Tesla, who was a refugee from the Aestii region. Bjorn Askå's father, Erik, was arguably more brutal than his son and Tesla feared his skillset would be manipulated through torture to fulfil only horror. Tesla managed to be smuggled to the RIA where the 35 quickly realised they had found a man who would revolutionise their country.

Tesla had discovered the ability to manipulate an electromagnetic current and turn it into a pulse, which rendered anything electrical to be completely immobilised. It was the perfect defence as it meant any attacks from the sky or sea caused chaos. It was also perfect for Tesla because the 35 gave him a home and paid him handsomely for his scientific expertise. The pulse Tesla created was refined into devices unobtrusive to any port infrastructure and, until Columbus arrived on the RIA's shores, they had never been used. Columbus's threats to the 35 in Spiro meant a very short meeting occurred where a Tesla Pulse was approved.

For Columbus, this meant he went from thinking he was about to receive a surrender to finding his ships lost all power, navigation and defence capabilities. This also meant that the surge of the Tesla Pulse caused surges in electrical devices on board Columbus's ships resulting in explosions. These explosions were like a domino effect for all three ships and as they were sinking and crew were abandoning ship, the 35 ordered torpedoes to finish the job. Again, the 35 were very concerned about how they looked to traders and tourists, but ensured the most efficient, hidden and deadly defences were available to them when necessary.

As Columbus abandoned ship, he continued to curse the 'backward Americans' but cursed his family name more, because an ancestor too had tried to conquer the RIA and ended up skewered. Columbus thought that he had the skills and firepower to prove his family wrong. He was the one who was wrong, though, and as he drowned he hoped one of the many gods he hedged his bets with had heard him and would give him mercy.

Chapter 7: The Missing Buzzing

"Interesting story," said Olivia.

"It's no story."

"I've just never heard about Columbus. And I don't recall Roman history ever mentioning him."

Newen smiled. "You think the Romans would mention such a glaring mistake in their annals? And I'm surprised you wouldn't consider Rome editing their history to ensure they don't look bad."

"Even after everything I've been through I seem to trust those in power to at least tell the truth, even when the evidence is completely opposite." Olivia sighed. "I trusted my husband to always tell me the truth and truth was a rather vague term for him, at times, so I don't know why I thought Rome would record everything objectively."

"I wouldn't admonish yourself too much. It's natural to trust. Human nature is to believe people are good and are only corrupted by the world."

"I met Maximus Nero, I know some people are born rotten. And not just rotten like an apple that has fallen from a tree and been left, but completely corrupted. When I met him I could smell the evil in him. It was like goodness had no place in him and the stench of his complete corruptness had no choice but to seep from his glands. Someone like him had never known goodness, even as a child," Olivia said.

"Did you ever meet emperor Nero?"

"No, one member of that family was enough. Although Boatman did share with me his experience of meeting him."

"What was his experience?"

"Boatman has met a lot of bad people in his time. He's killed a lot of bad men. I suspect he's killed a lot of good men too."

"Really?" Newen was surprised at Olivia's certainty.

"Of course. The price of war is that usually the good people are caught in the middle. And I know Boatman didn't differentiate if some of those good people happened to, misguided or not, believe the Empire was for the greater good. Boatman believed the Empire to be a stain on humanity and was dogmatic about it."

Newen said, "I'm not sure the Empire is a stain on humanity, but we certainly don't believe its ideology would be of any benefit to the RIA."

"Even that small level of sympathy would put you in direct conflict with Boatman."

"Well, I hope it never comes to that."

Newen indicated that they should turn around and make their way home, as they had been walking a while and the sun was starting to dip in the sky. He called Wicker and the dog came bounding through the bushes and trotted next to Newen whilst panting away. Newen told Wicker he was a good boy, and Wicker's tail wagged a little faster at those words.

When they had got back to Olivia's residence, Olivia said, "Thank you for the walk. It was genuinely nice to do something so normal."

"My pleasure."

"And thank you for not pushing me for information."

"Like I said, it's important you know that our primary goal is to keep you safe and give you assurances that you are out of the Empire's reaches here." Newen reached into his pocket and pulled out a card with his contact details on it. "And if you would like a walk with myself and Wicker again, just let me know." Wicker cocked his head, having heard his name, and wagged his tail again. Olivia crouched down and scratched Wicker behind his ears.

"That sounds good," she said and went inside.

Olivia closed the door and walked into the kitchen. She swore aloud at the shock of seeing Maverick sitting at her kitchen table. "By the gods, Maverick!"

"Sorry, I didn't mean to startle you."

"Well don't sit inside my house without telling me you're going to be here! What do you want?"

"I was just a bit curious about what that American had to say?"

"And what's it to do with you? We went for a walk. You know, what normal people do, Mav, instead of chopping people's heads off."

Maverick held up his hands, "And people say I'm tetchy."

"Fuck you, Maverick. You show no concern for me, only what's in it for Boatman."

"That's unfair."

"Is it? Your first question when you see me is trying to ply me for information? And you wonder why I'm cynical about you?"

"I've always focused on how I can protect you, Olivia."

"Let's not go round in circles with this, Maverick. Obviously I'm forever grateful to you and Tobias for saving me that day, but that doesn't mean I have to dismiss all the times Boatman has put his crusade above my wellbeing or my family's wellbeing."

"Some things were out of our control."

"What about my father? My mother? Molly?"

"I wasn't there for those."

"Exactly." Olivia sat down at the kitchen table. Tiredness seemed to be her permanent companion. "Why did you come round, Mav?"

"Because I honestly was worried for you spending time alone with a man you barely know."

"I doubt anyone here, even if it is their country, would risk the wrath of The Beast by harming me."

"Still, it looks a bit off?"

"Off?" Olivia knew what Maverick was implying but thought if he wanted to go down this road, he would have to bloody well say it out loud.

Maverick cleared his throat, "We don't know what's happened to Boatman, it seems strange you going for romantic walks in the forest with a man."

Olivia had learnt a lot of things providing therapy to Roman soldiers; the narcissists could never be reasoned with. It didn't matter how things were framed and how eloquently words were put, a narcissist would feign understanding and empathy, but completely dismiss everything said or agreed as soon as they left the room. Olivia saw it time and time again when she was in London. Now, she didn't believe Maverick was a narcissist, far from it. He was the epitome of selflessness when it came to Tobias and when he knew he would have to fight Boatman in the gladiator arena, he chose to sacrifice himself to save Boatman. Which narcissists would never do. No, he wasn't mentally wired in that way, but he was likely an appeaser of a narcissist. Olivia didn't like to believe her husband was such a thing, but the more she thought about his behaviour over the years and how he ploughed ahead, regardless of the emotional impact on her or those close to him, the more she wondered if those traits ran in him. She wasn't sure he was overtly aware like some she had met, but his actions and words at times made her wonder if there was something genetic in him which steered him a certain, selfish way.

Boatman didn't know much about his origins. He knew his mother was raped by a Roman soldier and died from the injuries and torment of that attack. He knew that the soldier would have been protected by the Empire as Boatman's mother was a cleaner, who cleaned up the blood and mess after torture sessions, so irrelevant to the soldier and beyond. He didn't know anything else, though, and it enraged him, that he might never find his mother's attacker and avenge the terror she went though. What Olivia was beginning to understand was that Boatman's father was likely a man who was rotten and unfortunately for Boatman, some of that might well have tainted him. And the other side to being tainted was Boatman's ability to charm people and bring them round to his zealous view. Maverick would die for Boatman and therefore struggled to see a viewpoint that greatly differed to his leader's. Which is why Olivia knew it was futile debating with Maverick, as Maverick was only thinking of his boss. With that in mind, she told Maverick she wasn't going to argue with him and he needed to leave her house. Which he duly obliged.

Before Olivia killed emperor Maximus, she'd believed she had a gift (or curse) from the gods. She had empathy that was almost painful for her. It was like vibrations running through her. She likened it to bees buzzing in her brain. Whenever someone close to her was in trouble she would feel this buzzing overwhelm her and know something was wrong. She felt it when Molly was abducted.

She felt it when Molly's mother was in mental darkness just before she died. The thing was, since she released her revenge on Caesar, it was like that empathy which had plagued her since she was a little girl had completely dissipated. She cried at night thinking about it because she wondered if fate or the gods had released her because of the torment she had endured: like that was her destiny. She had felt like she was a pawn in Boatman's game, but now when she experienced silence at night she wondered if she was a pawn in the gods' games. A mocking of her empathy, because now she was safe, she was all alone and wondering if her husband was dead or alive and the silence truly was too much to handle at times. She knew she was a hypocrite because of the anger she felt towards Boatman and she wasn't sure if she even loved him anymore, but she felt anxiety in the pit of her stomach not knowing if he was okay.

From the days of wishing the buzzing would go away, she now lay in her bed hoping buzzing would start again, just so she knew her husband was still breathing.

Chapter 8: Training Day

Boatman was breathing. And he was breathing hard. He had been training some of Aska's gladiator recruits for hours on end, days on end. Aska was determined to breed a fighter as good as Maverick Kirabo, and believed Boatman would be the route to that achievement. Even though Aska had destroyed his alliance with Rome, that didn't stop him from wanting to keep producing world-class gladiators. Aska's plan was to not only continue seeing gladiators entertaining the masses throughout the world, but especially in Rome, showing them a level of ferocity that The Beast used to have. He would march into Rome, take it violently, and then celebrate with the bloodiest games ever. Therefore he needed fearless and expertly trained fighters for the entertainment that would be coming. Aska was convinced, having not only seen Boatman fight but briefly engaged with him, that Boatman would not only instil something special in his young gladiators but maybe transfer the raw and almost supernatural side to his fighting abilities.

Aska's problem was forcing Boatman to do the training. Boatman wasn't afraid of death, so threats of violence if he refused wouldn't work (and a dead man couldn't train gladiators). Threats of torture were no good, because a tortured man would be of no use. No, violence against Boatman was a pointless path to take. He thought about violence against Faust as a threat: do what I want and I won't hurt the Roman. Boatman would have been unfazed by that, though, as Faust was an enemy, as was Askå's pet, Titus. Maybe a man who wasn't so hardened by battle and sanitised by misery would have sympathised with Titus; the thought of Titus losing another vital bodily part would be too much for some men. Boatman wasn't like some men. Boatman wasn't like most men. He believed in vengeance and was born from vengeance, so Askå knew idle threats about the welfare of men who Boatman wanted dead anyway were not going to wash. No, Askå knew he needed something much more potent. Or rather, someone.

Which is why Askå revealed to Boatman that Molly was now his ward and if Boatman didn't do what was required, then the young girl would be faced with unimaginable pain. Boatman was quick to agree, through expletives and rage, because Molly was his adopted daughter and almost a symbol of the only thread of connection he still had to his wife. Molly was the daughter of a soldier Boatman had abducted to use as leverage against emperor Nero II and also turn against the Empire. That didn't pay off and Molly's father died in the mess of Boatman's plans. Unbeknownst to Molly or Olivia, Molly's father died by Boatman's hand. Boatman felt he had no choice at the time, but lied to Olivia, saying the Romans had committed murder. In tragic circumstances, Molly's mother couldn't live with the pain and killed herself. It meant Olivia and Boatman took Molly into their care.

Either Molly was astute or, as a young child, viewed things simply, but she always blamed Boatman for her parents' deaths. She felt anger at Boatman that never went away, and when Askå found an opportunity to take her away, she didn't resist. She felt relief being as far away from Boatman as possible. And in the time she had spent with Askå, in his mansion, being given everything she wanted or needed, she was actually happy. Boatman didn't know this. Boatman thought Molly was being held against her will, and therefore the Aestii giant was able to bend Boatman to his will at the thought of the little girl being harmed. Even Boatman, in his callousness, was unable to sacrifice Molly out of stubbornness, and so relented and agreed to train Askå's pupils. Boatman made the point he could train them to kill, but having never been a gladiator, he didn't know about how to teach them to entertain. Askå had smiled and said that was nothing to worry about; he would sort the entertainment side of things.

Which is what he had done with Maverick.

Maverick, when he was a gladiator, was the perfect fighter. He entertained and he imbued fear in all who encountered him. He had been a teenager when Rome had ripped him away from his home town in Uganda. Even as a young boy, Maverick was ferocious and a number of soldiers were severely injured when they abducted him. Maverick's abduction was part of the Empire's strategy to falter any rebellion efforts by removing young men and women who could become rebellion fighters. Instead of rebellion fighters, they would be trained as gladiators and entertain Rome, not defy it. It was quickly established that Maverick, although talented, would defy his captors again and again. The only way to break him was to send him to the Aestii region and see if Askå could tame the Ugandan.

Askå was delighted to receive Maverick and knew, as soon as he met him, the boy didn't need taming, he needed unleashing on the world. Maverick reminded him of the wild tigers who roamed parts of Aestii in his majestic strength and ferocity, so

'The Beast' quickly became Maverick's nickname, which translated very appropriately. Askå knew, though, unleashing The Beast was all well and good when he was focusing his rage on opponents; it was a different matter outside of the arena. So Askå ensured Maverick feared the man who trained him. Askå, to this very day, was unsure if he could beat Maverick if the fear wasn't there, but it was a question he never had to answer because once Maverick was fully trained, he was shipped to Rome to be adored by millions as his fights were streamed around the world. Even with all that fame, Maverick never shook away the fear of his trainer and he carried a scar on his face which always reminded him.

Askå wanted Boatman to manifest similar levels of fear in those he would be training because fear filtered out those who would freeze from those who would fight.

And so, here Boatman was, breathing hard, exhausted from a relentless schedule to train young fighters to be Rome's next generation of gladiators who would possibly be paraded on every channel conceivable. When training had begun, fifteen new recruits had been put into Boatman's care. But care wasn't what this was. It was a brutal fight for survival. Boatman's knowledge of gladiator training was limited, but it had evolved into a sleek professional sport. Training for many, whether they were reluctant rebels or rich fame wannabes, was strictly managed to ensure no major damage was done before becoming a full-time arena gladiator. Training was performed with fake swords and computer-generated opponents so that technique was mastered no matter the fighting error. Computer simulations allowed gladiators to practice complex fighting manoeuvres again and again. Sparring was done with non-lethal weapons. With Askå, though, he believed that to be a great gladiator was to think you would die from the very first day of training. And for some, that was unfortunately the case.

When Boatman was presented with those he would be teaching, he expected the setup to be similar to what he already knew. What he knew was quickly torn up. When he arrived at the training arena and saw all fifteen new fighters holding real swords, he immediately video-called Aså, "There appears to be a mistake." Boatman said.

"And what would that be?"

"The students all have real weapons."

"And?"

"They're not ready for that. They'll seriously injure or kill each other." Boatman paused a beat. "Unintentionally."

Aså looked amused. "I'm sorry, dear Mr King, I'm not quite sure what your point is?"

"I'm here to train them, not watch them butcher each other."

"And that's what your expertise will do, Mr King: teach them how to fight without accidentally chopping their own hands off or the heads of their training partners."

"It's months and months before most gladiators use real weapons against each other during training!"

"Well then, I guess your pupils will need to be fast learners. Like Maverick was." Aså cut the call and Boatman swore at the blank screen. He put the phone back in his pocket as Aså wouldn't answer another call. The phone itself was useless apart from being a direct line to Aså. Boatman had tried to use it to contact someone for help, but the phone was like holding a tin can with string tied to it. It had been completely restricted so it was worthless trying to find a way to hack it. Boatman had looked over at the fifteen potential gladiators and he'd known from then: some of those young faces would be dead and buried very soon.

And he was right, because within six months the group was

only five.

This particular morning, he had been instructing the five to see if they could attack him in a combined assault. It was known for some gladiator bouts to involve teamwork before they had to turn on each other, so Boatman wanted to highlight the teamwork that might save their lives. Boatman was impressed with their improvement as they attempted to attack him, and it took him longer than he thought it would to render them all unconscious. It was certainly over five minutes.

"Bravo!" Askå stepped into the arena, clapping and wandering around the unconscious figures of his remaining five recruits. "But why are they still alive?"

"It's hard to make money out of dead gladiators."

Askå looked genuinely perplexed. "But you beat them, so they should be dead."

"As you can tell from only having five of them still alive, it's not very lucrative to kill all your apprentices, so maybe mercy makes sense during their training."

"Mercy breeds weakness, Mr King, which I'm sure you're well aware of," Askå said.

"It can also inspire untapped strength."

Askå snorted. "You sound like one of those stupid motivational posters Rome plasters around to make the masses feel less oppressed."

"I just don't understand your logic in wanting these people dead."

"Because they're a fucking disappointment, Boatman." Askå said, his contempt bubbling over. "And disappointment has no place in what I'm trying to achieve. I want to build at least one fighter who will make me proud, like Maverick did."

"Maverick's an anomaly."

"No, he was a good student," said Askå, "And you need to be

a better teacher." Askå looked around again at the unconscious victims on the floor, and said, "I'm not interested in reasoning with you, Mr King. I think you overstate how important you are. Or how much value I place on you. If you can't do what I need, then you are dispensable." He looked down at the students again and drew his battle-axe from the holster on his back. "Just as these poor excuses for fighters are dispensable." He raised his axe above his head to bring it down on one of the students, but before he could strike he was knocked down by Boatman.

Boatman stood over him with a sword to Askå's throat, and Askå raised his hand. Not in surrender but to indicate to his bodyguards that they should stay where they were. "Maybe you are more useful than I thought. It's been a long time since someone managed to catch me off guard. You're quick. The rumours about your strength and speed are clearly not rumours."

"These students have real potential, and I can bring it out of them. It's senseless to murder them now."

"Senseless to you." Askå swung his axe upwards, making Boatman parry the blow but stumble backwards. Boatman was exhausted from the relentless training he had to give each day and the fatigue made him uneven on his feet. He composed himself enough to prepare for another attack from Askå and managed defensive manoeuvres with his sword as Askå's axe came from every angle. The sound of mental clanging and grinding echoed throughout the arena. Boatman knew exhaustion had dulled his senses because he was keeping Askå at bay, but it was all defensive. He couldn't move to another gear and shut this fight down like he usually would. And Askå was a great fighter. A really great fighter. Boatman tried to feint and then land a surprise blow, but it was too obvious and Askå anticipated it. Instead of landing a fatal blow with his axe, he used the handle to strike Boatman on the side of his head. Boatman went down, dazed. He went to stand, but was sluggish, and another blow made everything dark.

Chapter 9: Boatman's Rage

Boatman woke up back in his quarters. To his surprise, he wasn't restrained. His head felt like it should: recently pummelled by a seven-foot giant. His next surprise was that his phone was on his bedside table. There was a message on it from Aská simply instructing him to call. Boatman obliged. He was curious why he was still alive.

"Good morning, dear Boatman."

Boatman hadn't looked at the time. By the gods, he thought, he'd been out cold for nearly eighteen hours. "Why am I still alive?"

"I wonder, what would it take for you not to be selfish?" Aská asked.

Boatman's head was pounding so that his captor's words sounded a little tinny. He squinted as he looked at the image of Aská on the phone. "I don't follow."

"No, you certainly don't. Selfishness, Mr King, it seems to be one of your strongest traits. I'm curious as to what would make you stop, even for a moment, to be selfless instead."

"I don't have time for this bullshit."

"On the contrary, you have all the time in the world." Aská's demeanour changed. "So you will answer my fucking question."

Boatman was rarely intimidated. He was rarely scared and Askå's outburst neither scared nor intimidated him. He knew he was trapped and he knew he was likely to die in this cold and god-forsaken place, but it didn't scare him. In fact, Askå's outburst merely confirmed Boatman's disdain for the lack of respect he was being shown. "You need to phrase a question which makes sense, you fucking cretin!" Boatman said.

Askå went red and looked like he might burst an artery. "And this is why people close to you either leave you or die. And that answers my question. I told you that your selfishness would be your undoing. You tried to usurp me and embarrass me in front of my people. I made it clear to you what would happen if you ignored my very generous conditions. And, well." Askå waved his hand in the air, dismissively, like there was nothing more to say.

That's when it dawned on Boatman. That's when it dawned on him, through his incessant headache, that he'd fucked up. That's when he felt fear and regret and the need to back track. "Hold on a minute. That's not fair."

"Not fair? You arrogant prick. I've been fairer than you've ever deserved. I've given you chance after chance. I've kept you in wonderful surroundings and presented an opportunity to be part of something historical, and you act like it's beneath you. No, Mr King, I have been very fair and all you've done is throw it back in my face." Askå paused a beat and then said, "And Molly's."

Boatman felt anxiety twist through his stomach. "She's an innocent little girl."

Askå pointed at the screen. "Exactly. She's innocent so shouldn't be subjected to the horrors that will inevitably follow her into adulthood. Especially the horrors that would follow her if she remained in your care."

Boatman was struggling to stay calm. "I'll do whatever you want, just let Molly live. Let her see what life could be like."

Askå laughed. It wasn't a laugh which evoked any humour. It was a laugh that Titus had heard before and made Titus cower for fear of what body part he would lose next. "Fascinating that now you will do whatever I ask. Fascinating that a child's life means something to you when you realise you're out of options to try and subvert me. Why didn't you think of Molly's life before you attempted to kill me yesterday?"

Boatman knew there was no way of negotiating with a sociopath. He knew he'd made a catastrophic error, but he hoped there was a way to save Molly. "Look, Molly is a needless victim in the crossfire of my ego, and for that I apologise." Boatman nearly vomited on the apology.

"Goodness. An apology from the mythical and indestructible Boatman King. I'm so happy I'm recording this little chat we're having!" Boatman bit his tongue, he knew Askå would want to keep gloating. "It's always a disappointment, isn't it, meeting your heroes? Not that you're my hero, but you have intrigued me for years. I watched the carnage you were causing in London and how much head-scratching the Empire were doing about you. It was like you were a ghost, and that made me giddy with excitement to meet you." Askå looked to the ceiling, thinking about his next words. "Which is why meeting you has been so underwhelming. And hearing an apology come from you? Pathetic. For that alone, the girl dies."

Boatman took a moment to process what Askå had just said. "What? Hang on. Look, I can do whatever it is you need me to –"

Askå cut the call. Boatman stared at his phone for a few

seconds and then the realisation of Molly's fate, combined with his exhaustion, caused him to collapse on the floor, clutching his chest like he was having a heart attack. Faust had been listening to the call from another room and came rushing in when he heard Boatman making guttural noises like he was in agony. He managed to get Boatman to his feet and put him back into bed. Faust tried to reassure Boatman that Molly would be okay but he knew the words were empty. He knew it because whilst he comforted Boatman, something happened that he never imagined would have occurred and been a scenario he would be a part of: former Legatus Titus shuffled around the doorway to the bedroom, making whining noises. And he made those whining noises because Aska had, long ago, eaten his tongue.

Chapter 10: Herr Faust

In the midst of Boatman being forced to train new gladiator recruits, Faust had wondered if he had been forgotten about. And if he had been forgotten about, then maybe he was worthless. And if he was worthless then, he resigned himself to a similar fate as his former boss, Titus. In the cruel irony of being in captivity, he was relieved he hadn't been forgotten and wasn't, in fact, useless, because that, for now, meant he had a bit longer to live and therefore a little longer to try and work out how to escape. He and Boatman knew the building they were captive in was bugged and therefore used code as often as possible to share any plans for escaping. Their code was, for the time being, rather useless as escaping appeared to be a futile endeavour.

Faust was sure Boatman was being physically pushed to his limits to stem any possibility of trying to escape, as Askå had seen Boatman's abilities and decided a physically exhausted man would pose little physical threat. He had worked this out quickly because Faust was mentally exhausted. He tried to find recharge and solace in his memory palace, but his captors did what they could to interfere with that without resorting to basic methods of torture. As a high-ranking officer in the Roman Empire, Faust was fully aware of and, on occasion, involved in torture. Torture, Faust knew, provided little useful intel but it did break the will of those in rebellion. Many, after being tortured and then released, were shells of the people they once were, and therefore flaccid instruments in the efforts of the rebellion.

Torturing Faust, though, that was a path of pointlessness because Faust was essential to garnering information about how to best overthrow Rome's establishment and install a new government. Yes, Askå was going to use force, but he knew if he didn't gain political support, even with all the brute strength in the world his influence would wane quickly. He had seen that with London. Augustus, Nero and Maximus had believed fear and awe would keep the rebellion at bay, but Boatman's ability to sow seeds of defiance caused endless headaches for the emperors. He managed to project a mythology around him and it made the public brave and soldiers fearful. No, Askå knew that to truly control Rome wouldn't be through bloodshed (as much as he would still enjoy that part), but through subduing the political classes bickering behind the scenes and ensuring they filtered messagesof compliance to the people they represented on the streets.

Faust was key to that happening.

Faust had been thrust into the role of Grand Protector after Titus went AWOL and Nero was assassinated. He was always admired for his superior intellect and also his social prowess. Faust's wife, Alypia, was the daughter of Frigus, the Grand Senator of Rome. Alypia was adored throughout the Empire. Whenever polling was performed, she always equalled the percentages of Caesar, which was quite extraordinary considering her polling figures didn't involve coercion or outright deception. Her popularity, along with her close ties to Rome's Senate, meant Faust was also privy to the inner workings of Rome's political wrangling. Caesar had the power, but the Senate had their ears to the ground when it came to public unrest. Alypia would spend many hours a week video-calling her father and, inevitably, discussions within the Senate would arise in their conversations. Only the naive would ever think confidential meetings and what was discussed in those were never leaked, accidentally or not. Faust never expected Alypia to reveal anything to him after she had spoken with her father, but snippets would come out in conversation as days went on, and it gave Faust enough to try and always stay one step ahead.

Alypia wasn't daft and knew what her husband was doing, but she had reached a point where she no longer dreamed of having a husband who simply loved her for who she was. She knew, as clever as Faust was, he was seduced by what most men were seduced by, no matter their intellect: power and adoration. She had become someone transactional to her husband so had looked to find genuine connections elsewhere. She reasoned that as long as they were seen as the ultimate power couple in public, she could at least experience genuine intimacy in secret with someone who wasn't bothered by her status. Alypia knew her husband down to the most mundane and subtle of changes in his mood, so was certain he never suspected her of her infidelities. Not that she saw her actions as infidelities because when you're paraded around the Empire as property and your husband uses you for information and access to your father, surely you're not cheating when your relationship is purely transactional?

On the day Faust was abducted by Aská, Faust almost learnt of his wife's extracurricular activities, but in the carnage of that situation he hadn't seen the true reality of that. In his naivety,

Faust had never suspected his wife of adultery, and even when she had left him on occasion for a few days at a time, his spies had never discovered anything to suggest she was seeing someone else. He had always assumed she had gone to stay with friends to spend time to try and cool off and reset. He had never pressed his spies too much on where she had gone; after all, Alypia was the daughter of the Grand Senator of Rome and married to the Grand Protector of Rome. He knew she had enough resources to lose anyone following her, but he also knew she didn't like that bullshit of deception, so trusted what she was doing on her own. He was wrong to trust her.

Not only was he wrong to trust her, he was flabbergasted that she had colluded with the rebellion. In the madness of the moment, when he had seen her standing next to Boatman he wasn't able to process the situation. Before he could even speak with his wife, violence and anarchy took over. He had found small windows to enter his memory palace before it was disrupted by Askå, but not enough to truly investigate what had happened with Alypia. He hoped she had been abducted and forced to show sympathy to the devil of the rebellion. If she had voluntarily joined the rebellion then he didn't believe he could forgive her for that, but he was also faced with very real threats against her safety and he wasn't sure he had the stomach to consign her to death. Not Alypia. She was his sweetheart, no matter what had been emotionally wedged between them.

It wasn't threats to Alypia, though, that forced him to divulge key information about Rome. It wasn't torture, and it wasn't the thought of dying. No, it was being in the presence of General Ira, Askå's second in command. Ira was a sociopath who Faust knew would never be appeased in traditional hostage/negotiator scenarios. Faust knew Ira had been assigned to Faust as his project to extract information from and Faust also knew about Ira's history, so when Ira had first arrived to question him, he was careful not to poke the bear, so to speak.

"I feel we're two very rare people," Ira said.

"I don't follow," Faust said.

"How many times do you think two men have stood in the same room and been Centurions with the personal ear of two different Caesars?" Ira snorted, lost a little in the thought of his former Lord, Caesar Augustus II. "He was a great man. Fucking clever."

"I never met him."

"Your loss."

"I'm sure you're right. It's hard to feel enamoured about the father when having experienced the son."

"Nero wasn't worthy to be his son. He had neither the class nor the brains."

"That's something I wholeheartedly agree with you on," Faust said.

"You don't need to play dumb with me, Herr Faust."

Faust bristled. He hated being addressed in such manner. If anything, he knew Ira had done his homework as Faust had done everything possible to distance himself from his Germanic history. Even so, Faust wasn't going to roll over. "One thing I never do is play dumb."

"How about ignorant?" Ira said.

"We all show ignorance when it suits us. Ignorance sometimes keeps us alive."

"You sound like a philosopher."

"You become philosophical when you're surrounded by death all the time."

"I should have a scholarship in philosophy then," Ira said.

"The confidence of Caesars and the blood of the people," said

Faust, almost to himself.

"I was banished because of the blood of the people."

"I heard differently. And it wasn't people's blood, but a woman's life."

It was Ira's turn to bristle. "She didn't die."

"So who's being deliberately ignorant now? Someone doesn't need to die to have their life taken away. Look at him." Faust pointed at Titus who was curled in the corner of the room.

Ira refused to look at Titus and held his hands up. "Okay, I'll own it. I have urges."

"Urges are when you rally fancy something sweet to eat, not attacking women."

"Grand Protector, sorry, *former* Grand Protector, don't pretend you didn't know about unofficial Roman code when it came to this sort of thing. Don't start trying to be self-righteous because you're now on the wrong side of history."

"Wrong side of history? You've kidnapped the ruler of the Empire, the whole might of Rome will be falling on your heads."

"Really? And when are you anticipating this to happen? Do you know how long you have been here? Six months, and no-one has come for you. And you know why no-one has come for you? Because no-one has any idea where you are."

"You underestimate the resources we have. It's been a long time since you served Rome."

"Maybe, but I still remember the great Augustus leaving many loyal servants of his to rot because saving them was too costly."

"Like I said, you underestimate my worth."

"And you underestimate the level of terror Askå will inflict on you in coming weeks. And if you need a reminder, then take a look at that thing in the corner and unless you decide to start giving vital information about Rome and how we will march on it, then you will soon join Titus as part of Askå's menu."

With that, Ira left the building and Faust became acutely aware of his surroundings. He was sitting in a giant, wooden chair that he was barely able to move because of its weight and size. And yet Askå would push it aside with minimal effort. The main living area was stone-walled and stone-floored, with a high-pitched ceiling and thatched roof. It had to be huge to accommodate the size of Askå. Sitting in the chair, at a giant oak table and in an enormous room, Faust felt very small and very insignificant. The silence of Rome, too, seemingly unable or disinterested in finding him, caused anxiety and fear to gurgle in his belly. He was always confident that his intelligence could find him a way out of sticky situations, but this was far beyond sticky. He was used to banal politics where he had to entertain senators with their requests and nullify their concerns by promising something that made them feel like their position actually carried some sort of power.

But now he wished those same senators had anything that would be beyond the banal and give him a way out of this terror. He knew Ira's chats were a psychological way of roughing him up, but they weren't anything other than gentle bullying. Faust knew that Ira's chats were to remind Faust that when it really became important, true torture would begin and Askå would join the party, and then he would have to think that this table, that he was sitting at, would be used for eating one of his body parts.

He attempted to retreat into his memory palace, to take up residence in a room which gave him comfort, but at every turn Ira and Askå stood there, smiling, blocking his way and the light that usually shone so brightly in his palace. Faust opened his eyes and looked over at Titus. He felt the fear of what would come press on him, and before he knew it he was bent over, shaking and praying for the first time in his life that the gods would hear him and save him.

Chapter 11: Legatus

Grand Senator Frigus stood on the balcony of Maximus's living area and felt disgust at all the blood stains on the floor of the arena Maximus had commissioned to be built. Maximus had used the small arena to make films reenacting scenarios he found particularly arousing. He was obsessed with recreating the moment he crucified Olivia King, but changed the ending so that he was able to finish the job. Maximus had used actors to act out Maximus's fantasies, but unfortunately for the female actors, the crucifixion element wasn't fake. Frigus enjoyed watching the Crucifixion Channel as much as the next man, but Maximus's efforts were grotesque, to say the least.

Not that it mattered anymore, now Maximus was dead. No announcement had been made. Yet. The Senate was still trying to figure out how to avoid riots and insurrection with two Caesars dying in less than two years. It was going to take intricate management of the situation to ensure Maximus's death was kept secret until it was deemed safe to release the information. But it felt as if there was never going to be a safe time. The religious zealots would say the gods had cursed Rome and their wrath was being unleashed. They would then call for a complete overhaul of the establishment and potentially cause riots throughout Rome and beyond. The remnants of the rebellion would be emboldened and Frigus was nervous that he didn't know the whereabouts of Boatman or any subsets of his ideology. And that brought him on to Faust, whose disappearance added petrol to the already out-of-control fire. If the population knew Faust was missing, and therefore Rome was completely rudderless, it would probably be the end of the Empire.

Askå's antics in London's colosseum had almost incited rebellion, but complete blackouts of anything online, along with strict and violent curfews, meant any boldness quickly turned to meekness. Still, it didn't answer what to do now that another Caesar was dead.

The Senate had been panicking about how to lead Rome through this and what type of leadership needed to be installed. The answer came when it was investigated who was technically the leader of Rome if the Emperor and Grand Protector had died (because it seemed safe to assume Faust had died). With Maximus and Faust dead, it meant there needed to be a Legatus of Rome. One didn't exist at present because Maximus certainly wasn't going to give someone in Rome great power to potentially rival his. Maximus knew about Roman history and read of the dangers assigning or sharing power gave, like with Crassus and Julius Caesar.

With Maximus gone, though, it was time to install a leader and therefore maintain a facade that the Empire still existed. Because, Frigus thought, that's all the Empire was, wasn't it, a facade? Yes, there were legions scattered throughout the world and laws and ideologies imprinted on countries and cultures across the horizon, but it was all bullshit. People obeyed because fear and tradition told them to. He saw how fragile certain countries were in Africa when a few decided they weren't happy with their leadership and the tsunami of opposition then sprang up. Rome was always blessed with two millennia of fear to make people think twice, and also a gargantuan media network to reach billions of people, but one ripple could bring the whole thing down and Maximus's death was a potential tidal wave.

And that was why Frigus was in Maximus's palace and why there was a knock at the door and a young Centurion was being escorted in.

"Hail Caesar," said the Centurion.

Frigus ignored the greeting as it was null and void to him nowadays. "Please, take a seat, Brutus."

"How can I be of service?"

"I understand you became Centurion just over a year ago?"

"Indeed. The youngest ever, I was told."

Frigus was looking at Brutus's employment history on his phone. He scrolled through and said, "That's right, you were. Two months younger than Grand Protector Faust when he was made Centurion."

"Wow, that's quite a name to be put next to."

"It is. And based on recent psychometric tests it would suggest Faust would have a rival in regard to IQ scores."

"I doubt I would ever rival the Grand Protector, he's like a god to most of us posted here in Rome."

Frigus's eye twitched at the hyperbole about Faust, which made what he was about to do a little easier. "Have you heard any rumours around the barracks recently?"

"Rumours?"

"Let's not talk about your intellect for you to play dumb all of a sudden, Centurion Brutus, hey?"

Brutus flushed a little and cleared his throat, "The rumours have been about the lack of activity around the emperor's palace, if I'm honest. Talk has been about how unwell he might be."

"Frankly, there's no smoke without fire."

"Is that why he's not here with us?"

"Yes."

"How unwell is he?" Brutus cleared his throat again, "If that's okay for me to ask?"

"He's dead."

"Sorry?"

"Don't insult your own intelligence, Centurion Brutus. You heard me the first time. I need you to tell me what the procedure might be on hearing Caesar is dead. After all, you are the top Centurion in the city."

Brutus's demeanour changed. He knew this was a test, he just wasn't sure what type of test. If it was for promotion, he was going to make sure he appeared as qualified as possible. "I don't know what the politics surrounding the Senate might be, my Lord, but militarily, if the emperor was dead and there was no apparent heir to replace him, which seems the case, then the Roman army would step in to preserve the integrity and protection of the Empire."

"That's good to know, because the Senate is relying on that."

"How does that practically look?"

Brutus went to speak, but then realised what the test was and enunciated his thoughts as they were hitting his brain. "Without a Caesar and heir to the throne, the military would be called to carry on the desires of the emperor as the Senate coming into power would potentially establish a republic."

"But an army is like a Senate, so how would you be different?"

"A Centurion would be elevated to Legatus legionis, and oversee command of Rome and beyond." Frigus raised an eyebrow. Brutus went back to flushing in his cheeks. "But that's what procedures were in place before it changed with the appointment of Grand Protector Faust." Brutus went a bit red from forgetting that part. "Is that why I'm here? What's also happened to Lord Faust?"

"The exact nature of what has happened to Lord Faust is confidential, but it is feared he is also dead and therefore you're the most talented Centurion in Rome and you're also the natural commander for the whole of Rome if emperor Maximus and Grand Protector Faust were to die."

Brutus was flustered. "I don't know what to say, my Lord."

"Remember your training, soldier. When you were appointed as Centurion in the city, you were given training about this possible outcome."

Brutus nodded and said, "I was, but it was never believed to be something that would ever be actioned."

"Well it is now."

"So it seems," said Brutus.

"Think about your training. What happens next?"

Brutus didn't need to think about it, he had daydreamed about this moment, even though he always believed it was a stupid daydream. "I would say the oath installing myself as Legatus legionis."

Frigus stared as Brutus. "What are you waiting for? Time is of the essence. There's no need to be coy about this."

"Of course, my Lord." Brutus looked around and six soldiers were present in the room. "What? Now?"

Frigus pulled out his phone and placed it on the small table in front of the sofa he was sitting on. He had pulled up a voice recorder app and pressed the record button. "We're now recording, which will act as a legally binding record. Please, go ahead, Centurion

Brutus and recite what you were taught."

Brutus nodded and said, "I swear that I shall faithfully execute all that the Empire needs, that I shall never desert or betray the service, and that I shall not seek to avoid death for the glory of Rome!"

Frigus stopped recording and said, "Congratulations, Legatus Brutus. You are now the leader of us all." Frigus stood up and poured himself a drink from the large array of spirits and wines at the bar Maximus had commissioned to be built. He offered Brutus a drink and Brutus happily took one, hoping it would calm his nerves. He opted for a whisky from Caledonia.

Frigus watched Brutus finish the whisky in a few gulps and said, "There's a slight problem with your appointment, though."

"In what way, Senator?"

Frigus noticed Brutus had immediately adjusted his language and didn't refer to him as *my lord*. The young man was going to take the role very seriously. "The death of the emperor was through treason."

"Is there any idea who it was, who killed the emperor?"

"It's been established that it was someone using his death to make a power play."

"A power play? How? Who?"

"The how part is easy. Kill the emperor and make the Grand Protector disappear and then fool a Senator into helping make you the Commander of Rome."

The sentence hung in the air for a moment as Brutus registered it. "Hang on, you invited me here. Before I entered this room, I didn't know Caesar Maximus was dead."

"You barely blinked at the news of his death and were installing yourself as the new Legatus in a heartbeat. I have the recording," said Frigus.

"This is a joke, right?" Brutus looked over his shoulder and saw the six soldiers were encircling him as he sat on the sofa. "I don't understand what's going on, but this is some sort of joke?"

"Assassinating an emperor is no joke."

Brutus stood up. "Woah, I did not assassinate an emperor." As he stood up, the six soldiers drew their guns. Brutus turned to the soldiers, "Put your guns down; I'm your Centurion."

"Correction, you're their Legatus," said Frigus.

Brutus turned to Frigus. "This is insane, Senator. I came here at your behest. I came here with no knowledge of the emperor's death."

Frigus raised his hands to the soldiers and ordered them to lower their guns. He then sat down, giving Brutus the permission to do the same. "Look, Legatus, we seem to be at an impasse here."

"An impasse? You're accusing me of killing the leader of the world…"

Frigus brushed the comment aside with a wave of his hand. "To be Legatus isn't simply to lead an army, commanding them to fight for the Empire. No, to be Legatus involves playing the game. It involves doing politics. And sometimes that political manoeuvring requires sacrifice."

"Willing sacrifice for the greater good of Rome is fine. Sacrifice without a choice isn't," Brutus said.

"No sacrifice is a choice. It's a necessity."

"Well, I'm choosing not to and I will use my role as Legatus as I see fit, not as you see fit." Brutus turned to the six soldiers. "As your commanding officer I am ordering you to arrest Senator Frigus for treason."

The soldiers didn't move.

"You all should think very carefully about your apparent insubordination as I am the Commander of Rome. Now, arrest the senator." Brutus hadn't noticed who all the soldiers were but spotted one of them as his close friend, Julius. "Julius? Listen to me and know that the best decision you can make is to arrest Frigus and you will be richly rewarded." Julius didn't move or respond but he looked down, unable to meet his friend's gaze. Brutus said his friend's name again but Julius kept his gaze downward.

Frigus broke the awkward silence. "I'm sorry, Legatus, I truly am. I wanted this to be as diplomatic as possible but it seems your oath has already been broken as you are trying to avoid death for the glory of Rome."

"How is killing me bringing glory to Rome?"

"It's sending the message that even if emperors are toppled, the Empire never will be and those who seek personal glory above the needs of the Empire will face the consequences."

"But you're mad, I haven't done anything of the sort."

"Your trial will determine whether that's true." Frigus looked at the guard. "Please take the Legatus into custody."

Before Brutus could try to resist, the six guards were on him and he felt punches from all angles. As he went to his knees, he managed to look up and see his friend, Julius standing over him, a sword raised. "Et tu, Julius?" Frigus said. Julius ignored the plea and brought the butt of his sword handle down, making Brutus's world go black.

As Brutus was dragged away, Frigus wondered if it was enough to keep the potential unrest at bay. With an apparent traitor arrested and the Senate showing their efficiency, it would just about stop the fraying threads of the Empire from snapping. But it was undecided whether to announce the emperor's death. The fallout from the announcement was hard to quantify, so Frigus saw the opportunity to stack the deck in Rome's favour. The arrest of Brutus was a power play in waiting. It could be used to frame Brutus for a

Caesar's death, or be used to frame him for the disappearance of Faust. Or simply used to invent a potential insurrection that was quashed. Either way, it was a distraction from the gaping hole of visible leadership in the Empire. If any enemies picked up on it, Rome could fall. Frigus needed a plan. Fast.

Chapter 12: Olivia's Loyalty

"I could get used to this."

"I'm bored."

"How? It's idyllic."

"It's boring."

"You need a hobby if you're bored."

"I have a hobby."

"Battering Romans to death isn't a hobby," said Tobias.

"Hobbies are meant to be enjoyed, and I enjoyed killing Romans, ergo, that makes it a hobby."

"Ergo? How long were you in Rome for?"

"It might be a strange concept to you, Tobias, but some of us know how to read."

"Can you read this?" Tobias stuck his middle finger up at Maverick.

"Mature."

"It is mature, because it's a universal language," Tobias said.

"So I assume there's a universal language where you understand to shut the fuck up."

"You say the sweetest things."

Maverick sighed. "I should have stayed in Rome."

"What, just to get your ass kicked by Boatman again?"

Maverick bristled. "I would have liked to have seen you do any better."

"I'm not stupid enough to get in that situation."

"No, of course you're not. You just decided to run straight at a giant and nearly have your head taken off by an axe."

"And you were there to save me," said Tobias. He reached out and took Maverick's hand in his. Maverick didn't resist. After a couple of seconds, Maverick squeezed his partner's hand.

"There's not a chance I'm letting anyone kill you because I'm the only one who's allowed to do that. You're a pain in my ass and no-one but me gets the satisfaction to take you out," Maverick said.

"You know, if we got married then the vows would mention about being together until death takes us, so you would be fulfilling your vows, technically," said Tobias. Maverick laughed and Tobias enjoyed the sound of the deep resonance that it emitted.

"But before we worry about how I kill you in your sleep when you're old and infirm, or when I've had enough of your bullshit, what do we do about Olivia?"

Olivia had been the focus of Maverick and Tobias's attentions for a few weeks since they had arrived in the RIA. She had distanced herself from them and also from Bella. It had been strange as there was a clear sense of separation between the core group. Most noticeably was how quickly and eagerly Olivia stopped engaging with Maverick, Tobias and Bella. She seemed to be sad in her eyes when she saw any of them, and that sadness appeared to compel her to avoid them. Maverick knew the pain and anguish caused from Molly's abduction, as well as Boatman disappearing, and not knowing if the Empire had released her mother meant seeing any of the original rebels was like reliving the nightmare. Maverick understood that and respected that. It didn't stop even the Beast from feeling hurt and disappointment. He remembered viscerally when he had to pull the nail from Olivia's wrist after Maximus had his way with her and the anguish that caused. He remembered the tubes protruding from Olivia and the beeping machine monitoring her vitals and although not a religious man, especially with the things he had done over the years, he still had quietly prayed for Olivia's recovery. He wasn't sure his prayer had been answered but even so, Olivia had woken up and he was thankful to have his friend back. He had always considered Olivia his friend because she was able to unlock the soft side to Boatman when needed. There would be moments Boatman wouldn't relinquish his opinion, as dogmatic as he was, and Maverick would want to scream in his boss's face. Olivia would find a way to break that stubbornness down, and it helped Maverick try to show Boatman a different approach to a problem. Olivia would take Maverick aside and remind him that unlike being a gladiator, in which brute strength found a way, diplomacy was necessary.

Olivia's recovery, though, it hardened Boatman. Maverick thought it would do the opposite, where the fragility of Olivia's life would make Boatman more fragile. Boatman, though, he became entrenched in retribution. Retribution which, at first, appeared to work, with the death of Nero. And in that desire for revenge, Boatman had managed to push his wife away, and now Maverick was on the other side of the world, safe, but watching Olivia potentially leave her husband forever.

"Why are you getting so worked up?" Tobias asked.

"Because she has a husband."

"She's not doing anything wrong. She's just going for nice walks."

"She shouldn't be alone with a man who isn't her husband." Maverick said.

"For a gay, black man who used to be a slave, you're being very backwards in your thinking."

"How? Look, Boatman might not even be dead and Olivia is having dates with another man."

"Dates? Did he approach the door with a red rose or did they walk down the road hand in hand? We're in a potentially hostile country, Maverick, being sheltered from an Empire, I think she's allowed to make a friend without you getting all huffy about it."

"I'm not getting huffy, I just think she should honour her vows?"

"At least she has vows to honour."

Maverick looked to the heavens, "At what point, Tobias, between me almost dying in Rome and you almost dying numerous times, did you think was the right time to get married?"

"In the time you've been obsessing over Olivia and her choice of friends, we could have got married and had a party." Tobias said.

"What is your fixation on getting married? You know we don't have that many friends, so there won't be loads of presents."

"I have plenty of friends, thank you. I can't help that my boyfriend growls at most people. Take Olivia's new friend, for instance. You might like him."

"I don't need new friends," said Maverick.

"Maybe I do, have you ever thought about that? All we do is fight, run, hide and fight again. It would be nice to have friends that don't talk about how many Roman soldiers they've killed in their lifetimes."

"Maybe that's what I want to talk about," Maverick said.

"Then that's why we need new friends, because you need to get out more." Tobias moved close to his partner and lowered his voice. "In all seriousness, Mav, we need as many people on our side as possible." Tobias placed a hand on Maverick's cheek and turned his face towards his so that their eyes met. "I've seen Phobos. I've been dragged close to Hades. I don't want to go there again. Maybe we need new friends. Maybe we need a way to stop running."

Maverick held his boyfriend's gaze. "Maybe." He kissed Tobias and let the kiss linger. "But maybe fighting is all I know."

Chapter 13: Askå's Apprentices

When Maverick was shipped to the Aestii region to be trained by Askå, most thought he would die. When Maverick was only 14-years-old, he weighed 15 stone and was pure muscle, but even so, no-one thought he would survive his time in Askå's presence. Not many young, potential gladiators did. Only a few ever managed to leave Aestii, and somehow their relief was to be in Rome and fight in the Colosseum. Those who survived training with Askå were fearsome and fearless. They were fearless because they had seen fear face-to-face and nothing compared. Being in Askå's clutches made anything most men would fear seem like child's play. Seem like something to scoff at, like when a child thinks a monster is under their bed. No, the world was not a scary place; only Askå's kingdom was scary. Being in Rome, fighting those who had never been subjected to Askå's ways, that was like a holiday.

But the flipside to that was that when you have become so desensitised to anything the world throws at you, you also become desensitised to life itself. And with that, many of Askå's greatest fighters were also some who died the youngest. They saw life away from Aestii as the end of their journey, not the beginning. They felt the relentlessness of life as an apprentice of Askå meant they had aged a hundred years. Being a fighter in Rome, therefore, didn't make them believe they were destined for glory for years to come, but somehow was the perfect way to mark their deaths. And mark their deaths they did with many of these fearless warriors choosing suicide in the arena.

They wouldn't do it initially or even in the first few months of fighting, but then something would clarify in their minds and they would decide life was no longer a preferred option. The first time it happened, it wasn't really noticed. It was thought maybe everyone mistook what happened and didn't see things correctly. Even when pundits discussed the fights in their television studios, they analysed it all so much they guessed the fighter made a terrible mistake and died as a result. The gladiator in question was Gabriel. He had been one of Askå's golden pupils. One who Askå put through hell in order to achieve the glory of Rome and adulation of the masses. And Gabriel did achieve that, for a while. He was adored for his smooth sadism. He killed efficiently and almost lackadaisically. The people loved watching him, and pundits ranked him amongst the best of the past decade and in virtual matchups against gladiators over the centuries, he was regularly considered to be one to be revered. Nevertheless, all the glory and adoration didn't change the time when he decided to kill himself in the ring. That is, he simply stopped fighting and allowed his opponent to cut him down.

The pundits explained away how he let his guard down to be killed, drawing expert opinion from across the globe, so that Gabriel would always be revered as a fighter, even in death. The truth was much more simple, and a note in his dressing room, which the Empire never released the contents of, revealed Gabriel was tired of living. He was bored of his existence and the gladiator arena was like having a job on a conveyor belt in a factory. He was out of adrenaline. He was out of serotonin. He was out of expectation. And because he was out of all that, he decided he should die. And when pundits in their studios slowed the footage down and analysed how the great Gabriel died, the moment before a sword plunged into his chest, it was very clear Gabriel was smiling. He felt true happiness for the first time in years, and it was liberating for him.

After Gabriel, many other of Askå's trainees did the same thing and decided life was flat when terror wasn't your close companion. Soon enough, the Gladiatorial Commission had to ask Askå to either sort his trainees out or they would be refused entry into gladiatorial bouts. For Askå, this was potentially calamitous as he earned great money from his fighters and the sponsors they advertised.

Askå was expected to go easier on his young recruits so that he didn't create fighters with desires to die, but Askå figured to go even harder. If his young fighters found the passion to end their own lives, then he wasn't doing enough to make them into emotionless machines. Once all emotion was gone, so too would be self-destructive thoughts.

Maverick was one of the successes of Askå's new plan. Maverick experienced hell and survived, such as proving his raw strength and desire to live against a wolf in the wild. Maverick was put into a place where his worth as an emotion-filled human was not needed or necessary. In the initial months of his training, as a teenager, Maverick cried himself to sleep and begged for the gods to bring him death. But death never came. Nor did mercy. Over the years, Maverick increased in scars from bouts and trials against the fiercest of nature. His empathy became less and less until it was a distant memory, an afterthought to another time and another life.

When Askå shipped Maverick to Rome, Askå soon reaped the reward and became very rich as The Beast's sponsor. Money, too, from advertising and the world's media desperate to interview the man who seemed indestructible. Maverick had become a killing machine who felt no empathy for his opponents, and he felt no remorse. He obeyed the will of Askå and Rome and performed his duty as the greatest gladiator with consummate efficiency.

What Maverick didn't share with a single soul, though, was how he did *feel* what was happening. He did experience very human emotions. Although he had been trained in the gates of hell, it didn't stop him from storing humanity in his heart. The key for him was that he would never let any of his 'masters' know that he still harboured humanity. The more they believed Maverick had become like a machine with human skin, the more their guards would be let down.

When Maverick turned 16, he knew he was never going to escape Askå or Rome. He knew his prayers were futile and his hope naive. He decided that to stay alive and not believe death was the best option, he would cram his love, hope and faith deep, deep down inside him, so that no-one would ever discover it. He would draw from it when desperately needed, but he would otherwise be the man he was trained to be. He knew that if he allowed his humanity to pick away at his brain in this situation, it would lead to him deciding to take his own life. He had seen it before and understood why.

No, he would wear a mask.

The mask he wore was one of obedience, and he knew that to survive would be to give Askå everything he wanted. If Askå wanted an emotionless killing machine, then he would get one. Maverick grew up quickly training to be a gladiator and vowed that he would eventually escape Aska and Rome, but it would be through patience, discipline and feeding on the spark of humanity buried deep within his psyche. He knew his chance would come one day if he managed to survive, and the day he faced the wolf was the day he knew The Beast had to emerge if Maverick would ever see the faces of his family again.

Chapter 14: Sharing

Maverick and Tobias sat on the sofa of the guest house watching an American film. They had never seen one before, as the Empire churned out hundreds of films a year and didn't allow films to be shown from non-Empire affiliated countries. It was fascinating viewing because the film focused on love and relationships. Its narrative drove towards hope and believing people could do better. Maverick and Tobias were very confused during it, as films circulating the Empire were propaganda-driven nonsense which over-exaggerated the glory of Rome. It was strange viewing for the men, but what it did was make Maverick pause the film and say, "I need to talk to you."

Tobias looked at Maverick, confused. In all the time they had been together, Maverick had never wanted 'to talk.' "Are you breaking up with me?"

"Of course not."

"Are you dying?" Tobias said.

"By the gods, Tobias, no, I'm not dying. Will you shut the fuck up for one minute so I can share something with you?"

"Now the grumpy man that I love is back in the room, of

course you can," Tobias said and smirked.

"I'm sure it's my time in Aestii that has given me the patience to stay with you and not kill you." Maverick held up his hand so that Tobias wouldn't make any sarcastic remarks. "And it's Aestii that I want to talk to you about."

Tobias shifted in his seat and said he would just sit and listen.

Maverick squeezed his partner's hand and said, "I've never felt the need to speak about it because it's always been part of my life I've compartmentalised and kept it locked away. Seeing Askå in the flesh, though, and almost losing you again, I feel like you should know some of what happened in the camp. And considering it became a massive part to my persona, it's only fair I tell you about how I became The Beast."

Chapter 15: The Beast

I was sitting in the camp, at a table, eating my breakfast with another trainee. Her name was Clara and I still remember her bright green eyes, like she had replaced her eyes with emeralds. She was tough. She had been taken off the streets of Rome, in one of Augustus's drives to clean the city up. She had been on her own since she was a toddler and so had learnt how to survive. She had clearly needed to survive because in Rome, on the streets, if you weren't killed for food, you were likely raped and killed by a solider looking to vent some steam after performing a crucifixion. She'd made it to the age of 17 so was more than adept at surviving.

And I knew she was tough because I was nursing a black eye she had given me the afternoon before. I had never met someone who could move so fast and the punch to the face was like a cobra striking. At breakfast when I touched my eye she called me a pussy and her more than anyone like Aska taught me to be careful when to show my vulnerabilities. She taught me how to mask. Aska taught me how to be a psychopath. I remember her finishing her breakfast and getting up from the table and saying, "Don't show them you're hurt." I had nodded and she said, "Promise me." I promised and then she said, "Happy Birthday." She turned and walked away and I was glad because I didn't know she knew it was my birthday. Hell, I didn't know anyone knew it was my birthday, so I blushed at the emotion of it and Clara would have been mad at me for that. I might have received another black eye for my birthday. I had vowed to ask her how she knew it was my birthday but that was the last time I ever saw her.

So it was on my sixteenth birthday that I promised not to show my weaknesses and it was on my sixteenth birthday I was called to the residence of Bjorn Askå where I was certain I would die.

"Good morning, Maverick. I trust you had a nice breakfast?" I nodded and said it was good. "That's great to hear. I like to look after my apprentices. Excuse me, I haven't quite finished my breakfast." He licked his lips and finished some meat on his plate. He took great delight in licking the juices off his fingers and then pushed his plate away. "Delicious!" He motioned for me to take a seat at the kitchen island he was sitting at and I perched on a stool.

Askå had looked at me for a while before saying another word. He seemed almost vacant in his eyes like he was somewhere else mentally and only his body remained present. If his eyes had rolled back to reveal their whites he would have been the land version of a shark. In a moment though, he had come back to the room and said, "I'm impressed with that shiner Clara gave you. You certainly let your guard down with her, Mr Kirabo." He laughed. It was a horrible sound. I attempted a laugh too and Askå abruptly stopped. "If that bitch can hurt you, imagine what would happen in the colosseum." I stopped laughing or smiling. I apologised for my poor performance. Askå waved his hand, "Apologies are like dust in the wind; irritating and fleeting." His eyes had taken the shark-like nature again, "How we survive is a true reflection of sincerity. Anyone can say sorry and anyone can believe they mean it. How about when it's literally life and death? That's a true reflection of humanity my dear Maverick. That's a true reflection of whether we really want to live. Wouldn't you say?" I had shrugged. I didn't know. I didn't know anything. I was 16 and scared. I was comfortable fighting, but sitting at a breakfast table, talking the philosophy of human survival? I didn't have a fucking clue. And I definitely didn't have a clue when I was talking philosophy with a true psychopath. My shrug wasn't satisfactory to him though, so I answered how all I wanted was to live and be the gladiator he expected me to be. Askå had laughed his horrible laugh again and said, "You're so lovely, my dear Maverick, always thinking about what I'm feeling." His face grew serious again, the shark manifesting itself, "But empathy has no place here. Empathy has no place in the arena. Just as careless mistakes like getting a black eye in basic training has no place in my school." I had gulped then, certain Askå was sentencing me to death. Instead he picked the final bit of meat on his plate, swallowed it in one, and smiled. He said, "And because carelessness and complacency has no place in my school, I will teach you the true meaning of survival. It's time you graduated, Maverick."

With that he rose from his seat and went round the island to where I was sitting. At the age of 16 I was tall, well over six feet, but Askå was a giant. More than seven feet high and almost as wide. I stayed frozen in position; I wanted to fight, I felt the adrenaline pumping through me, but the sight of him, a giant standing over me, with my lack of skill as a fighter, I knew it was futile to even attempt to hurt him. A predator like Askå saw the defeat in me and chuckled, "It's okay, dear Maverick, your time isn't yet. I have very high hopes for you. I can see what you will become. Even so, you still need to learn." I wasn't even able to lift my arm to protect myself when one of Askå's fists came down on me and blackness became my companion.

When I woke, I was in a forest. I had enough clothing to keep me from freezing to death, but not enough to make me comfortable. And next to me was a sword. To be precise, a Gladius sword. I was feeling groggy, the punch from Aská was like a hammer to the side of the head and I was surprised it hadn't killed me. It had taken me a few minutes to get my bearings, but even so, my head felt like something was loose inside. I had looked up and the moon was full, the light of it glowing on the forest floor. I'd felt the weight of my sword in my hand and initially guessed I was going to have to fight either Aská or one of his commanders here in the forest. Survival of the fittest or something messed up like that, but then I heard the howl and I feared it was much worse. I'd never heard a wolf's howl before and after that night never wanted to again. I had grown up in a rural life in Uganda so was used to sleeping outdoors and living with nature. My brother Damba and I loved it when our parents let us set up a tent by the shore of Nnalubaale or in the undergrowth near our village. I wasn't afraid of the outside, but a wolf's howl, when so exposed made my stomach twist.

I was in quite a large clearing and as my eyes adjusted to the darkness, the moon my only companion of light, I made out some silhouettes on the forest floor. I approached one and bent down, it was a human skull. I looked around and saw other bones, scattered. I realised I wasn't in a clearing, I was in a feeding area. A possible den. Then the wolf's howl came again, but this time it was close. Very close. I stood up and looked for a way to safety.

But it was too late. Only fifty feet in front of me was the source of the howl: a gigantic wolf. It stalked towards me, its hackles raised and each step cautious yet fearsome. The size of the wolf made me feel insignificant again, like in the kitchen next to Aská and, looking back, I wasn't quite sure which animal I feared the most.

I raised my sword, ready for the attack. The wolf made its move, teeth bared and a guttural growl seemingly bouncing off the trees in echo.

I had never fought a wild animal before. In Kenya, which borders with my home country, many young men gained their manhood by hunting a lion, armed only with a spear. Unfortunately for Kenya, the Empire used this by taking the adolescents and making them do it in front of television cameras, in artificially created environments. For me though, I had never been in a position to fight a wild creature. What I was experienced with was focusing my rage. When I had been abducted by the Empire I broke the arms of at least two soldiers as they tried to haul me away. Yes, Clara had given me a black eye, which landed me in front of the wolf, but that was down to her superior skills, technically. When it came to surviving this encounter with a wolf, the rage I felt that I was literally being thrown to the wolves made me fearless. It made me what Askå had wanted the opposite of: to have no regard for my own life and nonchalance at the thought of dying.

When the wolf came at me it snarled and I too snarled. At the age of sixteen, on my birthday, I was nowhere near the skilled fighter I would become but one thing about being young and inexperienced is that there's a confidence to take more risks and no true sense of mortality. So when the wolf came at me, I didn't shy away, I decided that I would be as much a beast and see which primal creature would come out on top.

I don't really remember the actual fight with the wolf; it was all teeth and blood and blur. And to call it a fight was probably a stretch as it was over in seconds. I do remember the aftermath though, staring down at myself and wondering what was my blood and what was wolf's blood. And staring down at the wolf, this majestic creature which must have weighed nearly as much as me. My sword was still in its gut, only the hilt showing, and blood was everywhere. I remember the overwhelming sense of guilt when I looked down on the dead wolf. It was a beautiful animal and deserved to be roaming the wild. But it had to go by its instinct and attack me. The rage I felt defending myself came back, but it was rage at Aská for finding life so inconsequential and amusing. I hated him and vowed to put my sword in his gut when I found myself back in his camp. I had debated skinning the wolf and taking its hide back with me, but I didn't know where I was or how far the walk back would be. Instead, although not religious, I said a prayer over the wolf and apologised for what I was about to do.

One thing I knew, because of what my father had taught me, was to use the sky to guide me home. The sun was high in the sky and therefore it helped me walk east. I knew the camp was east as when I had been abducted I took in as much as I could about the direction we were headed and where the camp was situated. I refused to believe the camp wasn't too far away because if I was victorious I was sure Aská would want to gloat about my achievement and produce some sort of narcissistic display of praise. I was right, because in a couple of hours walking I spotted the irrefutable spire of Aská's house. His mansion was huge and in the centre was a spire, made to look like some religiously iconic building. And hours later I was at the gates and guards were clearly prepped to look out for me as they let me in the grounds without too much fuss. I was escorted to Aská's mansion and led into the room he had built for sparring. Aská was in there, sparring with one of my fellow 'recruits'. Again, like the term fighting, when thinking about me against the wolf, was misleading, so too was the word sparring when watching Aská and his victim. It was a pummelling and I had shouted for him to stop before I knew the words were out of my mouth.

Askå did stop.

He climbed out of the ring and said, as he walked to me, "The Prodigal Son returns. Hello, my dear Maverick." He wiped a bead of sweat from his top lip. "I'm surprised you survived. Was it a cub you ended up killing?" He laughed at his joke. The few staff in the room laughed too. They knew better than to not. He walked up to me and I managed to stand my ground. I was tired, having walked for hours, but my adrenaline was still pumping from the thought of having killed a giant wolf. And if I could kill a giant wolf then I could certainly kill a giant man.

I had no sword on me, as that would never have made its way through security, but I did have something else. Askå came close; I still wake up in the night thinking I can smell his coppery aroma. He came close and said, "You're not as useless as I thought. Wow, you'll have to tell Clara that she might have to try a little bit harder to give you another black eye, my dear Maverick." Askå looked me up and down, taking in the blood and fur stuck to my clothes and skin, and wrinkled his nose, "You smell like rotten, wet dog. Go get washed and then you can spar with me."

Askå had turned away from me and that was my moment: I lunged at him and punched him hard in the back and then raked my knuckles down his spine. In my clenched fist were two wolf's teeth, and they sliced his back open. Askå arched his back and turned in a flash. I went to punch him in the face, aiming for his eyes, hoping the wolf's teeth would blind him, but my hand stopped like it had hit a brick wall. Askå had stopped my punch by managing to get hold of my wrist and then he twisted. I yelped in pain and fell to my knees. I remember thinking an axe would be bearing down on my skull at any moment but the axe didn't come. Instead, a kick had gone into my stomach and as I bent forward, winded, my arm was twisted again and I was on my back. Aska had then straddled me and pinned me down by my shoulders using his knees.

I had killed a wolf so do remember that arrogance of youth believing, even in this moment, I would be able to kill Aska, so I had spat in his face, hoping to disgust him and gain a split second to get free. As with the arrogance of youth also comes the naivety and Aska wasn't a wild animal. He was wild, but he wasn't easily distracted and didn't flinch, even as my spittle dripped off his nose and back onto my face. And my inexperience hadn't prepared me for when he grabbed my wrist and yanked my hand back, snapping a bone, and the wolf's teeth dropped to the floor. I cried out in pain and instinctively wanted to grab my broken wrist but I was still pinned in place. The pain made me woozy and I hoped I would pass out but a hard slap across my face kept me very awake and in full awareness of the pain pulsating through me. And that was when Aska smiled and I truly understood how much he enjoyed people's pain.

Aska had then brought his hand in to my eye line, and he was holding one of the wolf's teeth. "Something to remember me by," he had said and then he dug the tooth into my face, just below my left eye and dragged it down, slicing my face open. Only then did Aska allow me to pass out from the pain.

And after that day I made sure I would be the perfect pupil and I unleashed all the fury I had for Aska upon anyone who I faced in practice or my early fights. I imagined being the wolf and the one tearing Aska's throat out. Quickly, throughout the camp, people said I acted more like a beast than a human and it became my nickname which never went away.

Chapter 16: Dust in the Wind

"I always assumed you got your scar from a fight with Askå in the ring and it was his axe?"

Maverick shook his head. "No."

Tobias sat up straight on the sofa and turned to face his boyfriend. "Let me get this straight. You fought a wolf in the wild, removed its teeth and then got that scar from the teeth you removed?"

"Something like that," Maverick said.

"You do know how batshit that sounds, don't you?"

"Probably why I don't tend to share the story."

Tobias shook his head. "No, not batshit like you should be ashamed of the story, but batshit crazy that you have never told anyone that you fought and killed a wolf! That's mental! That's amazing."

"No, Tobias, it was traumatising, as was having Askå slice my face open."

Tobias held Maverick's hand. "Mav, you killed a fucking wolf."

"I think you're missing the point of the story."

"No, I think you're missing the point of the story."

"Tobias, I haven't ever shared what happened to me before, when with Askå, because he tortured and abused me. He gave me this scar with sadistic pleasure and then for years he took pleasure in my pain. It was hell," Maverick said.

"But you killed a wolf. In the wild," Tobias said.

"Are you trying to wind me up?"

Tobias squeezed his partner's hand. "No, my beautiful man, I'm not trying to wind you up." He leaned forward and kissed Maverick softly on the lips. "I'm trying to show you something."

"What? That you always miss the point of a story?"

"No, you grumpy git, that you have missed the point of your own story."

"I was there, Tobias, I think I know what the story's about."

"I don't think you do."

"You're starting to be the usual pain in my ass with this conversation, Tobias."

Tobias held his hands up, "Okay, okay." He took his partner's hand in his again. "Look, you were beaten down and degraded by Aska and I understand how you became The Beast, because of that and the way you felt like mirroring the wildness of the wolf you killed. Trust me, I get the point. But my point is, you fought a wolf in the wild. You had to be this wild beast to do it and yet, in all that, in all the torture and tribulations, at such a young age, you knew that you had to somehow store your humanity deep down, so that you never lost it. Because if you did lose it, then there's no way we would be sitting here now."

"I still don't think that's the point of my story."

"Then what's your point?"

"I was weak."

"Mav, you killed a wolf."

"I was weak. Aska scared me. He still scares me."

Tobias stood up and then moved so he could kneel in front of his partner. He took Maverick's hands in his. "And that's you proving I know the point to this story better than you. Askå scared you and he still scares you. Right now, here, in this safety of what we have, Askå still scares you." Tobias put his hand on Maverick's cheek, "All that you went through and still you know the very human emotion of fear. You learnt how to keep that humanity safe before being stripped of what makes us human: emotion. You might have earned The Beast as a nickname but Askå is the untethered, emotionless beast. And, like I said, you killed a wolf, Mav. You faced a beast, killed it and then felt remorse. You apologised to it. You did something brutally incredible and retained your core humanity." Tobias kissed his fiancé. "That's the point of the story."

Maverick looked deep into his partner's eyes and said, "I've always found you a sentimental motherfucker. But this time, I think you're right."

"Can you put that in the vows when we get married?"

"And an annoying motherfucker."

"Definitely put those words in the vows."

Maverick sighed and got up from the sofa, saying he needed a beer. Tobias watched him leave the room and thought how the man he had met, many years ago, when they were both AWOL gladiators, fleeing the Empire, was a cold and aloof man. Even after they'd fallen in love, there's no way Tobias would have dreamt of Maverick sharing his vulnerabilities like he just had. It made Tobias choke on emotion because although he knew it, it was wonderful to truly know that someone loved you deeply and unconditionally enough to share their demons.

Tobias got to his feet and called to Maverick to also grab him a beer. With the life they lived, these moments of normality were like dust in the wind so he was going to savour it.

Chapter 17: New Friend

Olivia sat in the small restaurant near the park's lake waiting for Newen to arrive. They had walked Wicker earlier in the day and Olivia had found herself saying yes to Newen's invite for an early dinner. The guilt that drilled through her made her want to cancel but the opposing rationale of having every right to enjoy herself in spite of being a pawn of her husband's vendetta against Rome weighed stronger. And she wasn't sure what the guilt was about. She hadn't done anything to betray Boatman or the sanctity of their marriage. She had simply made a friend. But Maverick's brutish invasion of her privacy had played on her mind. She believed she was right to admonish Maverick for daring to question her motives and her actions in regard to her marriage, but his words still grated on her. No, not his words, but one word, *off*. To Maverick and, in his thinking, to other people, Olivia's friendship with Newen looked *off*. She didn't want it to bother her. She didn't want to have to justify to anyone or herself about a friendship she had made, but that tiny word played havoc with her and that caused the guilt to flourish. Because if she did know Boatman was alive and did know where he was, would she engage with someone in this way? Would she do something others thought was a bit off? She didn't know. And it made her angry she was even debating it with herself because for the first time in years she went through a day without thinking about Romans and what they might do to her. It was liberating. And although she wasn't sure she would ever be able to tell another soul, she had some moments in a day where she didn't think about Boatman and that too was liberating.

She had no idea if Boatman was alive, but her last sight of him was charging towards a giant man she now knows as Bjorn Askå. That was underground in London and that was a memory she was trying to wash away. And Newen was helping her forget about the horrors of recent years. Horrors of being crucified and horrors of being a rebel. Newen appeared normal, like walking his dog and chatting about the weather were what people did. Now, Olivia wasn't dumb and as she had called him on it before, she knew he wanted information about Boatman and anything about the Empire, but he appeared to be doing more and more things to shift conversation away from the Empire. She had been the therapist of Roman soldiers and was the wife of Boatman King, she certainly wasn't naive about people's motives. She was tentative about her own motives too; had she become so entwined in the deception and gaslighting of living a rebel life that she wasn't even being genuine with Newen?

Olivia tried to put such mental gymnastics out of her mind because one thing she was sure of: she enjoyed Newen's company and she enjoyed not wondering if the Romans would appear.

"Sorry I'm late." Newen pulled her out of her introspection.

"I didn't notice that you were."

"Nice to see you're that interested in meeting up that you didn't notice I'm late."

"Is there such a thing as being late in this city?" Olivia asked.

"How do you mean?"

"No-one ever appears to be in a rush. It's so different to when I was in London."

"Rome likes to keep the masses punctual. It's part of their control strategy. Make everyone rush and be afraid of being late."

Olivia shook her head. "I feel like the British would be like that anyway."

"Why?"

"Because the British like order and routine."

It was Newen's turn to shake his head. "Boatman's successes make no sense based on that assessment. Rebellion is anything but order and routine."

Olivia felt herself prickle at the way success of the rebellion was attributed to Boatman and not the collective effort of the rebels, but let it slide. His myth was more the legend than the actual man, "The British have always been an oxymoron. The majority are submissive and apathetic to their subjugation, but a few break that trend. And it's enough to rally support."

"So what went wrong?"

Olivia cocked her head. "Wrong?"

"Why did the support falter?"

"I don't recall it ever did."

"From our perspective it seemed London's effort against Rome faltered massively," Newen said.

"An emperor was killed."

"And it propelled Faust to power."

"And where is Faust now?" Olivia said.

"True."

Olivia sighed, she was tired of talking politics. She felt like normality was something to be grasped but everything always seemed to circle back to the rebellion. Even conversations. "Can we talk about something else?"

Newen placed his hand near Olivia's on the table, but didn't try to hold it. "I'm sorry. I am genuinely fascinated by what you did in London. And you're right, you did do something no-one could do for generations, kill an emperor. The 35 were astounded. It's arrogant of me to criticise the aftermath."

"But you did believe it to be a mistake as events played out?"

"Hindsight is a wonderful thing," Newen said.

"In so many ways," Olivia said.

"But you're right, we should talk about something else. This is meant to be a place of relaxation for you. A place of recovery." Newen glanced down at the menu in front of him and said, "So, firstly, what do you like to eat?"

Olivia thought back to the all the fish and oysters she had eaten in the previous year and said, "Meat. I want meat."

Newen smiled. "Meat we can do. In the surrounding area there are wonderful wild deer roaming and this particular restaurant serves the finest venison."

Olivia smiled back. "My mouth's watering from just the thought of a venison steak. It's been a very long time since eating something like that. A lot of tinned goods in London."

"Well in that case I will get the cook to put together their specialty." Newen motioned to the nearby server that they were ready to order and asked for two plates of the cook's venison special. And a bottle of red wine.

"Red wine? Goodness, it's been years since I've drunk that too. Rome made point of subsidising the vineyards of Britannia and they only ever produced white wine."

"Wrong climate for red wine," Newen said.

"From what I tasted, it was the wrong climate for white wine too. And, what, you're a wine connoisseur on top of what you do? And what is it you do, exactly? Are you one of the mysterious 35?"

Newen shook his head. "I advise the 35, I'm certainly not one of the 35."

"And whilst we're on the subject; who are the 35?"

"It's really nothing that mysterious, Olivia. They lead America and represent the 35 districts of America. And to lead this nation, they obviously have to ask questions about anyone who may be a threat to a very peaceful nation."

"I'm a threat?"

"No." Newen had raised his voice a little. Not at Olivia, but more at the topic of conversation. "No." His voice had lowered this time. "You're not a threat. It's the people interested in you who are a threat."

"I would think Rome's interest in me is very low considering their Grand Protector is missing, and Boatman is also missing."

"I'm not referring to Rome."

Olivia didn't need Newen to mention Askå's name. "Why would he want me?"

"Why wouldn't he? I can't imagine Boatman would be particularly keen to share information. And if he did, I doubt it would be truthful."

"So, what, he abducts me and forces the information out of me? As if I actually had any information? It didn't do Maximus any good."

"We don't believe Askå will come after you, but we do believe he is interested in you. We have a very delicate relationship with him, but it is a relationship." Newen, this time gently rested his hand on

Olivia's. Olivia smiled and slowly removed her hand from Newen's.

"You have a relationship with the man who, at best, is holding my husband hostage and, at worst…" Olivia let her words trail off. She didn't need to finish the sentence.

"I feel I can be honest with you, Olivia. It's naive to think we wouldn't have a relationship with him."

"Fuck you," Olivia said. Newen was taken aback. Olivia wasn't deterred. "I'm not naive. I know these relationships happen and I know my husband is irrelevant. It makes me laugh that no matter what side of the world I'm on, all men are the same: they play with power, massaging egos, but publicly denounce the men they massage."

The wine had arrived and Olivia and Newen didn't hesitate in taking large swigs. The conversation wasn't necessarily heated, but it wasn't relaxed. "I understand that to keep Rome at bay we need to sometimes 'massage egos.'"

Olivia was quick in her response again, her face red with anger now, "Nothing needs to be massaged, Newen. Nothing at all. You play games with each other like it's artificial reality and of no consequence. You don't *need* to do that. It's not necessary."

"There's thirty-five leaders who would beg to differ with you on that."

"The majority view isn't always the correct view." Olivia said. "And my husband can attest to that, considering he did more to destabilise Rome than America ever did with making Aská its bedfellow."

"We haven't made Aská our bedfellow, but simply understand that without him we would be in a much weaker position."

"But he's insane."

"Insanity doesn't necessarily negate diplomacy."

"But it negates any sense of superiority when dealing with a man like him," Olivia said.

"Trust me, we've dealt with men like him before and it's about their narcissism distracting them." And Newen knew what he was talking about when it came to this topic. He knew very intimately. A decade ago a man, who had inherited riches from his Germanic parents decided he would attempt a coup of the 35. He had managed to grow quite a following of disenchanted Americans who felt their voices weren't being heard by the 35. The 35 were pragmatic, like the Romans, on the importance of multiculturalism. To grow as a nation they understood that bringing skills of immigrants in was necessary and enriching for a society.

Some disagreed and showed their disagreement with violence against those who had started a new life in the RIA. The man, Trump, who would eventually attempt a coup, saw the opportunity to make money out of discontent and drive up fear and loathing through sensationalist propaganda. The 35 had decided the way to dilute and destroy Trump's fear-mongering message was to counter with facts and truths about Trump. A man like him had dark secrets and the 35 were able to uncover them and display them to the nation. It seemed, though, that Trump's dark indiscretions only enamoured some followers and boosted Trump's support through wild conspiracies of the 35 faking the evidence. Even in the face of all the evidence and witnesses coming forward to attest to Trump's depravities, he still stood up, in the presence of thousands to say it was all fake news and he had never done what the 35 accused him of. With so many duped by his lies, the anger grew towards the 35 and Trump used it as an opportunity to subtly suggest maybe the HQ of the 35 should be stormed and a new government installed. Of course, Trump used all plausible deniability as he never directly said anything of the sort, but angry rhetoric was easily interpreted by the mob and thus the mob came together.

The 35 quashed the coup with ease but the greater problem of the cult that had formed around Trump needed to be solved. Pragmatism hadn't worked. Propaganda hadn't worked so that's when the 35 called upon Newen. Newen was specialised in silencing those who tried to usurp the peace of the RIA. Trump was going to be a bit trickier to silence because very quickly he had established a significant following with robust protection. It was agreed that to silence Trump Newen would need a way in and that way in would be through the skills of one of the 35, Omaha. Omaha could solve most problems and he had been one of the dissenting voices in the 35 who had believed Trump should have been silenced a long time ago. The 35 agreed they had been ignorant and asked Omaha and Newen to fix the problem. They duly obliged.

Newen was the blunt force but needed Omaha to direct that force in the correct manner. For Omaha there were two options: make it appear Trump had an accident or be very blatant in an assassination. He decided to go with the latter. Newen had questioned the decision and Omaha had explained how an 'accident' would be treated with such suspicion and wild conspiracy it would likely grow Trump's cult, not dissipate it. Whereas a clear and obvious assassination would most likely cause the angry followers to go silent. Omaha reasoned that most rabid followers are actually cowards and show some force, and show that their immortalised leader is very mortal, it makes cults go out with a whimper. Newen wasn't convinced. He'd killed enough people to know the reaction to the killings vary as wildly as his methods of elimination. He also knew he was being paid very handsomely so didn't make too much effort to question Omaha's logic.

The logistics of Newen's assignment were complex but Omaha's job was to make it appear very simple and that's exactly what happened. And the skill of Newen was to actually make it obvious he was killing

Trump so the news picked up on it and his supporters saw it with their own eyes. Because, for Newen, he was able to kill Trump and walk away from the scene without anyone even realising he had been there. So Newen did things exactly as he planned and killed Trump in front of his adoring fans. Omaha had nullified Trump's security by paying them a huge bribe to look the other way. And all of Trump's security happily took the bribe because Trump was a terrible businessman and had failed to pay any of his security for months, always making excuses about why the money never appeared. To be offered large amounts of gold which was paid upfront meant none of the security had any qualms about letting someone put a bullet in Trump's head.

Therefore, Newen was able to walk up to Trump, put a bullet in his skull and walk away. When a gun is fired most people either run or duck. No-one tries to apprehend the shooter. It's not fight or flight, it is only flight. So as people flew, Newen walked away from the corpse of Trump and disappeared into the panicking crowds whilst the security detail held down an innocent man. And in the commotion, the news reported on the innocent man as the shooter whilst Newen's identity remained a blur.

In the following weeks the cult of Trump dispersed. The bluster of the initial days after the assassination went quiet as the 35 made it clear anyone who would attempt a coup would be violently stopped. Many of those who showed aggressive support for Trump decided they weren't passionate enough to take on the might of the 35. After only one year, Trump's cult existed only in memory and his legacy was a little footnote on disquiet in the RIA.

So, yes, Newen knew what it was like to deal with narcissistic men like Askå and knew to try and topple him through pragmatism and facts didn't work. You had to get close to pull the trigger and the only way to get close was to feed his narcissism until his guard was down and a blade could be put to his throat. Aská thrived on his own sense of grandiosity. Aská, unlike Trump, was smart, though. He could see through most deceptions, so to charm him, to get close to him and kill him was difficult. He tried to convey some of this to Olivia but it was a hard sell to get her to see the logic.

"Maybe some within the 35 would be able to explain things better," Newen said, aware of Olivia's anger at the politics they were discussing.

Olivia eyed Newen whilst she had a drink of her wine. "What do you mean?"

"Sorry?"

"What do you mean by that?"

"I'm simply suggesting the 35 would be able to point out our position much better and more eloquently than I can."

Olivia put her glass down. "That's the thing that doesn't make sense. You talk of the 35 like some mystical group who are verging on omnipotent, and then you casually say we'll just wander into their presence and ask their views on our little political tiff, like we're meeting some friends at the pub. It doesn't make sense. What do the 35 want with me?" Olivia ran a hand through her hair and absently scratched her head. It was a tic that came through when she was frustrated.

Newen was impressed and surprised by the woman opposite him. He had read about her career as a therapist and the valuable insights it gave to Boatman and the other rebels to frustrate Rome. What he hadn't read about and was understanding, now he had met her, was that she wasn't merely observant because of her professional skills, she was an empath and she picked up on micro-behaviours and micro-expressions. She was displaying a hypervigilance where she could see a change in mood or hear a subtle change in someone's tone and astutely pick up what was going on. And she was currently reading Newen like a book because the 35 did want to meet Olivia and her empath skills were, in their minds, a powerful string to the RIA's bow. And so Newen told her that.

"I'm not going to be another pawn," Olivia said.

"I've read about how you were used like bait in the past. This isn't the case. We want your skills to help us proactively."

Newen thought Olivia would refuse the offer but instead she said, "So when are we meeting them?" She drank her drink in one and then said, "No time like the present?"

Newen laughed and held up his hand. "Take it easy. We can see them in a few days. Maybe just try to enjoy the evening instead?"

"I can try." Olivia said. "I assume decent company is arriving soon for that to happen?"

"Fuck me," said Newen, "You don't hold back, do you?"

"In a world of cowardly men who don't get to the point, I've always found honesty is the best policy."

It was Newen's turn to down the rest of his drink and then refill it. "That's fair enough and I hold my hands up for being one of those cowardly men." And Newen was being honest. He'd killed many times and felt no fear when it came to that, but he'd been naive and, if he was truly honest with himself, misogynistic towards Olivia by trying to somehow trick her into meeting the 35 or working for them. He's been scared to be honest and he wasn't sure why. Olivia scared him. In a good way. Yes, he thought, in a good way. "I won't ask you to trust me. Just yet. But we'll see the 35 and I would hope they will instil some trust."

"Let's hope so," Olivia said and raised her glass.

Chapter 18: The Roman and the Rebel

Boatman and Faust sat at the giant, oak table that Askå had had built and drank their coffees in silence. Well, silence was a stretch as Titus's whimpers never stopped, day or night. It had become white noise to them. Horrific noise, but white noise nonetheless. Eventually, Faust broke the silence. "Any decent recruits?"

"They'll all be dead within seconds when they get into the Colosseum," Boatman said.

"Your optimism shining through as always."

"What's the point of optimism when there is none?"

"By the gods, do you ever lighten up?"

"I'm not really in the mood to start telling jokes, Grand Protector."

Faust laughed. It came out like a sudden sneeze. He hadn't expected to laugh and was genuinely annoyed with Boatman, but hearing his official title whilst imprisoned in Askå's kingdom, well, that made him laugh. "Please don't call me that. It's rather redundant, wouldn't you say?"

"What would you prefer? Judging by your reaction the other

day, Herr Faust, isn't the preferred option."

"Augustus is fine," Faust said.

'Why the distancing from your Germanic heritage?"

"I'm not distancing myself that much, otherwise I would have changed my name to something more Roman."

"Don't dodge the question."

"I don't really think it's important."

Boatman huffed. "Best case scenario is we end up being prisoners for years in this place and therefore get to share a coffee each day. I'm not bothered by how important you think your family history is, I just think it might help distract from the shitshow we're in."

Faust took a sip of coffee and nodded his head. "Okay, fair enough. I'm not sure how clued-up on Germanic history you are, but my Uncle was called Heydrich." Boatman shook his head, so Faust continued, "Uncle Heydrich was one of Hitler's closest advisors, and had very extreme ideas."

"My Germanic history is very limited, but to hear you say someone had extreme ideas stinks of irony." Boatman rubbed his face. "Sorry, go on. I think I recognise the name, Hitler, but very vaguely. He wasn't someone taught about when I was younger."

Faust smiled. "That's interesting, as his name, and my uncle's, would have been much more recognisable if Rome had agreed to work with them."

"Why didn't they, then?"

"It was when Augustus II was a young emperor and boldly taking on new allies as well as enemies. He was overseeing most of Germania but there were pockets still resisting Roman rule. Hitler and Heydrich came to Augustus promising a way for Rome to secure the rest, but also break into more North eastern areas beyond Germania which had previously been elusive. Including Britannia.

Augustus had wanted proof they could help and within weeks Hitler and Heydrich had paraded dozens of anti-Roman rebels on the streets. Instead of having them crucified they had them dig their own graves, shot them in the head, pushed them into the graves and then they set the graves on fire. Heydrich said the rebels created their own hell, so they could burn in it. Augustus had been fascinated by the brutal efficiency of the Germanic men and the following they had garnered in their pursuit of a Roman alliance."

"So what changed?" Boatman asked.

"Augustus sent diplomats to spend time with Hitler and my uncle, to better understand their motivations and how an alliance could work. Augustus was positive about forming alliances with others because he believed peace and cooperation would keep the wheels of the Empire turning. He'd brokered a deal with India and was reaping the rewards so believed the same could happen with Germania. What he didn't know, and was fed back via his diplomats, was the depth of insanity that controlled Hitler and my uncle's philosophies. It disturbed the emperor."

"A Roman emperor was disturbed by someone's philosophy? I think my irony meter just exploded."

"As much as you despise Rome, there were ethics abided by and Hitler seemed almost opposite to them."

"You'll forgive me for currently siding with your uncle in this story."

"We'll see," said Faust.

"Rome got into bed with Askå, what did your uncle do? Refuse to bend the knee to the gods?"

"No, it was all about genocide for Uncle Heydrich and Hitler."

"Again, how would that be any different to Rome?"

"Come on, Boatman, don't be so deliberately ignorant. For all your hatred for the Empire, one thing that hasn't driven its rise has been genocide. There's always been an understanding that to grow Rome's presence it needs the conquered people to be a part of it, not destroyed."

"There's plenty of crucifixions which would disagree with that analysis."

"Again, your ignorance is lazy, Boatman. You know the Empire has succeeded this long because of the people Rome rules over."

"We'll agree to disagree on what we view as success. But, you're right, I'm being facetious. What was it your uncle was doing that disturbed someone like Augustus?"

"It wasn't what was being done, it was about what was wanted to be done. And the paranoia that went with it. The diplomats staying with Hitler and my uncle reported on events Hitler would speak at. He was eloquent and knew how to stir the crowd into a frenzy. He was able to say things that, if you heard those words over dinner, you would question his sanity. But on stage, in front of hundreds, sometimes a few thousand, what he said made sense to them."

"What was he saying?"

"Mainly, the reason why so many in Germania were struggling. He stoked fears and false information about why some were finding life difficult and instead of acknowledging complex socio-economic issues he went with the scapegoat method blaming a certain section of society."

"Which section?"

"Immigrants."

"Fear and hatred of others are powerful propaganda tools."

"I know."

Faust smiled, "Touché. The diplomats reported back to Augustus that Hitler and my uncle were stirring up a lot of unrest and there were reports of immigrants, who had made a good life in Germania, being attacked. Augustus was known for his pragmatism so instead of pondering and waiting to see what might happen, he sent a covert unit into Germania to uncover more information about Hitler's intentions. What they discovered was a plan to manipulate Rome's resources to perform genocide on an epic scale. A final solution to Germania's woes and it would place Hitler and my uncle at the pinnacle of world leadership. There were even plans on how to usurp the emperor and take his place. Hitler as a Grand Caesar and Heydrich as his Chancellor. As it's recorded, and I've already said, Augustus was a pragmatist so told the covert unit that they had permission to do what they were trained for."

"I can't believe I don't know about any of this."

"Grand plans mean nothing if they don't come to fruition. The unit Augutus sent in were swift and efficient. Hitler and my uncle were driving back from an event and because they were still political novices and arrogant they had no real protection. The unit had placed a bomb under their car and when the car was in a rural area it exploded. Hitler and my uncle were killed instantly."

Boatman shook his head. "I'm surprised I've stayed alive for this long."

"As am I," said Faust.

Boatman got up from the table and made fresh coffee for himself and his Roman cell mate. As he was stirring in some sugar for himself he said, "But if Heydrich was your uncle, how did you end up becoming a soldier?"

"Heydrich was my mother's brother and when she married my father, connections to my uncle were severed. My father hated Heydrich and made sure Roman leadership knew it. He even volunteered to do whatever Rome needed to eliminate my uncle.

So when I came of age and was drafted in as a soldier, my allegiance was never in doubt."

Boatman placed the coffees on the table and sat down again. "And now you're a deposed Grand Protector who is probably viewed as a traitor. Your uncle would be proud."

Faust laughed. "You'll certainly never be a diplomat, Boatman." Faust went serious. "But you are a leader."

"Was a leader. Or just a rebel. I'm not sure what it means to be a leader, if I'm honest. And being honest with you feels weird."

Faust always consciously went to his memory palace to either find comfort or find information but this time his memory palace came to him. It stormed his mind with such force he had no choice but to share what it was pressing on him. "I need to share something with you."

Boatman wasn't known for his empathy, but even he saw the change in his Roman friend's (he realised he was able to call Faust a friend, which made him think death wasn't far away) demeanour. "Judging by your face, I'm not sure I'm the person to be sharing with, Augustus."

"It's not about me. It's about you."

Boatman frowned. He wasn't stupid and having spent years preparing for the worst, he was pragmatic too. And being pragmatic, and intuitive, about how other people framed sentences and responses to scenarios, he could see that Faust was very nervous about sharing whatever was one his mind. Which meant only one thing: "What's happened to Olivia? She should be miles from London by now. What's happened to her?" Boatman stood up. His blood pressure was rising and his rage hard to control.

Faust held his hands up. He'd fought Boatman before and barely survived. He'd only managed to live because he'd studied

Boatman's fighting techniques and learnt from it. His memory palace enabled him to not get an upper hand, but have enough information to enable him to survive. When it was a planned fight. This was Boatman in a rage and very much unplanned so he wasn't going to be able to draw on anything apart from hope Boatman calmed down quickly.

"It's nothing to do with Olivia." It was too late, though, Boatman had seen red. Boatman moved so fast Faust barely registered it had happened before he was pinned against a wall by his throat. Boatman was squeezing the air out of Faust. His body inches above the floor. Boatman's strength almost superhuman.

Faust tried to speak but it was a gurgle. He went to raise his hand and Boatman's fist went into his side. If he could have yelped he would have, but the lack of air made it hard to even stay conscious. He managed to get the word "Please" out in a broken, croaky manner. He tried to pull Boatman's hand away but it was like he was being held by a vice. Faust began to panic. He could feel himself losing consciousness and every attempt at breathing was starving his brain of oxygen. The lack of air made him try to kick his legs out, to somehow get free and get air back into his lungs. His experience, way back in his brain, told him that staying calm was key to staying alive just a little longer, but the front of his brain was screaming for him to get away before his world went dark. Permanently. He croaked again and the name "Nero" came out of his mouth. It was enough to pique Boatman's curiosity, and he let go.

Faust collapsed on the floor, spluttering and taking in as much air as possible in ragged breaths. Boatman was pacing. He'd spared Faust but he was still raging. "What about Nero?"

Faust got to his knees but was still bent over, coughing and trying to regain composure. Boatman asked the question again, his impatience and prowling making Faust panic. He needed to answer the question before Boatman lost control again and there was no way out. He managed to whisper that he needed a couple more minutes and it was enough to appease Boatman. Ever so slightly. Boatman became aware of his pacing and sat down at the table, drumming his fingers. Waiting for the Roman to explain himself.

Faust got to his feet and poured himself a glass of water. He downed it and then said, "There's something about Nero that you will want to know about."

"He's dead, that's all I need to know."

"It's about his birth father," Faust said.

"His birth father?" Boatman squinted. "What the fuck is this, Augustus? I have no interest in Nero's father. The prick's dead and not sitting on a throne anymore. That's all the information I need."

Faust was still finding it hard to breathe and his face was glowing red. He took another swig of water and went to speak again. He didn't even manage to get a single word out of his mouth before the door to their quarters buzzed and opened. Three guards walked in, their hands holding electrified batons, ready to strike the Roman or the rebel if they stepped out of line.

"You, come with us," said the guard, pointing at Faust.

Faust stepped forward and Boatman's hand was on his forearm. "What did you want to tell me?"

"It will have to wait," Faust said. Boatman's hand fell away and Faust stepped forward. In usual circumstances, Boatman would have shown disdain for the guards and given at least one of them a thrashing. And he'd done that early into their stay. What transpired though, was that Aska would punish Boatman and Nero not by assaulting them but by abusing Titus. The poor creature that used to be Commander of Britannia would be subjected to more beatings and even more cannibalism. Boatman and Faust didn't need to say anything to each other to be of one mind about trying to keep Titus safe and away from the monster that was Askå.

As the back of Faust disappeared when the door to their accommodation closed, Boatman wondered what information Faust was sitting on and even more intriguing was what that information had to do with him. He guessed the likeliness of the information was that the Empire had solid evidence he was the murderer of the emperor, but a cold feeling went up his spine and he wondered how, even after all this time, Nero still managed to hound him.

Chapter 19: Ira's Little Secret

Faust was led into Askå's kitchen and was confronted with Ira and Askå sitting at the island in the middle of the kitchen. Askå was eating breakfast. Ira was sipping a coffee. Askå wiped his mouth with a napkin and said, "Augustus, my dear man, please, take a seat." Faust stayed where he was and then Askå said, "It's not a request, Herr Faust." Faust obliged and sat at the island opposite Askå and with Ira to his left. Faust glanced around the room, taking in information at a subconscious level that he would go back to if he needed to access it in his memory palace at another time. "Drink?" Askå asked the Roman.

"Do you have something stronger than coffee?"

Askå looked up at the clock on the kitchen wall. "Seems a bit early, wouldn't you think?"

"Early for who? Unless you know different, I'm not going to work today, so why not have a drink instead?"

"Surely you want to keep your wits about you?" Ira asked.

"Why? If you want me dead, I'll be dead. But either I'll be dead sober or be dead drunk. Either way, I'll still be dead." Faust looked Askå dead in the eye. "So, do you have something stronger?"

Aská smiled. "I can tell you've been spending time with Boatman. British sarcasm has a way of rubbing off on others. Even Romans with Germanic descent."

Faust smiled too. "Look, I just want a drink. Either you have one or you don't."

"What would you like? Vodka?"

"A beer."

Aská motioned for Ira to go get Faust a beer. Ira, for a split second, looked like he would object, but thought better and got off his stool and grabbed a beer from the fridge, opened it and placed it in front of Faust. Faust didn't say thank you and took a swig. He remained silent. He figured that if Aská and his lap dog wanted something it was for them to instigate a conversation. Faust waited and took another swig of his beer. Aská broke the silence. "We have a small favour to ask of you."

Faust coughed a little on his beer and chuckled. "And there's you commenting on my new use of irony. I don't think prisoners get to choose when to provide favours."

Aská bristled. "You have comfortable living quarters. I've sacrificed my bungalow for you to stay in. I would say you are living much nicer than a prisoner. Unless you would like that changed, Herr Faust."

"And clearly irony doesn't suit you," said Faust. "What favour are you wanting?"

It was Ira's turn to speak. "We know you know about Boatman's parentage. We want you to keep it to yourself for the time being."

Faust looked at Ira and frowned. Genuine confusion on his face. "Why do you speak like that?"

"I don't follow," said Ira.

"You're Boatman's father, why word it like that? Why didn't you say, 'We know you know I'm Boatman's father?'"

Ira was now the one to be confused. "I don't really know what your point is."

Faust smirked. "Now I understand why you phrased it that way."

Ira opened his mouth to speak again but didn't really know what he wanted to say. Aská stepped in. "My dear Augustus, I don't particularly have the time or patience to navigate through whatever that just was, so can you promise you won't inform Boatman that his father is this degenerate?" Aská pointed at Ira.

"Why?"

"Does it matter?"

Faust downed the rest of his beer. "Can I have another?" Aská looked at Ira. Ira rolled his eyes and fetched Faust another beer. Faust took a drink, wiped his beard and said, "What Boatman does or doesn't know will make no difference to him killing you both."

Ira laughed. Aská didn't. Ira stopped laughing. Aská spoke, "You get your arrogance from your family, Herr Faust." Faust froze for a millisecond, but Aská picked up on it. "What, you think I don't know the extent of your Germanic heritage?" Aská narrowed his eyes and lowered his voice. "And you think I don't remember you when you camped nearby, all those years ago?" Faust couldn't help but gulp. "You think you were clever? No, you're alive because I allowed you to be alive. You became *Grand Protector* because I allowed it."

Faust had a flashback to when he was a new solider and was sent to a camp in the Aestii region. He thought about the nights he lay awake and saw Aská enter where he stayed, taking young soldiers from their beds, for those youngsters never to be seen again. He thought about the way Aská would sniff their necks, like a hungry vampire. He thought about how he feared each night would be his last and he would be taken away by the giant that sat before him now. Then he thought a bit more and said, "Fuck you. You didn't allow me to live. You were instructed to let me live. You're as much a pawn for the Empire now as you ever were, Bjorn."

Akså stood up. Faust noted how long it took for Askå to reach full height. "For a man to become so powerful, your stupidity betrays you."

"And your arrogance betrays you. What, you're going to kill me now? You weren't able to kill me when I was a teenager and I'm sure you're not allowed to kill me as an adult." Faust pointed at Askå's food on the counter. "You can eat all you want when there's no repercussions, but I know for a fact that your hands are tied. As much as you want to be the next big thing, you are still someone's bitch." Faust wasn't sure where his words had come from and if he was even right, but his mind was giving him enough to take a punt.

"You're good," said Askå. "Really, fucking good." He pushed his plate aways, "But you've overstretched yourself." Askå grinned. "That big brain doesn't always get things right. You are correct about your own fate. You're not dying soon. That's not because I'm someone's bitch, though, that's because I'm going to enjoy breaking you." Askå moved round the table. Faust tried not to react to the intimidation of the man's size. "And I will break you."

Askå moved away from the Roman and slammed his fist on the countertop. Faust tried his hardest not to flinch but failed. He repeated again that he would break Faust, and Faust believed him. Askå left the room but before he was out of sight he said, "If you say anything to Boatman, remember what I will do to Titus." And then he was gone.

Chapter 20: Fear Not Hope

When Faust returned to his living quarters, Boatman asked what had happened. "A show of power really. And a show of futility."

"What do you mean?"

Faust shrugged. "It was like they enjoyed pointing out how trapped we are. There's no escape and no point us trying to do anything about it."

"Well that's depressing," said Boatman.

"It's like they were just flexing their muscles and reminding me not to step out of line."

"Did it work?"

Faust thought about Aská's promise to break him. "I would say Aská can be very convincing."

Boatman looked over at Titus, who was sleeping in the corner of the room; how Aská could make the mighty fall. "So, what did you want to tell me?" He looked back at Faust.

"It's of no real relevance," said Faust.

Boatman narrowed his eyes. "It seemed relevant earlier."

"Everything seems relevant when you're having your life choked out of you."

"You mentioned Nero's father." Boatman wasn't going to let it go.

"I heard whispers that he's still alive."

"Any idea who he is?"

"No. Just rumours that he wasn't killed."

"Why the need to suddenly tell me?" Boatman wasn't convinced. There was more to this conversation than Faust was letting on.

Although Faust was a solider first, he was also a politician. That's how he had become the leader of Rome, and therefore lying was sometimes easier than telling the truth. "I thought we could use him as leverage if we found him. We don't have any cards left to play. Thought this was a way to deal us back in to the game."

"Quite the optimism considering our current situation," said Boatman.

"I think that's the way we get through this. If we lose hope we'll end up like him." Faust nodded in Titus's direction.

"But is false hope any better than hopelessness?" Boatman looked at the clock on the wall and saw it was almost time for him to train the gladiator recruits.

"I do know one thing, and that's how fear consumes. At least hope motivates and doesn't destroy."

Boatman frowned. He wasn't so sure. And the fear he saw in the eyes of the gladiators he trained meant they stayed alive a bit longer. Although, he had to silently admit that the fear he did see in his pupils' eyes would be their eventual downfall when they faced an opponent who feared nothing. If they ever faced someone like Maverick then their young lives would be cut very short.

The doors buzzed and opened with guards standing there ready to escort Boatman to the training arena. Before he left he had a thought. "Earlier, when you started talking about Nero's father, within moments we were descended on by guards. This time we were left to our own devices. And considering any conversations which were even slightly dissident in their topic in previous months have been brutal in their consequences, I'm curious why Askå or Ira or whomever is listening let this one go."

Faust held Boatman's stare. "You're asking me like I have access to their deranged thoughts."

"I am, aren't I?"

Faust didn't say anything. Boatman thought about saying something else but the crackle of the guards' batons made him reconsider and in a moment the doors buzzed shut. And Faust breathed out.

Chapter 21: Slippery

Aská settled in his office and fired up his computer. He had two screens on his desk and a giant screen on the wall facing him. His office chair wasn't one of comfort. It was handmade out of oak from Britannia and built to be able to accommodate his size, but also deliberately made to be uncomfortable. Aská had an identical chair built for his outbuilding, which Boatman and Faust were the current occupants of. For Aská, the point of the chairs was to remind him that he could never be comfortable, because if he ever got comfortable then that was when he would potentially get sloppy and complacent. In a world where he was on the verge of ruling it, he was not going to get complacent. The chairs were so heavy it took three men to carry them and so uncomfortable a normal person could only spend a few minutes sitting in it before getting a backache. Aská liked the pain though, as it focused his mind and kept him sharp. Because, for Aská, the pain meant he didn't switch off and was always focused on any potential threats. And it also meant that when he was in his office and speaking with his allies and enemies he never relaxed and therefore saw through any lies.

Aská placed a call and it started to connect on the big screen on the office wall. In a few rings, Grand Senator Frigus answered. "Good afternoon, Lord Askå."

"Afternoon, my dear Senator."

"How are my newest assets coming along?"

"They're learning. Fast," said Askå.

"Fast enough?"

"They'll be ready when you asked for them. There's no need to doubt my ability to get them ready. Your predecessors would never dare to micromanage me, Frigus."

"Clearly I'm not my predecessors, am I?" Frigus took a sip of a drink he had on his desk. "Because I'm still alive."

Askå laughed. "You found a pair of balls, Senator! I'm impressed. Tell me, would you be so brave if we were face to face?"

Frigus didn't stutter. "If we're ever face to face then I would like to think it's because politics has overcome barbarism and you're on a crucifix."

"The irony of those words, Senator," laughed Askå.

"The only way for a system to change is from the inside and excuse me if I take some delight in that transition."

"Transition. You thinking of usurping your Caesar?"

"Not at all. But even Caesars understand the need for change to ensure their empire survives," said Frigus.

"How is Emperor Maximus? I note his usual egotistical propaganda monologues haven't been aired recently. I'm missing his robotic voice to put me to sleep," said Askå.

"The Emperor sends his regards, but is focusing on restructuring the leadership throughout the Empire with the Grand Protector missing and presumed either dead or a traitor. And, incidentally, you know nothing about that?"

"My dear Frigus, how very hurtful of you to suggest such a thing."

"You did plant explosives in the Colosseum, it would be obvious for me to think you're behind Faust's disappearance." Frigus sighed. "Some within the senate are incessant over the fact we're still doing business with you."

"Ah, you see, that's the key word, isn't it? Business. Without my business you would be poorer."

Frigus frowned. "But you sabotaged a good relationship."

"Relationship?" Aska laughed, hard. "Relationship? There's no relationship. Only transactions. And I saw an opportunity to improve my business opportunities by ensuring the greatest rebel leader in a generation and arguably the greatest gladiator of all time stayed alive. Because, dear Frigus, them being alive is much more financially beneficial to all of us than some petty desire to kill."

"Judging by Caesar's condition, I would say it's much more than a petty desire," said Frigus.

"Judging by Caesar's little temper tantrums, I would say petty is his legacy," said Aska.

"I would be careful of your words, Bjorn. We have been more than forgiving after your actions recently."

"And yet here we are, still doing business. How about, instead of empty threats, you tell your Caesar that if he wants to keep ruling the world, then he needs my gladiators and the information I'm getting from various sources. If he was too short-sighted to see that having Boatman and Maverick fight to the death was a terrible fucking idea, then that's his problem, not mine. But, regardless, please pass on my best wishes to Maximus as I need something decent to fall asleep to."

Frigus bristled, but the diplomat he was raised to be took control. "I will of course pass on your wishes."

Aska wasn't feeling diplomatic, though. "How's your daughter by the way?"

"I'll hear from you when the gladiators are ready," said Frigus, not taking the bait, and cut the call.

Aská smiled. He enjoyed the pain he saw in Frigus's eyes. And he enjoyed the fact that the Grand Senator didn't know where his daughter was. Alypia was the Senator's daughter and Faust's wife. Aská had seen her getting shot back in London, and then a few moments later, saw the whole tunnel network that Alypia was in with other rebels explode. It appeared Alypia and her captors (or allies, Aská wasn't sure) died in the explosion, but Bjorn never made assumptions. He'd made that mistake too many times before when he thought he'd managed to manipulate the Empire. If Alypia was alive, then it meant Maverick was alive, and that excited him. It was quiet, though. Maverick operated on vengeance and retribution and if he had survived the explosion he would have appeared in Aestii by now. Not only would he have appeared to hunt Aská down for the explosion, he would have done anything to rescue Boatman. Maverick adored having a leader so he knew he would be raging about Boatman's treatment. But as the weeks went by, Aská guessed Maverick was dead. Maverick didn't sit on revenge, he went straight for the jugular. Again, the signs indicated Maverick and his rebel friends had perished, but he wasn't going to assume. He stayed in his chair a little longer, to really work his back and remind him the weakness of complacency.

After another twenty minutes of pain, Aská was about to get off his chair when a video call came through. It was encrypted, so Aská knew immediately who it was. He answered the call, "Good morning, Omaha. You're up early."

"Politics never stop."

"Indeed. And what politics do you need me for?"

Omaha cleared his throat. "I've been gathering intel for months now, so wanted to be sure, but it appears the rebellion in London had been exterminated. You did what the Romans couldn't."

Askå grinned. "Oh really? How coincidental. I was just thinking about that. How can you be sure?"

"Empire channels haven't reported anyone of interest coming out of London or trying to escape Britannia," said Omaha.

"I'll concede, I've heard nothing too." Askå put his hands through his hair and adjusted his ponytail. "And you haven't had any asylum requests?"

"We're very wary of any asylum requests connected to rebellion activities. And we certainly haven't had any of those. We tend to deal with many more from the Aestii region," said Omaha.

"And I'm grateful for you providing safe keeping for those cowards. Saves the expense of hunting them down."

"You don't hunt them down because we pay you," said Omaha.

"Like I said, it saves me any expense of hunting them down."

The 35 had never resented taking in refugees from the Aestii region and they certainly didn't regret paying Askå. Although Askå thought he was somehow extorting the 35 in exchange for his benevolence, the 35 were actually happy to pay because the benefits those who came from Aestii brought were immeasurable relative to what Askå thought was a good price on their heads. The 35 saw that people who escaped a country in fear were passionate about giving their country of solace all the skills they could offer. And the rewards financially and socially were the reason why the RIA flourished.

Askå cricked his neck. "So, apart from telling me the good news about the rebellion, what pleasure are you calling me for?"

"We're concerned about your intentions for Rome."

"My intentions? And what would you know about my intentions?"

Omaha breathed deeply. "After your antics at the Britannia Colosseum it's clear you're trying to unsettle the establishment in Rome."

"I think that's always been clear, my dear Omaha."

"Even so, my dear Askå, you're clearly making a move and I thought we agreed you would wait."

"Wait for what? The implosion of the Empire or the death of the Emperor? Because both are on the verge," said Askå.

"We have to choose the right time. We agreed that the natural death of Maximus is the most logical timeline, and after his death, we can install a new power structure. You saw the polling," said Omaha.

"Ah yes, the polling. I seem to remember Faust polling very well and now he's missing."

Omaha knew he had to tread carefully. "And I assume you don't know anything about that?"

"I know a missing man doesn't poll so well," said Askå. "And I do seem to remember you being with him in London just before he went missing."

"The 35 don't do abductions or assassinations," said Omaha. "Which I think is quite the opposite of your policies."

"Is there a full moon because it seems everyone today believes they can disrespect me without any consequence," said Askå.

"There's no disrespect, Lord Askå. It's a simple stating of facts. You are making a move and it's important we know your intentions. After all, we provide you with a rather generous allowance.

"You provide me with a generous allowance? Don't patronise me, Omaha. I do well enough without you."

"But you do even better with us," said Omaha. And he knew he was right. He didn't know what Askå's financial situation was but he was receiving reports of Aestii operatives abandoning provinces, so although he didn't know how financially stable Askå was, he knew Askå was moving his pieces regardless. He wasn't going to get information out of Askå, but he did still need to ensure the psychopath was on his side, so he changed tack. "And we also do well out of you. I'm not here to bust your balls, Bjorn, but over the years we have worked amicably and it's been beneficial to both our kingdoms staying independent."

"I remember meeting Emperor Nero a few years ago. He wasn't the slightest bit intimidated by me. Even when we stood face to face. It was like I literally meant nothing to him. Fascinating man. Complete lunatic, but fascinating nonetheless. I recall the only conversation we ever had and he asked me some probing questions about my allegiance to him. I managed to answer diplomatically and he called me slippery with my response. Apparently he liked referring to people as that. He liked the imagery of an eel. But I say that because your response just then would have been classed as slippery by Nero. I'm not so sure your desire for amicable relations is your motivation."

"I stand by what I said," said Omaha with a smile.

Askå smiled too. "It's good speaking with you." Askå cut the call.

Askå was suspicious of Omaha's assertion that none of the rebels had survived and opened up a video which had been sent to him. It was CCTV footage of when Askå had been in London. Askå had done a flying visit into London to grab Boatman and Faust. To achieve abducting them, though, he'd had to travel into the underground network. The mission was a success and Askå decided to ensure no-one would follow and try to rescue Boatman, so he instructed his team to burn the underground tunnels. Igniting a fire in the tunnel network meant no escape and as Askå watched the CCTV footage he saw why, as an explosion tore through the tunnels and fire and smoke erupted from the entrance to the tunnels. It was caused by a backdraft, which was likely because rebels had opened a door. Although Askå was happy with the footage, he kept watching. Patiently. Thirty minutes after the explosion, and after Askå and his team had escaped with Faust and Boatman, Askå saw something curious. A figure appeared through the smoke. It was grainy and hard to make out who it was, but the figure, it seemed, pulled out a phone and made a call. Askå paused the footage. He had no real way of telling who it was, but it confirmed one thing for him: someone survived. And if someone survived, the rebellion was still in play.

"Like I said, very slippery of you, Omaha," Askå said to himself.

Chapter 22: Belle of the Empire

"How are you feeling?"

"It still aches at night, but I'll live," said Alypia.

Bella kissed Alypia and said, "Do you miss it?"

Alypia was lying on the grass out the back of the house they were staying in, courtesy of the RIA. "Miss what?"

Bella was lying next to her. "Being the belle of the Empire?" Alypia laughed at the question, but in a genuine and amused way. Bella adored the sound. She also realised how little laughter she heard in recent years. Everything and everyone were so serious and laughter seemed almost forbidden.

"'The belle of the Empire', hey? I've never heard that one before. The bitch of Rome was used plenty of times behind my back."

"Who by?"

Alypia had her arm over her eyes, shielding from the sun, and waved her hand dismissively. "Anyone and everyone. Especially in the higher ranks of Rome."

"Jealousy?" Bella said.

"Maybe. Most of the time saying shitty things was a natural element to being in the establishment of Rome. Praise you to your face and sell a story to the press with some awful rumour behind your back," said Alypia.

"Did that happen often?"

"Weekly. Most of what was printed about me or mused about me on some late-night gossip show, was that: gossip. Augustus used to go mad and try to bring some sort of punishment against the lies, but no-one listened to him. He was just a Centurion back then. A respected and famous Centurion, but ultimately a foot soldier that the Senate praised but ignored."

"But what about your father?"

Alypia scoffed. "My father has always put Rome before his family. To the outside world he's always looked like a loving, doting father, but he never really cared about me. I don't particularly remember him when I was a child. His path to senate glory always came first. He was always up before dawn and home after I had gone to bed. If you asked me for a memory of my father, when I was a child, I would struggle to give you one."

"But all the shows I watched and all the articles I read about you being proud of your father? Of the legacy your father has built as the Grand Senator? I remember reading an interview with you where you spoke passionately about the work your father was doing in Rome and maybe you would follow in his footsteps," said Bella.

Alypia laughed, but this time it wasn't a pleasant sound and it wasn't a laugh that warmed her soul. "When you're on the cover of every magazine and when you're seen as not only an ambassador for women, but an example of a strong family unit, and you know what you say has very significant consequences, so of course I'll talk about my father like he's some sort of hero."

Bella turned on to her side and held Alypia's hand. "Not to be devil's advocate, but surely some of that was him working so hard to provide for you?"

Alypia tightened her grip on Bella's hand but stayed flat on her back with her other arm covering her face from the sun. "One of my most vivid memories from when I was a child was how hungry I was. It was strange because we had plenty of money, or so I believed from where we lived and the many, many people who were our staff. So I remember not being confused by being hungry, because as a child what you have in front of you is normal. Why question normality, right? So there was no sense of confusion or injustice around, but the plain fact that I was always so hungry. I simply wasn't fed enough. And there were no regular meal times where, as a family, we would sit together and eat, so meals came when it fit around when someone remembered to feed me. And that was made stark, when I look back now, by the fact that when I was at school I would scrounge for food. The most telling moment for me, now, was during break times between classes when I was only seven or eight years old. Before my father became a Senator of Rome we lived in a coastal village a few miles west of Rome. My school was near the water and it was quite beautiful to grow up in such a place. What sticks with me though, is how being in a coastal village meant there were lots of seagulls. Big, big gulls that were always looking for food. They would circle the school hoping for scraps from the children and I noticed them because I saw them as a threat to my own sustenance."

Bella squeezed Alypia's hand and said, "Sorry, I've lost you. What do you mean?"

"Bella, I was so hungry as a child, when it was break time I would pick food off the playground floor and eat it."

Bella's eyes widened. "Of course you didn't. You must be remembering wrong."

"I'm not."

"But that's so awful, Alypia. You were raised in a rich household. I don't understand how you were so hungry you were doing that."

Alypia teared up a little, she rubbed her eyes. "It sounds crazy, I know. It sounds like I'm making it up. But, Bella, I'm not. Nothing meant more in my household than work and public perception. And I can't even explain it, all these years later, but I remember the hunger and I remember picking food off the playground floor before gulls got to it, and I remember it feeling completely normal." Alypia rubbed her eyes again, trying to keep back the emotion. "Sorry," she said and got to her feet and went to the bathroom.

When she returned from the bathroom, Alypia managed a smile and said to Bella, "Sorry, I didn't mean to share so much."

"You don't need to apologise. And you can never share too much with me."

"We'll see. The hunger story is only tip of the iceberg."

Bella laughed but stopped quickly. "By the gods, you're not joking."

It was Alypia's turn to laugh and Bella felt relief that it was a genuine laugh. "I'm afraid not. If you can face it, there's a lot more stories where that came from."

"If it's cathartic for you, I will always listen," said Bella.

Alypia cuddled up to Bella and thanked her. Alypia wasn't sure how much she wanted to share as it was hard for her to be too vulnerable. She felt something so deep for Bella that she couldn't help but follow the path her heart was taking her, but the voice niggling at the back of her mind was one questioning Bella's loyalty. Could Bella be trusted? Only a few months ago Alypia was in London and having an affair with Bella. She'd met Bella in one of her favourite restaurants in the city and although Alypia had never really analysed how she felt about women, in regard to sexual attraction, Bella had grabbed her attention one evening. Bella had made her feel seen which, Alypia thought, was something she hadn't felt in a very long time. Sharing her story of hunger with Bella reminded her that she was so invisible as a child, she was picking scraps of food off the schoolyard floor. She felt so invisible as a wife that she was eating lobster in one of the finest restaurants in London and this time was searching for emotional scraps, which Bella provided. It was no surprise, now Alypia looked back, that she was magnetised to Bella. And now she knew so much more, it was no surprise that Bella was assigned as the one to infiltrate Alypia's life.

Alypia had fled from Bella when Bella revealed she was a rebel and needed information about Rome's plans for London. Bella hadn't wanted to reveal her identity to Alypia, but Boatman had forced the situation, saying that time had run out. The hate Alypia initially felt for Bella's betrayal was immense, but what came in the following weeks shocked her. Alypia had returned to her husband who, although one of the most intelligent men in Rome, failed to pick up on his wife's infidelities. Often Alypia would leave Faust for a time, angry at his neglect of her, only to return when the questions about her whereabouts became too loud.

For Alypia, the questions from the press weren't the main reason for her returning to her husband. It bothered her because it had been drilled into her since she was a child to have a good public persona, but no, the main motivation behind her always going back to him was that she felt guilty. Faust, she was sure, loved her. He did. She knew he would always protect her and provide for her, but he easily forgot about her, too. Other things in his life would take priority and she would become an afterthought. Just like the way her father treated her. And she knew, when she thought about it all, she must have subconsciously chosen Faust because of the similarities he shared with her father. Even so, she felt guilty because she thought that maybe she wasn't trying hard enough with him, and needed to show him more affection and more understanding about his job and what he was doing. Of course, it never transpired like that and all the fawning in the world didn't change Faust's (or her father's) level of attention.

Alypia had also been conditioned to view the rebels as scum of the earth. They appeared to be doing everything to create unease and never did anything to bring unity. All she heard about in rants from Faust at breakfast or broken conversations of Centurions whilst they drank wine at her house in London, was death and destruction from the rebels. She heard of when Maverick and Tobias tore through a young legion, leaving one man with his jaw torn off and another man with more bones broken than intact. She heard about a time when Boatman destroyed a house with a Roman family in it. So, for Alypia, she had little sympathy for the rebellion and when Bella revealed she was a part of the rebellion, it made her feel sick. So sick she had to leave Bella with the idea of never seeing her again, because surely she couldn't be with someone who was part of that terrorist outfit?

But she couldn't stop thinking about Bella. And she couldn't stop thinking about how Bella made her feel seen. And if this woman made her feel seen. And loved. And cared for. Then maybe this woman wasn't part of something so heinous. Because Faust was still coming home, sometimes covered in blood and talking to people on the phone about how some crucifixions took longer than he was happy with, which was clogging up the execution list. And sometimes Faust would talk on the phone about how he wished there was a method to execute lots of people at once like his uncle used to talk about. And then it made Alypia wonder where the right side of history was and then she thought about Bella's soft laugh and sweet touch and it made her think she had been mistaken again.

She had been mistaken throughout her childhood about her own worth. As a child it is easy to think you are worth a damn. You are discovering your identity and abilities and when you realise you can do something, that you think is pretty cool, you want to tell the world. "Look at me, Daddy," as you jump off a step. "Look at me, Mummy," as you twirl in a circle for the first time. It's liberating and exciting to discover your abilities. For Alypia, she had staff who would praise her as a child, so her worth was manufactured. As she analysed her past, she realised her parents were never there to praise her for her talents and achievements. And when she announced her achievements, the praise never came because it was seen as boasting. She never stopped believing in herself as she grew up because, like she had seen so much in her life, like being so hungry, it was normal not to be praised by your parents. That was part of what it took to grow up as a strong woman.

But, now she was a woman and she saw the brutality of the world around her, she saw that praise and validation were part of what kept you sane. She saw that edification meant a difference between believing you can do something and then trying to do that thing you believed in. She saw that encouragement went a very long way to growing from a child of hope into an adult of action. And she saw how the child of hope who she was never became the adult of action.

People would have mocked Alypia for saying she never became an adult of action as one of the most famous people in the world, but her fame and fortune came from nepotism and narcissism and those were not things of encouragement or belief. They were things of fawning and side doors being opened. For a moment, Alypia had looked at Bella in the same way: someone accessing her because of what she was, as opposed to who she was. Something beyond that stuck with her though, because she was unable to shake the feeling that Bella, dear, sweet Bella, was actually infatuated and looked at Alypia as Alypia. This was something Alypia had rarely experienced so she saw it starkly, as when the sun bursts from behind a cloud. She saw it so much like that, she couldn't shake her mind from that of Bella and had to see her again. She had to see her in spite of who Bella was; a traitor. But that didn't distract her. Bella was like a drug and she needed another fix. And when she got that fix she decided she would have to be dealt that fix for the rest of her life.

Bella pulled Alypia back to the present. "What about your mother?"

"Maybe we should start on an easier subject and leave that to when we've had a few bottles of wine."

Bella leaned in and kissed Alypia. "Maybe we should have some wine anyway." Alypia nodded and they both left the garden and went to the kitchen to see what was in the fridge. As Alypia was opening a bottle of RIA sparkling wine, Bella's phone chimed. She answered it and it was Maverick. "Hey, Mav, you okay?"

"Boatman's alive. And so is Faust. Meet outside in ten minutes." The line went dead.

Bella stared at the phone and then Alypia brought Bella back to reality. "You okay? What did Maverick want?"

"I think we need to drink that bottle fast," said Bella.

Chapter 23: A Hunch

"How do you know Boatman's alive?"

"It's a hunch," said Maverick.

"You made it sound like you were sure," said Bella.

"I am sure."

"You just said it was a hunch, so you need to make up your mind."

"My hunches are as good as knowing for a fact," said Maverick.

"I love my partner, he's so modest," said Tobias.

Bella ignored Tobias's comment, "Can you be more specific about your hunch?"

"We've been watching Olivia and her new friend."

"Not in a creepy way," said Tobias.

Maverick turned to his partner. "Why did you need to add that point, Tobias?"

"Because it sounds creepy with the way you say it. Diplomacy isn't your strong suit."

"My strong suit is putting my foot up your ass," said Maverick.

"Like I said, diplomacy isn't your thing."

Maverick went a little red in the face and said, "Look, we've been monitoring what's been happening between Olivia and her new friend, because I'm certain the 35 are using Olivia for information."

"That goes without saying," said Bella. "We've come closer to dismantling Rome's power structures than anyone. They would obviously think Olivia has something of use to them."

"But why not ask her outright?" Maverick said.

"How do you know they haven't? Have you asked Olivia?"

"The last conversation I had with Olivia didn't go down well."

"As I was saying, my boyfriend, the great diplomat," said Tobias. Before Maverick could go a deeper shade of red, Tobias continued, "We're pretty sure Olivia has been sharing innocent information with her new friend. And there's no reason to think that's a problem. After all, the RIA has provided us with refuge and it's no secret what they think of Rome. It's just that it appears there's some frantic activity going on around the 35's headquarters and we saw Olivia go there. It seems like there's an urgency, which makes Maverick think something else is going on, like Olivia's information is immediately vital. Which means it's possible Boatman is alive and therefore they're looking for a way to retrieve him."

"That's quite a leap," said Bella.

"Not really," said Maverick. "The RIA is fortified. Any attempts at invasion have been futile. If they wanted information from Olivia to simply continue adding to their intelligence on Rome, they would garner that bit by bit over as long as it takes. There's no immediate threat from Rome, especially after London's antics with Askå and trying to contain that. But this urgency from them means they're thinking of doing something in the immediate. I'm sure of it."

"Why do you think that means my husband is also alive?" Alypia said.

"That doesn't," said Maverick, "But I spent time with Askå, he takes pleasure in people like Faust. He would want to drag that pleasure out."

"I'm not sure how I should feel about that," said Alypia.

"You shouldn't have to feel anything," said Maverick, "At the moment I have a strong hunch, but what we do next is a big unknown."

"I would think the next thing we do is see if we can get a meeting with Omaha and find out what's going on," said Bella.

"Will he see us? I haven't seen him once since we arrived. It's like we've been settled and that's it for us."

"Not at all." Everyone turned around to where the voice was coming from. It was Omaha.

"Now that's creepy," said Tobias.

Maverick bristled and stepped towards Omaha. "Have you been following us?"

"Of course," said Omaha, "And you would be naive and a little stupid to think we weren't. You're the famous London rebels!"

"He's got a point," said Tobias and he put his hand on Maverick's shoulder. Maverick allowed his shoulders to relax, just a little. "You could have just asked."

Omaha smiled. "And I'm sure you would have told me everything I wanted to know. All your tactics and methods for causing Rome such a headache all these years."

"Again, he's got a point," said Tobias.

"But you're right, Maverick, we do think Boatman and Faust are alive and it's time to ask for your help to plan our next steps, as both men are vital to finally breaking Rome's back."

"What do you want from us?"

"The 35 would like you to come and meet with us tomorrow morning and we'll explain all."

"What about Olivia?" Tobias said.

Omaha had already started to walk away and didn't stop. "Her role is, shall we say, a little more complicated." Omaha didn't give any of the group a chance to ask him to elaborate.

"Well that was suitably cryptic," said Tobias. "I don't know about you, but I need a drink."

The group made their way back to Mav and Tobias's house and spent the evening theorising what the next steps could be, but always coming to the conclusion that their cosy time in the RIA was most certainly coming to an end.

Chapter 24: Olivia and the 35

Indeed, Olivia had been to see the 35. She had met Newen at the entrance to the building in the morning and been led into their chambers. The headquarters of the 35 was surprising to Olivia. She assumed she would walk into something reminiscent of the Roman's headquarters in London, the HoC. There, it was a constant bustle of people. On occasion she had been to the HoC to provide counselling to officers if they weren't able to get to her place of work on time. Whenever she signed herself in it was surrounded by soldiers and civil staff arguing and rushing around, trying to get control. She knew her husband was part of why everyone seemed so harassed most of the time, but it didn't, in her mind, change from the fact that the disorganisation at the grass-roots level originated from the very top. She was consistently amazed at how successful the Empire was considering its unhinged leadership in Rome.

The 35's headquarters, though, was a place of serenity. And hardly anyone was around. They walked into the foyer where they were greeted by reception and then another person escorted them though some double doors, down a corridor which had numerous doors on each side. At the end of the corridor, double doors opened to reveal an elevator. Olivia and Newen stepped in and the doors closed. They travelled up ten floors and the doors opened not onto a corridor but onto an expansive room.

Olivia walked out of the elevator and was met with an impressive sight. The room she had walked into was circular and had enough space to seat two hundred people, with room for standing. The walls were lined in dark wood and there were semicircular desks, also made of dark wood, scattered about the room. When the 35 were questioned about how apparently random the desks were, they always replied that leadership wasn't formulaic but best when apparently out of sync, which is why their room for meeting looked out of sync too. The roof of the building was the most impressive thing to see. It was a glass dome which was slightly hazy, to stop direct sun light but allow a wonderful, uninterrupted view of the sky. Newen informed Olivia that at nighttime the dome gave a stunning view of the night sky, with stars as far as the eye could see.

Olivia had wondered if the 35 were actually thirty-five people, and it appeared their name was based on something that simple. Omaha saw Olivia and Newen and crossed the room to greet them. "Good morning, Olivia. Thank you for taking the time to speak with us."

"I'm not sure what I can offer you," said Olivia.

"It's not about exchanging of goods, Olivia, like you're giving us something. It's more about how we think you will be able to help save some lives."

"Whose lives?"

Omaha breathed out. "Hopefully, your husband's."

Olivia felt her heart in her chest. She was convinced people would be able to see it beating. "Boatman's alive?"

"We think so. He's too valuable to kill." Omaha rubbed his eyes. "Sorry, Olivia, but Boatman is no longer a thorn in the Empire's side but a pawn in Askå's game. As a pawn we can get him removed from the game without too much damage, but we will need you to convince Askå that it will be okay. We need you to somehow get him to give Boatman up."

"Shall I flash my tits?" Olivia said. "By the gods, you men, with all your wrangling and self-assurance, you need me to wink and flirt with a man to save the world?"

"You think poorly of us, Olivia," said Omaha, "In spite of our hospitality?"

Olivia laughed that dry and humourless laugh again. "I should be groping at the hem of your garment for having a place to stay?"

"That's not what I meant."

"Then what did you mean? I'm not grateful? I remember what not being grateful meant in the eyes of Maximus."

Omaha blushed. "I'm not a misogynist, Olivia, and I'm not someone who sees you as a token to get us what we want, but I am an opportunist and you know full well that, regardless of your gender, we are in a position where we might have a way to make an avenue to save your husband."

"But what does that mean to me? I still grope all you men for appreciation? I thank you for allowing me to be here? And then you decide I have to show my thanks by asking a psychopath to spare my husband? It's so messed up. All of the time."

"We need to find a way to save Boatman. Why not you?"

"Because saving Boatman isn't my responsibility."

"You're his wife."

"And that makes me his saviour?"

"No, but at least his guardian," said Omaha.

"Really? And when was Boatman my guardian whilst I was being raped?"

"I can't comment on that."

"But you can comment on my perceived role in this, even though I didn't choose it," said Olivia.

"We don't know for sure, but we believe Askå is moving pieces to come for us."

"That's what you get for making your bed with the devil."

"You might be right," said Omaha, "but the devil has been useful to us for many years."

"But now you're panicking and out of ideas."

Omaha clenched his jaw. "We're not panicking, but we see a way forward with saving Boatman and keeping Askå at bay."

Olivia laughed. "You really think Askå will simply give up my husband because I flash him a smile? Are you really that naive?"

"No, we're not being naive. Askå sent one of his closest friends to the RIA to spy on us, but we caught him and imprisoned him. We're willing to do an exchange."

"Why do you need me for that?" Olivia was confused about why the 35, with all their diplomatic power, would ask her.

Omaha blushed again. "Look, we need to be honest with you. Since capturing Askå's spy, he has revealed various things about the giant and one thing is that Askå had, shall we say, a rather unorthodox relationship with his mother."

"So?"

"You have a rather uncanny resemblance to her. If he saw you and you offered an exchange we think it would throw him enough to agree."

Olivia shook her head. "That's messed up."

"We know," said Omaha. "But we think it might be the best

chance we have at rescuing your husband." Omaha looked around the room. The 35 were standing around, listening. "We have enjoyed safety and security for a millennia, but if Aská manages to align himself with Rome, or worse, we could find it difficult to stop him. I'm not going to underplay this. Boatman is a force to be reckoned with. He destabilised an Empire and killed an emperor. We need him. And we think you can help us achieve that goal."

Olivia sat down. "I've been face to face with enough monsters, I'm not sure I want to face another."

Newen crouched down next to Olivia. "You'll have me close by. If it's too much we will cut the call."

"I need to think about it," said Olivia. Newen looked up at Omaha and he nodded at Newen.

"No problem," said Newen. "Sleep on it."

Chapter 25: Olivia's Guilt

Olivia and Newen walked back to her house. Olivia was in a daze. She was processing the thought of potentially speaking to Askå to try and save her husband's life but it felt out of body and not part of her lived experience. She thought that maybe she was viewing everything through the lens of another person, like an unconnected observer. Like a voyeur sitting in a darkened cinema watching events play out on the big screen. She had become detached from herself and it felt unreal to be thinking about her husband because her husband had become so unreal to her.

After she had been abducted and abused by Maximus Nero, Olivia had never been able to shake, not a feeling but a rage of injustice caused by her husband. She had argued with Boatman, countless times, that his dogmatic approach to everything in his life would be his downfall, but most likely not his direct downfall but the shrapnel flying from his actions impacting those around him. And she, Olivia, surmised, would be the one caught by the biggest shrapnel. And she was right, because in Boatman's unrelenting desire to shatter Rome's throne, he forgot about those not on that throne, and Maximus breezed into London, sought out Olivia and almost killed her. Boatman failed to see the threat, promising her exposure wasn't possible and any worries were paranoia, and yet, now she regularly felt her skin graft, from where she was crucified, itch or swell in the heat. No, there was no paranoia, only knowledge that Boatman's vendetta caused her chaos and Boatman an unjustified path of revenge, because he was the reason she had almost died.

Olivia was confounded by guilt because she wanted to save her husband, because that's what a wife should do, but she didn't want to save her husband out of love. No, all the sacrifices she had made in her life, to support his freedom fight, had ended her freedom, and also ended his. She resented Boatman for causing so much chaos and yet never resolving any of it. Her peace was coming not from something Boatman had done but something Boatman had not done. Boatman had not killed Maximus, she had. Boatman had not found her a way out of London, Omaha had. No, Boatman wasn't present when she needed salvation again. Now she was in a place she found comforting and peaceful and with a person who seemed to respect her need for calm.

And that's where more guilt came from. She liked Newen. A lot. They had lovely dog walks. Wicker was a beautiful dog, so free and friendly. It was strange for her because she had spent so much time underground or on the run that to do something so mundane as walking a dog was as alien to her as Newen would have found life in London. It was soothing for her soul, though, to walk through the woods, being able to listen to the birds chirrup and the leaves rustle. It was wonderful and it made her feel like she could be healed and live out of the shadow of her trauma. Being in Boatman's presence always reminded her of her trauma and of the abuse she went through. Outside of that, away from that, in a world so unrelated to that, she found she was content. And so when the 35 asked her to save her husband, it wasn't because she was afraid of Askå that caused her anxiety to spike, but the fact that her husband was the epitome of all the pain she had been through. To be away from him was to avoid the toxicity that he represented and this is what she told Newen.

"It's like he's the one who crucified me," said Olivia.

"Surely not," said Newen. They were sitting in Olivia's garden, sharing a bottle of white wine.

"I know it sounds harsh, but everything, for years, has always been about Boatman's crusade. When the shit hit the fan and the people he claimed to be fighting for were the ones most hurt, well, yeah, it felt like he was the one doing the torture."

"Did you tell him?"

"Have you been married, Newen?"

"Yes. We were young. She wanted children. I wanted a dog."

"How did those honest conversations about what you wanted go?"

"They didn't. I got a dog and she got a divorce," said Newen.

"You know what it's like not to speak honestly with the person you're married to, then?"

"I know that I didn't have the courage to say how I felt. So leaving things unsaid made a wall between us."

Olivia sipped her wine and blinked hard, remembering something. "I remember, when I was in the medical wing, after Maverick and Tobias had saved me, how I was trying to focus on not having a panic attack about even being alive. It's funny when you almost die and believe you will die, it becomes traumatic to then survive. It's like you have reconciled yourself to death and then death is torn away from you, leaving another scar. You're scarred in life and death. But I'm lying there, in the medical wing, trying not to have an anxiety attack over the fact that I can hear myself breathing when Boatman walked in. He walked in and kissed me on the forehead. It was a simple gesture but made me feel sick. It made me feel sick because at no point did he question whether he should do it. He arrogantly walked into the room without knocking and kissed me. I had been raped and crucified and he didn't even take a breath to wonder if any of that would impact how I would feel being physically touched so soon after such an event."

"To be devil's advocate, surely your husband only did what was natural."

"Maybe he did, but I can't help thinking about how natural to Boatman it was to never think about others."

"And you don't think he ever thought about you."

Olivia nodded. "And I reached a point where I didn't know how to ask him if he did." Olivia felt her bottom lip go. She was exhausted from grieving her relationship with Boatman. She struggled to remember the moments when she had felt that giddy excitement of new love. All she remembered now was pain. Newen held her hand and electricity seemed to come from it. She looked at Newen and saw a pain in his eyes. An empathy to her suffering. It was strange for her because she struggled to remember when someone looked at her with empathy. Boatman looked at her with pity or an objective calculation. That was who Boatman was. When they first met she remembered the ferocious passion he had and how his eyes were, in the most cliché way, a gateway to his soul. And she saw an integrity and gorgeous pathway to love. But then the obsession with the Empire, the hatred that he felt for Rome, it overwhelmed him and became his true love. He no longer looked at Olivia with ferocious love, but looked at footage of Nero with obsessive ferocity which, Olivia felt, bordered on being besotted.

She remembered the day Boatman killed Nero, and it was disturbing for Olivia, not because of the death, but because of how upbeat Boatman was to begin with and then the next day it was like he was grieving the emperor. It disturbed her now to think about how her husband appeared to grieve the man he had murdered. And when she tried to talk to him about it, he closed down even further. She had no idea what he was thinking, but knowing her husband enough, she saw a sadness in those eyes she knew so well, and that sadness was more prominent than when he looked at her when she was in hospital after being attacked by Nero's son.

But now she was looking into the eyes of a man who was hurting because she was hurting. It made her body move before her brain could engage, and she was kissing Newen without thinking about what that even meant. And the kiss was good. And the kiss felt right. And then she felt guilty. She pulled away from Newen and he said, "I'm sorry, that wasn't appropriate."

"You don't need to say sorry, I kissed you."

"But I could have stopped you," said Newen.

"Honestly, you don't need to apologise, I wanted to kiss you. But I shouldn't have. I have a husband."

"Who I'm trying to convince you to try and save."

Olivia laughed and this time it was a laugh with humour. "How messed up does that sound?"

Newen shifted how he was sitting so he could face Olivia. "Look, Olivia, I obviously like you. I've never given Wicker so many walks."

"And I've never had so many walks. I don't even like walking." Olivia laughed again

"I assumed you liked walking."

"Well you can't read people very well, then," Olivia said.

Newen laughed this time. "Clearly. And let me guess, you don't even like dogs."

Olivia shook her head. "I love dogs. Humanity doesn't deserve dogs. There was a beautiful dog in London, called Gordon, who belonged to a homeless man. He would make us laugh because his owner, Mikey, could make Gordon, on command dry hump any solider that went past them. Gordon was soppy and loving but seemed to know that Roman soldiers weren't right, so would hump them, making them so uncomfortable they would leave Mikey alone."

"Weren't you worried the soldiers would kill the dog?"

Olivia thought about it. "Not really. There weren't many soldiers capable of killing a dog in cold blood."

"They killed plenty of people in cold blood."

"I guess it seems worse killing a dog," said Olivia. "Like I said, we don't deserve dogs. And Wicker is proof of that."

"He is my best friend," said Newen.

"Well if Wicker likes you then I guess my judge in character isn't too bad."

"I wouldn't trust Wicker's judgement too much. After all, I kissed a married woman."

Olivia's face darkened and Newen apologised for the crass joke.

"Please, don't apologise." She reached out and took Newen's hands in hers, her thumb stroking his. "I enjoyed the kiss. And I want to kiss you again. But we know the fury that will come if Boatman ever escapes from wherever he is and found out."

"I've only heard rumours about your husband."

"The rumours don't exaggerate enough."

Newen squinted. "C'mon, the rumours about Boatman are almost like he's some sort of demon."

Olivia shrugged.

"He's just a man," said Newen.

"A man who killed an emperor," said Olivia. By the gods, Olivia scolded herself, she always went into some sort of boasting session about Boatman whenever someone mentioned his name when, in fact, she despised all the violence and brutality that he represented. She didn't know why she did it, and she said as much to Newen.

"It's okay," he said, "You've been married a long time."

"But I defend him to others when I don't necessarily even feel he deserves defending."

"Like I said, you've been married a long time." And those words hurt Newen because he'd fallen for Olivia. He'd fallen hard.

Newen saw in Olivia someone who gave newness to life. He saw in her someone who provided hopefulness with pragmatism. Even through all her pain she was someone who radiated healing. It was strange and it was alluring and he was besotted. Olivia snapped him out of his thoughts. "I don't know what this means," said Olivia, "But it's confusing."

"Be as confused as you need to be," said Newen. "Just know that I'm here for you and anything you need." Newen held Olivia's hand. "Anything." He held her hand a little tighter. "And I swear I'm here. You don't have to feel like you're fighting everything on your own. The loneliness in a crowded room doesn't have to apply to you."

Olivia felt her heart beat a little faster. "Thank you," she managed to say. She'd been looking at the floor, unable to meet Newen's eyes. The kiss made her feel guilty and elated at the same time, and it was troubling for her. But now she looked him in the eyes. "I do really appreciate you." Newen nodded, but was astute enough to know there was a 'but' coming. "But," she continued, "I can't be thinking about kissing you when I'm talking to a man who could decide to murder my husband."

Newen said, "I completely agree. I honestly do." He stood up and said, "I'll let the 35 know you're willing to speak to Aska and we'll work out the details so you're as prepared as you can be." Olivia nodded. "Trust me, Olivia, I'll do whatever I can to protect you and make whatever happens next as safe as possible."

"Thanks, Newen," she said.

Newen excused himself, knowing Olivia needed time to process everything, and he also found it bittersweet that he had kissed her and now he wasn't able to kiss her again. He needed to get out of her house, take Wicker for a walk and maybe scream into the forest. For a moment he'd felt unbridled elation as Olivia kissed him, and now he felt pain as she said she couldn't do it again. Newen was a pragmatic person, and had to be considering the work he did for the 35, but even though he was forty, he still had a feeling like he was a teenager and that butterflies-in-the-stomach feeling having kissed Olivia. And he hoped he would be able to kiss her again. But then he thought of Boatman and the myth around the man and wondered what carnage that would bring.

Olivia hadn't moved since Newen left and was still trembling a little after kissing him. She hated herself for doing it but also couldn't help but feel a smile caress her lips at the thought of the kiss. And then she thought of having to try and negotiate her husband's life with a monster, and a tear caressed her cheek. "You fucking idiot," Olivia said to herself, got up and went inside. She was exhausted from the guilt and exhausted from feeling guilty for feeling good.

Chapter 26: Roll the Dice

Olivia sat in front of a laptop, at Omaha's desk inside the 35's HQ. She was in a blank room. No paintings, pictures or any object to give a sense of the personal. No, the room was just empty, apart from a desk and laptop. It was depressing and didn't help Olivia focus any positivity about how to handle the video call. "You'll be okay," said Newen, his voice reverberating in her ear, as if he had read her thoughts. "Askå will scare you with charm. He will speak like he adores you but the words will be menacing."

"You're not bringing me much comfort," said Olivia.

"I think realism, not comfort, is what you need," said Newen.

"I think not doing this is what I need," said Olivia.

"You will be fine. You will have the upper hand, trust me."

"Let's just get this over with," said Olivia. Her anxiety was almost choking her.

"Just press the call button," said Newen.

Olivia tapped the red button on the screen and it initiated a call to Bjorn Askå. It rang and rang and Olivia was about to cut contact but Newen whispered in her ear to wait a bit longer, then the screen went from black to an image of Bjorn Askå. Askå was smiling but when Olivia's face materialised as the call connected, he stopped smiling and, for a moment, looked stunned. On another day Olivia said to her friends that he mouthed the word 'mother', but she couldn't be sure. Aska was adept at adapting and although Olivia's face knocked him off guard he composed himself quickly and said, "Hello my dear. I'm confused, I thought the intriguing Omaha was calling me, but instead it's a rather wonderful vision of beauty."

"Hello, Mr Aska."

"My goodness, I don't know who you are, but you can certainly call me Bjorn"

"Okay. Hello, Bjorn. My name's Olivia."

"Olivia?" Aska then let out a laugh. A booming laugh. "By the gods, the 35 are ruthless bastards."

"What do you mean?"

"Using Boatman's wife to call me? They don't give a damn about who they manipulate." Aska leaned in to the camera. "I assume that's why your face is on the screen? Because they think I have your husband and you'll somehow see him? Am I getting warm?"

"You're warm."

"And what did Omaha say to you about how this conversation should play out? I assume Omaha is lurking in background listening in."

Olivia was married to Boatman King, the man who slayed an emperor and made soldiers talk about him like he was a demon from the underworld, but Aska was terrifying and Olivia found it hard not to speak the truth to him. "He assumed you would be caught off guard by me."

"Oh, really? That is fascinating, dear Olivia. And why would that be?"

"Because I look like your mother."

Askå laughed and it reminded Olivia of herself because of how completely devoid of humour it was. The difference though was that Askå had a disturbing grin through it, so it was unnerving and another layer of terror to Askå's demeanour. "Indeed, you do look like my mother. And my mother was the most beautiful creature to grace this barren earth. And to see you did throw me off. For a moment. But not enough, because when I look at you it reminds me of something my mother used to say to me."

"Which was?"

"She said to me that I can have the world and once I have the world the gods should be scared. And if I'm going to scare the gods, then a little act of psychological trauma isn't going to stop me from getting what I want."

Olivia could feel her anxiety tunnelling through her chest but remained calm. "And what do you want?"

Askå spoke calmly but it was like he was shouting. "Some fucking respect."

Olivia had no response.

"Exactly," said Askå. "Where is the respect? What? You come online, flutter your eyelids at me, evoke some Oedipal longings in me and I just roll over like a horny dog and give you your husband? Is that what the plan was? Is that what the 35 thought would work in saving your husband? How disrespectful is that? And also, whilst we're on disrespect, you're being manipulated by them to try and manipulate me, even though, my dear, I can see you are not someone used to this sort of behaviour."

"So you have my husband?"

"We should stop dancing around each other. After all, you're the one with the courage to speak to me. Your apparent friends in the 35 seem happy to hide behind you."

"Is that a yes?" Olivia asked.

"Indeed it is," said Askå

"Can I speak with him?"

"Oh my dear, of course you can't. I need him focused on the task in hand."

"The task in hand?" Olivia found it strange that Boatman was being controlled by someone else. She'd never known a time in her life where she was genuinely unsure if he would make it out of a situation alive.

"Why, yes. Your beautiful husband is helping me train the next generation of gladiators. I must admit, his teaching skills have a lot to be desired, but he's finding me the next Maverick, so I can't have him getting all smoochy with you on a video call."

"I just want to know he's okay."

"No, you want him home."

"Of course I do. So let him come home."

"Why?" Askå asked.

"Because he's of no use to you."

"Did you not just hear what I said?"

"I heard you say his skills as a gladiator trainer were to be desired." Olivia looked behind her at the door out of the room and thought of Omaha and Newen listening in. She rolled the dice and said, "Instead of wishing for someone to be Maverick or train to be like Maverick, why not have a Maverick?"

"Olivia King, not only do you look like my mother, you are, it seems, as devious as my mother. Throwing The Beast to the wolves, are you?"

"I just want my husband back."

"Do you?"

"Of course," said Olivia.

"What if there was an alternative?"

"To what?"

"Your husband, my dear," said Askå.

"I don't know what you mean."

"Let me phrase it this way: I can offer you your husband. I will pay for his flight over to the RIA once Maverick has been delivered to me. Or?" Askå let the question hang.

"Or what?"

"Or you get Molly instead."

Olivia had been plagued by something for most of her life that resembled bees buzzing through her mind. She had such a strong sense of empathy that when she felt someone's pain or their future pain it was like a buzzing tearing through her brain. When she had first met Molly she had felt Molly's pain and the pain of Molly's mother, who decided to take her own life. It had been a brutal and disturbing journey with Molly. Molly had become like a daughter and Olivia had vowed to herself that she would love and protect Molly as much as she could from the evil of this world. But Olivia felt she had failed. She had failed because Molly had been abducted from Olivia's care when they were trying to escape the Empire and get to the RIA. Someone had taken Molly and Olivia had assumed it was the Empire and had either killed her or thrown her into slavery. Olivia had agonised because she had thought she would feel the buzzing of Molly's pain, but failed to pick up anything. From the days where she wished for the buzzing to stop, when it came to Molly she heard no buzzing at all and cried because it meant either Molly was dead or Olivia had lost all empathy for the girl she had vowed to protect and mother.

And now, here she was hearing words about Molly from a

monster and the desire to save Molly above anyone else, including her husband, caused a clarity in her that was as pristine as glacial water. She didn't not care about Boatman's redemption from Aská, but her primal desire to reunite with Molly and atone for her failings for the girl overtook everything else.

"You're lying," said Olivia.

"My dear, I am many things, but one thing I am not is a liar. Molly is here with me."

"Let me see her."

Aská wagged his finger. "It doesn't work like that. Give me Maverick and once he is in my care, dear Molly will be returned to you."

"Fine, it's a deal."

Aská grinned. "You know, it's a shame really, I will miss the girl. We've become rather close and she even shares some of my appetites."

"I just want her back with me."

"And she will be, oh doppelgänger of my mother, just bring me The Beast." Aská cut the call and Omaha and Newen stormed into the room.

"What the hell was that?" Omaha said.

"What you asked. I'm saving a life."

"That wasn't what we agreed. And you haven't saved a life, you've potentially condemned thousands of lives."

"How?"

"How?" Omaha was incredulous. "If we actually agreed to your 'deal' Aská would have three of the most influential men in the Empire in his custody! It would be like polishing the Caesar's throne and engraving Aská's name on it. Who knows what Faust and your husband have already told the Aestii maniac, but if Maverick was with them, then it would make the RIA highly vulnerable. And you have no right to shift the terms on what we agreed. And there is no way we would agree to this. What use is a young girl to us?"

"It's not *her* use, it's about saving her life."

"Saving her life and sacrificing many others? Of what good is that?"

"We can save her! And you don't know it would cause what you're saying," said Olivia.

"We have enough experience," said Omaha. "The hypothetical gives us that confidence."

"Molly isn't a hypothetical," said Olivia.

"And neither is your husband," said Omaha, "But it seems he is to you." Omaha left the room muttering he needed to consult with the 35.

"That was pretty reckless," said Newen. "And you can't be sure Aska even has Molly.'

"I have to believe he does. I can't live with the thought of having the chance to save Molly and refusing it."

"But saving Boatman would potentially mean a way to save Molly too if we could get rid of Aska completely."

"Don't patronise me," said Olivia, "I know what it means, but Molly is just a little girl. To leave her in the arms of that monster isn't an option."

"But it wasn't an option up to you, Olivia. You're not negotiating on behalf of yourself, you were negotiating on behalf of a country. I can't believe the 35 will agree with that."

"If the 35 choose to leave Molly to her death, then I understand who the 35 truly are," said Olivia.

"They're good people, Olivia, I just think you overstepped. Molly's absolutely important, but there could have been another way." Newen put his arms around Olivia and she didn't resist.

"There's always another way."

"It just doesn't feel like that."

"I know. But sending Maverick to Askå to save Molly feels more like you chose that because of how you feel about Maverick than it does about the situation itself."

"I'm not a bitch."

"I never said you were, but do you really want to give Maverick up to Askå?

"Boatman can look after himself," said Olivia and pulled away from Newen.

"I'm sure he can. And I'm sure he would relish seeing Maverick again. But surely that should be his choice."

"Well when I see him I will see if he wants that choice," said Olivia and she stood up and told Newen she was done. Newen nodded and left the room with her. The tech guy on the other side of the mirror in the room stopped recording and the entire interaction in the room was uploaded to the RIA's archive.

Chapter 27: Senator Frigus

Grand Senator Frigus descended into the depths of the Colosseum. The arena was full with spectators who were cheering and chanting getting ready to enjoy the Redemption Event. It was promised to be a day of bringing the best of the past, the best of the present and the best of the future into the world's greatest arena. It was about redeeming Rome from the difficulties of recent years and showing the world why Rome was the greatest place on earth. A warm-up act was on, playing some of the greatest hits for the Colosseum. For the past hour, to also warm the crowd up, the big screens had been playing some of the greatest gladiator bouts in modern history. With no surprise, many of the highlights were showing Maverick 'The Beast' Kirabo's most epic kills. The crowd were giddy watching some of Maverick's most brutal and famous moments.

The crowd went even more wild when the Colosseum announced there would be surprise entertainment before the main event. For years, the team involved in making the Colosseum even more spectacular had been working on technology to truly reflect the grandeur of the arena, which had been entertaining the masses for two thousand years. Since its construction in AD 70 it has seated millions of people keen to watch the blood and glory of Roman entertainment. Originally able to seat fifty thousand spectators, Caesar Pius in the early 1800s extended its capacity by making it taller and adding another ten thousand seats. It was Nero II, though, obsessed with being praised and considered the greatest, who added another fifty thousand seats to the structure. It was work which took five years and turned the Colosseum from a circular amphitheatre into an oval arena. Stonework from the original structure was replicated, and it was rebuilt in exactly the same style. The finished work was breathtaking to all who saw it and Nero was praised for his ingenuity to have the arena built in such a way. Nero wanted the arena where he lived to be the greatest in the Empire, not overshadowed by any other entertainment venue.

Whilst Nero was still alive he had another idea and even after his death the team carried on working on what was Nero's dream. Now Frigus was the one in charge and implementing what had been worked on. Nero had fantasised about what it would be like to see the greatest gladiators in history compete against each other. It excited him to think of Maverick gutting Spartacus. So Nero gave the greatest technological minds in the Empire the task of realising this dream and before Nero could see the dream become reality, he was assassinated by Boatman King. Frigus, though, he got to see what had been imagined and today would be the day it was premiered to the public.

Frigus got to the lowest level in the Colosseum and walked along a tunnel which took him to some holding cells. A facial scan recognised his face and double doors swooshed open. Frigus entered a reception area where a guard was standing to attention. Frigus acknowledged the guard and another set of doors opened, taking Frigus into a cell which was four metres by four metres.

A bed was at the far end of the room and sitting on the bed was Legatus Brutus. "Good afternoon, Legatus."

Brutus scoffed. "It seems redundant to use that title for me. I was stripped of it as soon as I received it."

"A title is a title," said Frigus.

"Should I address you as Liar Frigus, then?"

Frigus frowned. "Are you naive enough to believe your career was purely based on integrity and hard work? Come on, Brutus, your parents lobbied the Senate with so much gold, and I seem to remember your father's tongue far up the emperor's ass many, many times."

"Fuck you, Frigus, I worked my way to where I was."

"Did you? How much battle did you see, Centurion?"

"I was assigned as part of the guard to protect Rome from any invasion. My credentials are as good as any solider who has seen battle."

"Yes, I'm sure they are," said Frigus dismissively. "But nevertheless, here we are, with you as the attacker of Rome."

Brutus rubbed his head in frustration. "Why are you doing this? I've done nothing wrong!"

"We've all done wrong, Brutus, and it's just admitting to that. After all, the greatest honour is to die for the glory of Rome."

"But where's the glory in lies?"

"Rome was built on lies," said Frigus. "Rome was built on maintaining its power through lies."

"Only a Senator would say that. The Senate has always been jealous of the Caesars," said Brutus.

"Not jealous. Wary. And I'll let you in on a little secret. Well, not a little secret, a rather momentous secret, but it doesn't really matter if I tell you, does it?"

Brutus felt a surge of anxiety rush through him and he wondered if he was going to have a heart attack. As soon as Frigus's words left his mouth, it confirmed for Brutus that his life was going to be coming to an agonising end soon. If Frigus wasn't concerned about sharing Empire secrets with him then his life was no longer of consequence. It made Brutus do everything in his power not to throw up. "How about you tell me in a few days' time," said Brutus, barely able to keep the bile burning his throat from ending up on Frigus's feet.

Frigus chuckled. "Very good. Always thought you military types had no humour."

"I don't want to or need to hear some dirty Empire secret. It is literally of no consequence to me."

Frigus pulled out his phone and started scrolling until he made a happy noise that he'd found what he was looking for. He turned his phone round so Brutus could see. "This is your father, may the gods protect him in the afterlife, standing with Nero. Nero has his arm round your father in a very embracing manner, which, we know, was rare for Nero. If Nero touched you, it was likely you were going to die. You father, though? No, he had a wonderful relationship with the emperor. Really beautiful."

Brutus shrugged. "That's nothing to do with me."

"Of course I know that, *Legatus*, but what's interesting is that your father was Commander of the Aquitania Region, yes?"

"You know he was."

"And yet he had no experience of commanding and organising such hugely complicated logistical operations."

"He was part of a family of commanders. Our family have been involved, militarily, for hundreds of years," said Brutus.

"Indeed you have. And I am thankful for your family's service.

But your family have only ever been part of the City Guard. Your father's promotion was an eye opener to most circles in Rome."

"Like I said, our family have a strong military legacy."

"I don't deny that. You're, what, generation six of City Guard Centurions in your family?"

"Generation eight," said Brutus.

"I'm sorry, generation eight is incredible. Did you know, the chef who oversees the Senate kitchen is generation twelve of Senate chefs? It's quite remarkable. His ancestor, I can't even recall how many great grandfathers, created a dish using lamb leg, which is absolutely divine, and the chef still uses that same recipe to this day. It's astonishing to me, because I thought it would need adapting and improving, but it's basically the same dish as Romans were eating hundreds of years ago."

"What's your point?" Brutus said.

"I'm sorry, I digress. I just think out's fascinating that your father, generation seven of City Guards, who carried on doing what his ancestors were doing, like my good friend in the Senate kitchen, suddenly became someone so popular with a rather unpopular Caesar."

"You obviously have an answer lined up, so why don't you get straight to it," said Brutus.

"Okay, I will. I think your father knew things that Nero didn't want others to know. Which makes me think you knew things."

"I don't know what you're talking about," said Brutus. "My father never shared anything with me. He never even hugged me. So if he had some special relationship with Nero, it was beyond my radar. If this is some sort of interrogation about my family, you will be very disappointed because they shared nothing with me."

"So you say," said Frigus.

"So I know," said Brutus. "I know as much about Nero as whatever anyone is willing to reveal about him. If he had a good time with my father, that's between them. And I have no interest in any of your secrets."

"Really? Because I think your father knew what I know and that's why Nero was so welcoming to him. And I think that is also why your father had such a significant promotion and, most importantly, why he died in such a terrible 'accident'. Frigus did the inverted comma sign with his hands.

Brutus sat up. "We were told it was definitely an accident. They said there's no way it could have been anything else. Why are you suggesting otherwise?"

"I'm sure your father was planning to reveal what he knew about Nero."

"Well, what did he know?"

"That Nero wasn't the true heir to the throne. Nero was a bastard and Augustus took him in."

Brutus took a moment to absorb the information and then still didn't know what to say. "But I don't understand what that means? We had no emperor?" Brutus's mind was whirring. "I don't understand what that's got to do with me? Why not tell the world about Nero?"

"Leave the politics to the grown-ups. Telling the world about Nero would be a catastrophe."

"Oh, of course, because scrabbling to keep it a secret is going so well for you," said Brutus.

"It's going fine for me. For you? Not so much."

Brutus seemed to deflate. Everything in him wanted to rage and go for Frigus, but a sense of nihilism overwhelmed him and Frigus's arrogant words somehow drove a dagger of hopelessness through Brutus. What was the point? He was in the dungeons of the Colosseum, about to be executed for the assassination of an emperor he'd never met. It seemed futile to even fight. He had seen his own friend turn on him with barely a flicker of remorse, so knew that to be part of the Empire was to sacrifice all sense of self. The clarity hit Brutus with such force he started to silently cry. His tears came and he felt shame at the tears in front of his executioner.

"Look, Brutus, I'm not going to create a narrative of sympathy around this. You know the glory of Rome comes before everything else. And betrayal? That's part of what makes the Empire so strong. Obviously we won't share what your father knew, but we will share that you followed your father's footsteps in trying to blackmail the Empire and therefore your betrayal has meant you have to die. And your betrayal almost led to a coup of the Caesar's throne, so today's entertainment is to highlight that no-one can overcome the might of the Empire.

"Someone will find out the lies."

Frigus laughed. "Really? You really think anyone will care enough to look too deeply into the end of your short life? And if anyone does try to dig, what will they find? Tell me, I'm curious."

Brutus didn't have an answer because he knew Frigus was right. There would be no-one looking to unearth the conspiracy against him. He had no family anymore. His father was dead. His mother was dead. He had no siblings. And being a career soldier, he had no friends because no-one particularly enjoyed spending time with a City Guard. And what Brutus found particularly jarring was that his job was at its strongest when the masses were duped. Peace reigned when everyone believed a scapegoat had been identified and sacrificed to appease the gods and maybe make their lives better. And now Brutus would be that scapegoat.

Brutus had been hanging his head, unable to even look at Frigus, but he had learned from seeing so many people crucified that it was important to look at your executioner, so he looked at Frigus. "How am I dying?"

"You'll be crucified."

"But that could last for days."

"It will end quickly, don't worry. I'll give you that comfort."

Brutus scoffed. "Comfort."

"I apologise, that is a poor choice of words. I give you that assurance that you will be spared a long death."

"You'll forgive me for not saying thank you."

Frigus made a show of looking at his watch and said it was time he had to go and that guards would be collecting Brutus in about an hour. As Frigus left the cell, he felt his anxiety spike because he believed in his role as Grand Senator, but he had shifted in his position from diplomat to tyrant. His shift, too, brought back to him how his daughter, Alypia, always called him out as a hypocrite, and now he was fulfilling her words. He was also no longer acting as a Senator, because he had vetoed any objections to the event happening and he had installed himself as the temporary Grand Protector. He had become what he despised, and what made his anxiety spike was that he really enjoyed it.

Chapter 28: Simulation

If the organisers of the Redemption Event were worried about the uptick in public interest before the day, their fears subsided when they saw the crowds descend on not only the Colosseum but in the streets and green areas around the Colosseum. It was like the public needed something to entertain them and then have a release. There was unrest in the Empire because the Grand Protector was missing, presumed dead, and the emperor hadn't made a public appearance in months. Although the Senate had arranged press releases and statements from the emperor, some conspiracy theorists online mused that Maximus was dead and it was all a ruse to hide the truth about his death. The conspiracy theorists were generally made to appear stupid with Empire propaganda showing footage of Maximus alive and well. There were theorists deeply entrenched in the idea that the Empire had technology to fake the emperor's appearance and theories about body doubles were thrown around.

Even so, with all the rumblings of the Senate having performed a coup and assassinated the emperor, it didn't stop the crowds flooding to see what entertainment was planned for the Redemption Event. The questions buzzing through Rome revolved around what it meant for the event to be called Redemption. And that was the draw that Frigus knew would work; not curiosity but people being damn nosey and unable to deal with other people knowing or enjoying something they weren't. Frigus noticed it time and time again that there was a jealousy of others having a slight upper hand in life. Even if it was only a perceived upper hand. People would always believe they were missing out and therefore if they saw anyone doing something they didn't know about, they would make sure they were part of it. And that's what made the Redemption Event so popular, in Frigus's mind, because the mystery surrounding it meant no-one in Rome was willing to miss out.

And Frigus was confident no-one would miss out.

The Colosseum was heaving in the stands and security were advised they were allowed to let extra people in, so it was estimated over 150,000 people were in the Colosseum, with thousands more surrounding the arena and setting up camp on the various green areas where big screens were placed. It was believed that well over one million people were in the vicinity of the Colosseum on the day. It was probably the biggest turnout for an event at the Colosseum in decades and much of that reason was because of the mysteries not only surrounding the event but also surrounding the establishment of Rome.

Frigus realised that one way to quash insurrection and disquiet was to give a few people wild theories to share online and then counter those wild theories. The cauldron of disinformation meant that when 'official' information was shared, it drove the public and press wild. It was a perfect way to make the public believe they were unearthing truths, but they were ultimately being controlled. Feed the masses but keep them hungry. It was easy to do and Frigus felt since he had assumed his position of ultimate power that he was wrong about democracy. Democracy seemed to only allow people to think about things they weren't educated about and therefore didn't have the authority to comment on. He found it frustrating when visiting his local bar and listening to people talk with little knowledge on subjects they were so confidently espousing. And listening to such conversations increased his belief that the general public weren't to be trusted with the fate of humanity. Some people were blessed with a river of intelligence and although Frigus wasn't sure the gods were listening or enacting his prayers, he did believe the gods bestowed intelligence on those they ordained should oversee humanity. And now Frigus was plunged into the position he was in, he believed the gods had ordained him to be the guide of Rome. He felt he was right in those beliefs because he had been instrumental in the organisation of the Redemption Event and all he saw were people flocking like sheep. And sheep were easy to control.

Frigus had left Brutus down in the depths of the Colosseum and taken his place on the balcony overlooking the arena floor. He refrained from sitting in the throne of the emperor or the throne of the Grand Protector because optics were everything. The vastness of the crowd was exhilarating, and he was excited about the reaction of the crowd when the two main events happened. He was confident that this day would be noted down in the annals as one of the greatest in this arena's history.

One thing Frigus wasn't confident of and was jealous of people like Faust for being able to do was public speaking at such a grand level. He was able to address the Senate with ease because he knew most of the old bastards. It was a stuffy room, with people he knew better than his own family. They saw each other all the time so when they stood up to speak, it was like speaking into a mirror. Debating in the Senate was verbally masturbating and it became so sanitised Frigus forgot why they even did it. It was only when Maximus was murdered and Faust disappeared that Frigus remembered why he had sworn an oath as a Senator. And with that oath he remembered how he was seen as an eloquent and influential leader of society. He also remembered that as a Senator he was seen as someone who was able to speak to the world with ease and clarity, but that certainly was not the case. So when it came to Redemption Day, Frigus made a lot of effort to deflect the expectation that he would be the one presenting and commentating on the day. He knew plenty of great speakers and he also knew of talent who would enjoy a few minutes of fame to be given the opportunity to be on camera to the world. Therefore he recruited the talents of an actor who had recently starred in a film about the assassination of Nero. It was a propaganda piece depicting Nero as a bloodied and fearless fighter who was eventually stabbed in the back by Boatman King. It was pure nonsense and many of the population knew it was nonsense, but it didn't stop the public flocking to watch the film on the giant screening venues around Rome and the Empire.

The public liked to wallow in a narrative that was false but gave them entertainment that made them feel like history was different. It happened again and again and was popular with the masses. An alternate version of history made many people escape the reality of the now. Nero depicted as a martyr, bravely resisting Boatman until the very end made the Empire's film industry a lot of money and there was already a follow-up film in the works exploring the relationship between Nero and Boatman and how Boatman was always jealous of his friend. Pure fiction, but it would make the Empire even richer.

Frigus couldn't help but grin when his actor recruit announced the first event and the pleasure of being part of the Redemption Event. And the first event was spectacular. It was a fight between Maverick 'The Beast' Kirabo and Marcus Attilius. Attilius was a fighter from two thousand years ago who voluntarily became a gladiator. He believed he was talented enough to beat anyone in an arena, so opted to become a fighter. And he was right in his beliefs, because in a very short space of time he became famous for how efficient he was as a fighter and brutal as a killer. He showed little mercy and won nearly all his bouts even though no-one really knew who he was and if he had any talent. He was like a stealth fighter who moved through the arenas picking off fighters, until one day Rome noticed this man Attilius, who was winning all of his fights against some of the most talented gladiators in the Empire. When his death came, it was inevitable. He never wanted to die of old age, believing he would never be satisfied wasting away in some vineyard, pretentiously reliving his greatest moments as a gladiator. No, he wanted to die where he found his glory. After all, he voluntarily entered the arena to risk his life, so he would enter the arena one more time and have his life end there.

And that's how it happened.

Attilius was sixty when he stepped foot into the Colosseum (or any arena) for the very last time. He had been fighting in the odd event for a number of years, but because of his age he knew he wasn't the prime fighter he was when he burst on to the scene four decades before. And that stopped him in his tracks, to think about how he had been a gladiator for forty years. Rome knew he wasn't the fighter he once was but his name and appeal meant every now and then they invited him to fight because the crowds demanded it. But, of course, the fighter he was pitted against was nowhere near the calibre of Attilius. And Attilius knew this. What Attilius also knew was that although he won his fights, these subpar fighters were much harder to beat than he dared to admit. After the fight, he would boast that he dragged the fight out for entertainment purposes, but truthfully he was scared this fight would be his last. Attilius was, he was ashamed to admit, also a subpar fighter because time had finally caught up with him.

One morning, Attilius woke up and decided it was time to die. He was tired. He never believed life should be long-lived and that's why he became a gladiator. He entered the arena with a wish he would die. Since being a young man he had always been tired. He had been tired of the way life was just so tiring. It felt like being alive was a fight. He couldn't pinpoint why and if someone asked him why he found life so tiring he would have struggled to explain it. But, still, he was tired.

He was fortunate enough to have enough gold to last him, what he thought, a short lifetime, because his family kept him comfortable, so he had decided that being a gladiator was the way to end life on an adrenaline high and end this tired feeling. And if he won a few bouts, there was no financial pressure with paying for entering a few more. So the years went on and on and he kept winning fights and kept making money and then he was fifty years old and the short life he predicted had become a long life in anyone's eyes, let alone a gladiator. He was still tired.

Reaching sixty years old was a shock to him and he wondered how it was even possible. He had believed the tiredness he felt about life would have caused him to, one day, allow someone's sword to make that fateful blow, but each time he was in an arena he enjoyed the buzz of the crowd and the buzz of winning. The fatigue of life subsided and he enjoyed winning and feeling alive for once. He was also surprised at the relief of avoiding death when those moments of mortality had come. Maybe he had defeated the tiredness? It was when he was home, alone, pondering his existence that the tiredness came back and he felt like darkness was forcing itself on him. For decades this cycle happened so that, when he did reach the age of sixty he decided he really was too tired to play this game anymore.

Attilius had made Rome believe he was fighting people far less talented than himself, but who were stretching him to the lengths of his skills because of his age. He decided this was the perfect moment to end his life and to do it by choosing a fighter to mark his birthday. He would choose a fighter way beyond his skill level but, on paper, of equal ability to him. Attilius saw a way to die with dignity and adrenaline. Attilius chose a fighter for his birthday fight, which caused huge interest, who would give him a great fight without it being one-sided and would make Attilius look good. After all, he didn't want to die in the arena in some sort of easy massacre.

When the fight came, Attilius gave a great fight and was impressed with his own prowess at his age, but as he was fighting he knew he wasn't up to the standard of his opponent, and as he enjoyed the adrenaline of going blow for blow, he found the enjoyment of not fighting the tiredness anymore. He realised he was going to welcome the blow that would end him, but he wouldn't make that final blow easy for his opponent. In fact, Attilius's final fight ended up being recorded as one of the greatest of his entire career. The fight lasted for nearly an hour with each fighter giving it their all. Even though Attilius was sixty he fought like a man half his age and put to shame the gladiators touted as rising stars. When Attilius met his end it was through him making a genuine swing with his sword, but through his fatigue, failing to see his opponent had feigned an attack, and then Attilius found a sword lodged deep in his belly. As Attilius dropped to his knees, blood pouring from his gut, he managed to smile at the death he had always wanted. He also managed to look at his opponent, who was scared to have fatally wounded the greatest gladiator in generations, and signal to end his life quickly. His opponent understood the respect of doing such a thing and plunged his sword through Attilius's throat. Attilius died the way he had always wanted. And with that death, he went down in history.

Of course, this was two thousand years ago, so how Attilius was fighting a very alive Maverick 'The Beast' Kirabo was a wonder of the Empire's new technology. Because, also, The Beast wasn't present. He was in the wind with the Empire clueless where he was, so it was an added mystery how two of the greatest gladiators of all time were fighting in the Colosseum at the Redemption Event.

When it happened, the crowd went silent. It was a surprising silence because it was almost impossible to achieve in an arena of over one hundred thousand people. The silence did happen, though. The silence happened because in the middle of the arena, when the MC announced each name, Maverick and Attilius appeared. They not only appeared, but appeared in much greater clarity than anyone could have believed. They also appeared at a much larger size than humanly possible. Both men were standing there and at least triple the size of their namesake. The silence continued until the famous MC explained that Maverick and Attilius were projections, created by advanced Empire technology. Not only were they projections but they would be fighting to the death according to how the audience believed they should. And with that, the crowd were asked to vote, via a scan of their reactions. A thumbs up was for Maverick and a thumbs to the side was for Attilius. The cameras in the arena would scan and count the votes and then the projections would fight and the outcome would come from the crowd's votes.

It was still astounding the crowd to see these two famous gladiators projected onto the arena floor and appear to be physically there. And when they started to fight it made the crowd even more astounded because it seemed like two real-life gladiators were fighting. The projections the Empire had created were so advanced it was impossible to know the men fighting weren't real. It was only their size and the fact that one of the men had been dead for two millennia that confirmed what was being watched wasn't real.

As the crowd realized that they were involved in something innovative, they started to cheer on the fighters, although they knew, in the back of their minds, the projections' actions were not motivated by the crowd's cheers or jeers. Even so, the arena was electric with watching these behemoth fighters bruise it out. Part of the technology that was created was that the fighters would fight based on how close the votes deemed the bout. It appeared it was very even, as the fight went on for almost thirty minutes, with each fighter almost ending the 'life of their opponent until Maverick lunged at Attilius with his famous technique, but as he did it he stumbled slightly and Attilius took that moment to step away from the blow. Maverick stumbled even further and Attilius plunged his sword through the base of Maverick's skull. The Beast was defeated for the first time ever. The crowd went wild.

Frigus laughed at the fact that the crowd had voted for Maverick to lose his first ever simulated battle. He'd assumed everyone would have wanted Maverick to win, but it appeared the consensus was a curiosity about what it would look like to see Maverick die. After all, Frigus thought, no-one actually liked someone who succeeded all of the time. If there was a way to see them fail, the majority tended to enjoy that. Interestingly, after the match ended and Attilius and Maverick's images disappeared, the crowd started chanting, "The Beast, The Beast!" The world adored Maverick, even if they wanted to see his simulation die.

Frigus found it fascinating how fickle the masses were and it made him excited to see what the masses thought of the next act of the Redemption Event. He hoped the reaction would boost not only his polling, but give him even more time to work out how to keep Rome from falling apart. Frigus's MC called for the crowd's attention and announced the main event.

Chapter 29: The Brutality of Brutus

After the crowd hushed, the floor in the centre of the arena started to open. The floor had a secret platform beneath it and as a hatch opened, a platform raised up with the figure of newly appointed Legatus Brutus on it. The crowd remained silent and confused for a couple of reasons: firstly, no one knew who Brutus was. He had been appointed as Legatus, overseeing the army of Rome, but it had never been made public. Secondly, an unknown man strapped to a chair was very strange in the context of anything, let alone on the Redemption Day. It seemed like an age with the crowd so silent, but then the MC spoke. He informed the crowd that the main event today was the spectacle of seeing the man before them held to account for high treason. Some of the crowd murmured and some even clapped, but it still remained generally quiet in the arena. So the MC continued to explain that, unbeknownst to the public, the man before them was appointed as Legatus of Rome, replacing, for now, Grand Protector Faust. But, in his new appointment, he used it as an opportunity to try and usurp the emperor and have him killed. Today was a day of reckoning and it was Redemption Day because Rome's authority would be redeemed. The crowd livened up with this news. The MC carried on, encouraged by the crowd responding, today this traitor, he said, would be crucified and bring order to the Empire and glory to Rome and Caesar Maximus. The crowd cheered. Blood lust was always bubbling below the surface with the mob.

"LIES!" Brutus screamed. "IT'S ALL LIES!"

The crowd hushed. The MC spoke again and said to turn on the traitor's microphone, which was attached to his clothing.

Brutus was shaking with fear and anger, he spoke softly this time, now he knew he would be herd throughout the arena. "It's all lies. I'm being set up. They're lying to you. Emperor Maximus is dead, and I had nothing to do with it."

Laughter came from the main balcony, it was Frigus. "Our Caesar is alive and well, traitor Brutus, your lies won't save you."

"You told me he's dead," said Brutus.

The crowd murmured, but Frigus laughed again and said, "Your elaborate lies only make you look worse, if that's even possible."

"Then why hasn't anyone seen the emperor in months?"

A few of the crowd shouted in agreement with Brutus but then everyone went silent when another voice spoke up. "I am alive and well," came a robotic voice. Everyone's eyes went to the various big screens throughout the Colosseum, There was an image of Caesar Maximus on the screens, sitting in his wheelchair in what looked like a grand room of a villa. "I think you can stop with the fanciful stories, traitor Brutus."

Brutus's mouth opened, but no words came out. He felt disorientated. He was certain Maximus was dead, the Grand Senator had said so, but now he could see the emperor on screen, talking to him. The emperor continued speaking, "I'm sorry I can't be with you today, celebrating Redemption Day, but I have been travelling through our grand Empire building on making Rome's glory even more prominent, so I want to thank you all for your support. But rest assured, I am very much alive."

"Impossible," said Brutus.

"May the glory of Rome be upon you all," said the emperor and then the screen went black. A few of the crowd started chanting, "Maximus, Maximus!" In moments, most of the arena were chanting the emperor's name. Brutus kept shaking his head muttering that it was impossible.

"People of Rome," roared the MC, "In honour of Caesar, let the main event begin."

Brutus had been looking down, shaking his head, but the roar of the crowd made him look up and he saw two soldiers walking towards him. One of the soldiers was carrying a nail gun. Brutus panicked and tried to move but he was strapped to a post. Next to him, another hidden platform appeared and out of the floor raised up what Brutus had been dreading, the crucifix he was going to nailed to. He tried to speak, to plead his innocence, but his microphone had been switched off, and so his protests were unheard amongst the cacophony of noise consuming the Colosseum. When the soldiers reached Brutus, they had to shout to be heard over the noise of the crowd. "It's time, Legatus Brutus." Brutus tried to reason with the soldiers and still tried to command them to stop as he was their commanding officer but they pretended they couldn't hear him because of the volume of the crowd jeering and cheering. When pleading failed, as the soldiers untied Brutus to drag him over to the cross, he tried fighting. The soldiers were prepared for this, though, and the one holding the nail gun used it to punch Brutus in the stomach. Brutus keeled over and both soldiers grabbed him, shoved him on his back and dragged him over to the cross. The soldiers pulled out cable ties and fastened Brutus's arms to the cross. Brutus tried to kick out and the nail gun met one of his knees with a crunch. Brutus cried out and then the fight went out of him. The pain shocked him and travelled up his body, making him wilt. He'd been transported into a powerful role in the Roman army but the realisation that he had no true fighting ability or resilience sucked hope out of him.

Once Brutus had been subdued on the cross, the soldiers nodded to the grand balcony where the MC spoke again. "People of Rome! On this, the Redemption Day, we celebrate the redemption of Rome, saving it from the treason of Brutus and potential assassination of our divine emperor. We welcome the chance to show the gods that Rome's strength is like granite and Rome's power is formidable. No-one will stand against the destiny of Rome and its Caesar, and today is an affirmation of that." The crowd erupted in applause and cheers and chanted for the death of the traitor. Brutus felt his body turn to jelly and as he looked around the arena, all he saw were faces of hatred, spewing out vitriol and demanding his death. He tried to focus on the hope that this was fiction, that a mistake had been made, but all he could do was think about the moment he went from elation at his promotion to despair that he had been set up. He'd prayed to the gods for a reprieve but they appeared to be silent on his destiny.

The soldiers received the green light from the balcony and Brutus's image was displayed across the arena on the big screens. The soldier with the nail gun walked over to Brutus's right-hand side and with one hand held his arm in place and with the other hand placed the nail gun over his wrist. The soldier looked up at the balcony and Frigus gave a thumbs up. With that, the soldier pulled the trigger and a nail shot through Brutus's wrist, pinning his arm in place. Brutus screamed at the pain as the nail tore through bone and tendon. The soldier moved round to the other side and Brutus begged and pleaded for the soldier to stop and think about what he was doing. The soldier refused to acknowledge his victim shot a nail through the other wrist. Next, the crucified man's feet were positioned on a ledge and nails were driven through them. Brutus cried out, blood flowed on to the floor.

Once the nailing was complete, Frigus raised his hands and the soldiers stepped away from the cross. Frigus pulled out his phone and opened an app. He then pressed a button in the app and the cross started to rise. It was on a hydraulic hinge which powerfully raised the cross into the upright position. But it didn't stop there; once the cross was upright, Frigus then pressed another button and the cross moved higher. The platform the cross was bolted to rose until it was thirty feet high. This meant Brutus was suspended at a height of more than forty feet. During the process, the jolts from the hydraulics had made Brutus cry out in pain as the movements tore at his wrists and feet, blood making a steady stream down the cross. Usually, recipients of crucifixion were hooked up to a saline drip, to drag out the agony, but Brutus was drip free. Frigus had promised a quick death and due to the lack of drip and huge height Brutus was suspended from, the pressure on his lungs and heart was likely to cause a much faster death. Even so, a speedy death by crucifixion still meant agony for a few hours. Frigus wasn't interested in dragging it out for a few hours. He motioned for the MC to announce the next part to the event and the MC welcomed on to the stage a band singing some of the Empire's favourite songs from over the years. The crowd erupted with glee. They had all been plied with free drinks and discounted drinks to get them in the mood. The Senate had agreed that the cost of the Redemption Event was justified so that it took attention away from the questions being asked about various aspects of the Empire. Distracting the masses was as important as ever.

Once the crowd in the arena was singing in sync (and mostly in tune) and their attention had moved away from Brutus hanging from the cross, Frigus made a call. It was to one of the snipers on the roof of the Colosseum. He said a couple of words and hung up. The sniper got into position and with little effort took a shot when the music was at its loudest so the crack of the gun wasn't heard. A bullet went into Brutus's chest, lodging itself in the metal cross, killing him instantly. By the time anyone noticed Brutus was dead, no-one particularly cared. The traitor deserved what he got and they'd all enjoyed his pain.

When the event finished, the crowd were tanked up and boisterous. They'd had a very cheap night out and been treated to a crucifixion, a fight between two of the greatest gladiators of all time and a message from Caesar. If it meant the masses were distracted and happy for a few weeks, then Frigus would be happy.

All he needed now was to hope those few weeks of distraction gave him and the Senate ideas about how to navigate the issue of having deceived the world into thinking that Emperor Maximus was still alive.

Chapter 30: Maverick's Discontent

"Did we all just watch the same fucking thing?"

"It wasn't real."

"I don't care if it wasn't real. It was a load of bullshit."

"You need to chill out, Mav, it wasn't anything to take seriously," said Tobias.

"How would you like it if what was broadcast to the world was a fight between you and that prick, Cornelius, and it showed you getting your ass kicked?" Maverick said.

"Who's Cornelius?" Bella asked.

"That's not important," Tobias said, "But it's very, very certain that he would not have never kicked my ass."

"So it's certain that this Attilius would have kicked my ass?"

"I didn't say that," said Tobias.

"What did you say then?"

"Look, Mav, you're taking this very seriously. It was a simulation. An impressive simulation, but a simulation nonetheless."

"Who the fuck is that stupid to think that poor excuse for a fighter would have been able to beat me?"

"It seems about a hundred thousand people are that stupid,"

said Tobias.

"Do you want me to kick your ass?"

"You always say the sweetest things."

"Tobias, you're not helping," said Maverick.

"Helping with what? It was like a computer game. No-one will care and if they do, so what?"

"I care," huffed Maverick, "I was undefeated."

"I've never seen Maverick so sensitive," said Bella.

"I'm not being sensitive."

"Your bottom lip says otherwise," said Bella.

"Don't you get involved," said Maverick.

"It just seems you were less put out when Maximus held you hostage," said Bella.

"I just care about facts," said Maverick, "And facts would clearly state I would have won that fight." Maverick mumbled something and got up from the sofa and went to the kitchen to get another beer.

Maverick, Tobias, Bella, Alypia and Olivia were sitting together in Mav and Tobias's house. They had arranged to watch The Redemption Event together to try and analyse if there would be any clues as to what Rome was planning next. The simulation fight involving Maverick had distracted them from some of the more glaring moments; particularly the crucifixion of Brutus.

"Did you know him?" Bella asked Alypia.

"Not personally. I knew of his family. His father was very close to Nero."

"Does it make sense that he would have tried to kill Maximus?"

Alypia shook her head, "Not at all. He was a career soldier, like his father. Augustus would rage about how the Army of Rome was led by men who had never experienced battle. These men inherited their roles because of family connections to the emperor.

For Brutus to try and throw that all away and do some sort of insurrection without any real military knowledge is weird."

"So he was a patsy," said Tobias.

"A patsy for what?" Bella said. "The emperor did a live stream and addressed Brutus directly. Why would a man who had a career gifted to him decide to to try and kill the emperor?"

"He didn't try to kill the emperor," said Olivia.

"How do you know?" Bella said.

Olivia had been sitting on an armchair in the corner of the room, sipping a glass of wine, but had since stood up and paced whilst trying to compose her thoughts. "I don't know what I just saw, but that does't take away from knowing that Brutus didn't kill the emperor." Olivia was on edge. If she had been outside of her body she would have seen that she had been triggered and was struggling with the emotions that had manifested. She was struggling to stay composed and Bella went over to her and placed her hand on her shoulder, "Olivia, what's going on?" Olivia started to cry and Bella pulled her in close. The tears turned to sobs, with emotion pouring out of Olivia. She thought she had got control of her tears when another wave overwhelmed her. Bella led over over to the armchair and gently eased her into it. Tobias had brought over a glass of water and eventually Olivia took it and took tiny sips. After a few minutes the tears subsided and Olivia was able to formulate her thoughts and words again. No-one said anything or even pushed for her to talk.

"Brutus didn't attempt to kill the emperor," said Olivia.

Still no-one spoke.

"And the emperor isn't alive."

Tobias desperately wanted to speak but Maverick jabbed him in the ribs.

"The emperor is dead and I don't know how they did what they did in the Colosseum, but he's dead."

The silence in the room was the kind of silence which made everyone uncomfortable and desperate to break it, but they didn't push Olivia. She was going through something difficult and even mentioning Maximus wasn't only painful, but heart wrenching and traumatic. She needed to speak though, she needed to share what was happening and she was in the safest space she could do that.

"I know it's not making sense," said Olivia, "But trust me, that monster is dead."

Bella felt she could ask a question, "How do you know? Sorry, I know this is hard for you, but what have you found out?"

Olivia laughed, but the humour was painfully absent, "I haven't found anything out." Her words caught in her throat again but she was able to compose herself, "I know he's dead because I killed him."

Everyone in the room glanced at each other and then Tobias spoke before he really knew what he was saying, "Are you sure you're not confused?"

Olivia looked at Tobias, her stare hard and hurt, "You might get confused about all the people you've killed, Tobias, but I'm certainly not."

Tobias looked down and then Maverick spoke, "We all remember our first," he said. "When?"

"When we were in the safehouse in London."

Tobias opened his mouth but Maverick jumped in again, "How did we not realise?"

"I don't know," she said, shaking her head, "It's like everyone was watching for who might come to the safehouse, but no-one was thinking about who might leave the safehouse. I also thought that I had somehow become invisible like I was the day Maximus took me."

Maverick looked down, shame bubbling. He still felt responsible for not keeping Olivia safe and for the trauma she went through. "Sorry, Olivia."

"I don't need your apology. In fact, it made it almost too easy for me."

That silence dominated the room again.

'How did you do it?" Alypia spoke up. She didn't know Olivia particularly well so wasn't afraid to ask what her friends couldn't quite manage.

Olivia looked at Alypia. "A pillow over his face. He couldn't move. It wasn't difficult."

"Where?" Bella asked.

"The hospital." Olivia got frustrated. "Look, what does it matter? I know he's dead, and whatever they managed to construct on those screens wasn't him."

"Does anyone else know?" Maverick asked.

"Like who?"

"Like your new friend," said Maverick.

Olivia shot Maverick a look. "No, I haven't told anyone else. Including him."

"We need to keep it that way until we work out what to do."

Alypia had found her confidence to speak to the group. "What to do? I don't understand."

Maverick smiled at Alypia. "Tobias and I were arguing earlier about whether we were going to try and find your husband in Askå's kingdom. Now the argument is going to be about whether we do a detour past Rome first, because it seems they have no leader."

Olivia spoke up. "I don't think you're going to have a choice about that."

Maverick squinted at Olivia and took a moment to observe her. "What have you done?"

Olivia looked straight at Maverick. "I'm trying to save people."

"Right, Olivia, you have never been someone to skirt around words or talk shit, so tell me what you have done," said Maverick

"Askå has Molly and is willing to give her back to me."

Maverick had spent his life in a gladiator arena and knew how bluffing worked. "Bullshit," he said. "What's actually going on?"

Olivia didn't break her gaze with Maverick because she wasn't ashamed of the deal she had negotiated, but she was still guilty about the fact that it had come to this. "He'll release Molly back to me if I give you up to him."

"If you give me up to him? Sorry, Olivia, how would you be able to give anyone up?"

"I agreed to help the 35."

Maverick clenched his jaw. "If you agreed to help the 35, that would suggest I'm a hindrance to them? And then I would like to know how the hell I'm a hindrance?"

Olivia held out her hands. "You're not a hindrance, Mav, I just —"

Maverick cut her off. "Don't you dare 'Mav' me. You've sold me out, haven't you?"

"Molly can't be left with that monster."

"But I can," said Maverick. "Olivia, what have you done?"

"What's right," she said.

The windows to the lounge blew, shattered glass blasting across the room. Everyone ducked except for Maverick, who stood tall, not giving a fuck at the pain and also knowing that attackers were most vulnerable when they thought the victims were vulnerable.

So, as everyone was ducking, the team of RIA soldiers came bursting through the now glassless windows, expecting to crowd in on crouching bodies, but what two of them found as they came gliding through a window was a giant black man who was angry as hell and roaring in rage. As they planted their feet on the carpet of the lounge, they were met with their throats being throttled by Maverick and then being pummelled into the floor. After that, well, darkness came and later they would be thankful for that because the rage Maverick had was used on the soldiers who dared to try to fight him. One soldier forgot to pull out his gun and hit Maverick in the side of the head with his baton, thinking that kind of blow would bring this saga to an end. Maverick turned to look at the solider who was holding his baton like a limp sausage. Maverick took the baton and reciprocated the blow. The soldier's head caved and as he fell, Maverick wondered how Maximus had managed to survive such a blow. Another soldier came at him and Maverick brushed the attack aside by elbowing the soldier in the throat. The soldier crumpled and then it became a blur of bodies as soldiers piled on Maverick. In amongst the blur of soldiers fighting for their lives, as they had never encountered a man so strong, they also had to contend with Tobias doing his upmost to protect his husband as another man not quite so strong but still, very strong. And maybe the 35 thought their elite teams would take the room out quickly, nullifying the strongest and then cancelling out the weaker, but their intel was wrong because with most of the team focussed on Tobias and Maverick, that didn't account for how skilled and deadly Bella was as she incapacitated the soldiers on the fringes. All of a sudden, Bella was standing over unconscious soldiers and then pulling Tobias off others. Maverick was punching his way out of a pile of bodies like a kid with a piñata stick.

Then a second blast came. It was a stun grenade and it floored the room, regardless who was in it. Ears rang, eyes blurred and even Maverick collapsed. The second wave of soldiers came in and Maverick's rage was silenced.

Chapter 31: Boatman's Legacy

"Tell me, if you were emperor, what would you seek to achieve?"

"Not being emperor," said Boatman.

Askå laughed. "And what would that entail? Peace, love and happiness?"

"Equality. Liberty for all," said Boatman.

"Oh my dear Boatman, how fascinatingly naive you are. You think that equality comes from giving everyone this liberty you speak of?"

"Of course it does."

"Why?"

"Because everyone deserves their chance to forge their own destinies. Which is what I have always aimed for," said Boatman.

Askå looked at the ceiling. "It's frustrating to hear this nonsense from your lips, Boatman. I would have thought you would have been much more pragmatic about the reality of this world we inhabit."

"And what is this world we inhabit? In your view? Boatman asked.

"It's certainly not one of freedom and liberty. Look at your situation. Look at the world we're both trying to change," said Askå.

"Change? Replace one tyrant with another? That's not change, it's just your desire to be at the top and pretend there has been change."

"My dear Boatman, you misunderstand me. And you misunderstand true power. Tyranny isn't oppression."

"That's something a tyrant would say," said Boatman.

Aska ignored the jibe. "Tyranny will always be misunderstood by those who don't ever get to stand at the pinnacle of rule. People can't be trusted. They throw away their liberty with a nonchalance that is disgusting. It's easy to watch people descend into madness at the flick of a switch. Did you see what happened recently in Britannia? Not in your precious London, of course, but in a city close by.

"I think you'll find I've been slightly away from current affairs."

Aska held his hands up. "Apologies, I have been neglectful of your needs. I have you here as a guest and therefore you should still see the world's news. And if you did it would remind you that your path isn't as righteous as you would believe."

"Tell me," said Boatman.

"I don't need to tell you," said Aska, "you can see for yourself." Aska picked up his phone and selected an app. The app projected a video onto a massive screen on the wall of the room they were in. It was news footage. It was news footage of an incident in Britannia, and Boatman recognised the city as that of Colonia, the city close to the outpost of Meresig where he had grown up. Colonia was seventy miles northeast of London.

On the footage it showed riots in the streets with looting and chariots being set on fire. The news report was detailing how the riots had broken out after residents were originally protesting about a group of people who had settled in the city after fleeing unrest in the Aquitania region. Originally organised as a protest, it quickly turned violent, with people from outside of the city using the protest as a smokescreen for their bigotry. With Nero's death and then Faust's disappearance, Britannia had become very unsettled and it opened the door to a group of people with hugely anti-immigrant views who wanted nothing more than to expel anyone they deemed non-native, whatever that meant. Anyone who tried to debate with this group pointed out that their objections were ironic considering a lot of people over the decades had come to Britannia because of Roman colonisation, so it was weird for them to then be against others seeking a better life in Britannia. The sensible arguments fell on deaf ears as bigotry only seeks violence, and the violence was personified in Colonia.

"You see," said Askå, "Tyranny brings peace and order. Topple those building blocks of order and disorder thrives. Which, it seems, is thanks to you."

"You can't blame me for people's idiocy."

"Really? You were so determined to usurp the Empire you didn't think about the fallout. When you behead a beast, the vultures come scrounging."

"From what I can see and have always seen, the beast has many heads. I'm not finished beheading yet."

"Let me ask you a question," said Askå, "completely changing the subject, or not. Depending on your perspective."

"Okay," said Boatman.

"What if your ideology was changed or challenged? What if your sense of perfectness was less perfect? Apologies for the poor choice of terminology."

"Obviously this question is loaded, just ask it."

"I just wonder, my dear Boatman, what would happen if your belief in loyalty went out the window? What if loyalty was replaced by revenge? Or redemption?"

"Redemption? What the hell you mean by that?"

"Think about it. You have spent a rather sad part of your life trying to overthrow an Empire and then you managed it. You then had to deal with the fallout. You are now someone looking for redemption. You're looking for someone to tell you you're actually okay."

Boatman waved his hand, "Of course I'm not."

"Not even Olivia?"

Boatman went to raise his hands but they were restrained by chains. The clink rattled and Boatman tried again with no success "Take my wife's name out of your mouth."

"Touchy," said Aska. "You know that your wife isn't as precious about you."

Boatman paused, just a second, enough for Aska to pick up on it. "You don't know, do you?" Aska said. "Your bitch wife has given you up."

Boatman had always believed he was cursed. He had believed his life was one that had been consigned to the depths of pity and despair. Boatman had believed he was a failure. Even in the moments of killing an emperor and almost overthrowing the Empire, he still believed he was a complete failure. But then he had Olivia. Olivia who believed in him. Who gave him a sense of humanity. And it was hard for him to share that with anyone. Sharing personal stuff was difficult as a leader because everyone believed you were a perfect human. Then trying to be slightly vulnerable and a rebel leader, well, that was like being the weakest of them all. But Olivia made him feel safe. Olivia made him feel like it was possible not to be alone. And by alone, he meant, alone even when you were around others. He found, with Olivia, someone who gave him a sense of existence. She made him feel like a teenager, that butterflies in the stomach and nervousness about seeing them again kind of feeling. She tore his heart out of his chest by leaving him for even a day. She was the perfect night, she was the culmination of matter versus anti. She was what it means to live and to die. She was everything and he would do it all to protect her and to be all she needed.

But now he wasn't.

Now he was a poor imitation of who he believed he was.

Now he was someone who others would laugh at.

"Look at you," said Askå. "Pathetic. You really don't know, do you?" Boatman struggled in his restraints. Askå continued. "Your wife has decided your life is worth less than some orphan."

Boatman took a moment to register who he was talking about. "Molly?"

Askå laughed, "Indeed, dear Boatman. Poor little Molly. Poor little orphan Molly whose parents you killed."

"Who told you that?"

"Why, little Molly, of course. She told me lots of things about the infamous Boatman. You're not quite the saint you like to believe."

"Molly's a child, imaginations run riot with children," said Boatman.

"And that is why you clearly don't understand children," said Askå. "Children are the gatekeepers of truth because they don't subscribe to any bullshit. She believes you killed her parents and I believe her."

"Her mother killed herself."

"And her father?"

"He was betrayed by Rome. I offered him safety," said Boatman.

"Ah yes, as noble as you like to believe you are, you are as slippery as any politician I've met. An answer that isn't an answer. You offered him safety but stabbed him in the back nonetheless?"

Boatman yanked his restraints in frustration. "This is pointless conjecture, what have you done with Molly?"

"Pointless? It's all connected, my sweet Boatman, because I actually care about Molly and her future happiness. If I hadn't mentioned her, would you have even remembered her existence?"

"I don't need judgement from you, of all people, about people's existence."

"I'm not judging, simply pointing out the fact that Molly has been safely here with me and, might I add, very happy, and unless your wife decided to strike a deal, you wouldn't have even passed a second thought at Molly's safety or whereabouts. Like I said: pathetic."

Boatman struggled in his restraints but to no avail and Aska called him pathetic again. "And let me elaborate a little, as I like this part of the story, dear Boatman, your wife didn't only give you up, she offered you up like a sacrifice. Like a lamb to the slaughter. With little remorse it seemed."

"You're lying," said Boatman.

"Oh, come now, Mr King, you know I'm not lying. I'm taking a lot of delight in this being completely true. We had a lovely conversation via video call. Giving you up was all her idea," laughed Aska.

Boatman felt his entire sense of self crumble in a moment. Olivia was his constant. His anchor that kept him attached to reality and sanity, but if she had given him up, it was like his heart had been torn from his chest. And the pain was horrific. Aska could see the pain and he delighted in it and laughed his booming laugh. For Boatman, the laugh ignited his rage, as the laugh represented betrayal and a complete loss of all he had held dear.

And so Boatman's rage hit a level it rarely had. The last time he felt his rage overwhelm him was when he was cornered in London one time. He had gone looking for Simone, a young man, only twenty years old, who had defected from the Empire's army to join the rebels. He was passionate and he was intelligent and he saw the futility of Empires and the promise of freedom. Simone had rejected his entire way of life to join Boatman's resistance and accepted the reality of never seeing his family again. His parents were offshore Senators based in Britannia and reported to the Senate about recommended changes in laws to be suited to Britain's culture. They were loyalists and were devastated when Simone defected to the rebellion. For Simone, he felt like he had become an orphan, but believed it was necessary in order to uphold his integrity. He lost a family name but gained a family and looked to Boatman as a father. Boatman was cold and terrifying, but Simone felt a warmth for him in that paradoxical way that he hadn't felt for his biological father. Unfortunately for Simone, being the son of such high-profile figures in the Empire meant he had a target on his back. Boatman had urged Simone to lie low and, once the dust settled and Rome was bored, he would be able to be more present in the front-line activities of the rebellion. Simone, for a time, had agreed but then he had grown frustrated and needed to join the rebellion in their effort against the Empire. Without Boatman's knowledge, Simone had tacked on to a mission with Maverick and Tobias, aiming to take out a sentry on the outskirts of the city. All would have gone to plan but for Simone's naivety; he detached from the group, thinking he could make it easier by appearing to be alone and therefore undetected. It took moments for soldiers to detain him, identify him and then exact retribution on him and later claim it was self-defence. Simone's body was found by Boatman, crudely crucified to the gates of his parents' political headquarters.

Boatman had set out to find the soldiers. He found them quickly because boasting about horrific executions was normal within Rome's army throughout the world. It only took a little research online to find posts boasting about the execution and then a little bit more investigation into location meant Boatman identified the soldiers easily. And then it only took basic baiting for them to think they had cornered and captured Boatman. And when Boatman was, in their eyes, cornered, Boatman unleashed his rage. He had seen how Simone had been executed and it was brutal and harrowing. The soldiers weren't experts in crucifixion so their attempts meant nails had been driven into Simone's hands and had ripped out under the weight of his body. The agony he would have gone through until they had managed to get it 'right' was unimaginable.

The rage Boatman felt about Simone's suffering caused him to forget all morality and all sense of mercy. The soldiers had thought they had cornered and captured Boatman but all that ensued was a massacre. Boatman took the lives of the soldiers with such brutality that when the bodies were discovered it was only by dental records that their identities were known. And if being torn from limb to limb was a metaphor, it no longer was in regard to how Boatman understood it. Boatman's rage was like a ghost story, and moments like that showed how horror-filled his rage was. And also how superhuman his rage was. Not only was his speed superhuman but his strength was, too. It was almost like his rage gave him something more than most human beings.

And so, sitting chained to a chair with Aská calling him pathetic, lying about his wife and the life of a girl Boatman had tried to save, a rage only the unfortunate had seen erupted. Boatman roared and it made even Aská flinch. Boatman roared, and he thrust his arms up, breaking the chains he was in, and flew out of his chair and attacked Aská.

Aská wasn't prepared for the attack and wasn't prepared for

Boatman to be so powerful. Askå was used to being the strongest of them all. He was used to being the man that no-one dared challenge and no-one ever managed to defeat. He remembered when Maverick came of age and posed a slight threat and he was excited about meeting Maverick at full strength but other than that, he was never worried about another person. In fact, he had wished there were gods who would come to earth to challenge him. Now, though, now it appeared a god had fulfilled his wish as he was being attacked by Boatman, who appeared to have the strength of a god.

Askå had briefly fought Boatman on a couple of occasions and been impressed by his strength and skill and thought that this man would be a worthy foe, but the sheer force and rage coming at him now made him reconsider everything he knew. For one, he was confused how Boatman had broken free of the restraints. It would have taken the strength of a tiger to rupture those chains. And then, how he had leapt over the table so fast to be on Askå. It was absolutely confusing. Everything happening to him was bizarre and yet here he was, having his ass kicked by a man who was meant to be a myth, as the Romans had their propaganda make the world believe.

Aakå was used to being attacked, but most of the time it was from preordained positions, like a gladiator arena. Or, like when he had last encountered Boatman and had been holding a battle axe. This time was different because it was via surprise and Askå was seated. Boatman had leapt onto Askå, knocking him off his chair and landed on top of him. Boatman proceeded to pummel Askå with his fists and Askå felt his nose break. The attack was relentless and Askå's instinct took over; he kicked his leg up whilst managing to grab hold of Boatman's arm for a second and threw Boatman over his head in a judo-style move. Boatman clattered into a bookshelf standing against a wall. He was quickly to his feet, though, and onto Aska again. Boatman knew Aska had the advantage in size and strength so had to rely on his speed and endurance. And in close combat like this, because of Aska's size, it was awkward for him. He didn't have the freedom to move like he would in an arena and Boatman stayed close, unafraid of the closeness, which threw Aska off, psychologically. Boatman had never fought someone so large before and even though he was landing blows, and knew they would hurt, it felt like he was punching a wall. He was expending a lot of energy with each swing and yet Aska wasn't budging. His surprise attack had worked in throwing Aska off balance, but now Aska was standing firm. Boatman threw punches into Aska's sides, aiming for kidneys (and also because punching up was tricky considering the giant's size). Aska deflected some punches and also raged at his own frustration from the close combat. Aska blocked a punch from Boatman and then brought his fist down on the top of Boatman's head. Boatman sprawled on the floor, stunned by the strike. Aska saw his opportunity and moved in on Boatman, grabbing him by the throat and with incredible strength, picked Boatman up. Boatman choked under Aska's grip but then stabbed Aska in the eye with his finger. Aska let go and stumbled back, the dirty blow blinding him. Boatman wasted no time and did another dirty blow, kicking Aska squarely in the groin. He always knew that when it came to fighting men much bigger than him, there were always weak points: throat, eyes and groin. The kick was vicious and powerful. Aska made no sound but crumpled forward, the pain immobilising him.

Boatman wasn't one for ceremony and wasn't one for mercy and stepped over to Aska who was hunched forward in pain, blinded in one eye and in excruciating pain from the kick to his groin. Boatman walked up behind Aska and kicked him in the groin again; Askå sprawled forward in agony. Boatman then walked round to Askå's side, and looked down at the giant who had degraded Titus and feasted on human flesh and his rage fired again. He lifted his foot and with all his might stamped down on the back of Askå's neck. The crunch sounded alien and Askå went from agony to silence, his neck broken and life stamped out of him. Boatman stared at the body for a second, coldly observing another contender to Rome's throne now disposed of.

He searched Askå's pockets and found a phone and keycards to access the buildings across the entire grounds. He smiled, now there was a plan for escape. He opened the door to the room Askå had brought him to and found he was in Askå's main mansion. Askå had been arrogant enough to bring him here to try and torment him. It had wildly backfired. Boatman looked around and the mansion was quiet. He guessed Askå's arrogance meant he had waved away any guards who could have helped him. After all, why would a giant need assistance with a prisoner who was chained? He closed the door and the electronic lock went red. To be sure, he smashed the unit for the lock so no card could be used to unlock it. Boatman then made his way out of the mansion; he needed to get to Rome. If Olivia had made him a sacrifice, and Maverick, too, then the RIA wasn't the ally he thought they were. Rome was vulnerable and this was his chance to break its back.

Chapter 32: Like Father Like Son

Faust was sitting in his quarters at the kitchen table, opposite Ira. Ira had realised he'd hit a brick wall with interrogating Faust. Faust wasn't going to give any relevant information up that would be useful to him understanding how to infiltrate Rome. Ira had been Augustus's trusted bodyguard, but that was twenty years ago so what he knew and remembered of Rome was irrelevant. Faust was the key to breaking into Rome and exposing their weaknesses so he and Askå could storm it and rule, but Faust wasn't playing games. It was considered whether basic torture would work, but Faust had endured some probing methods of torture through sleep deprivation and waterboarding, and the results were useless. It was as if he didn't actually know anything. For Faust, he was able to regress his mind into his memory palace. When torture came, he took himself deep into his memory palace so that pain didn't exist. During one particularly brutal session of water torture, Faust was in the wine cellar of his memory palace enjoying a rather beautiful wine from the Aquitania region. His body was convulsing and struggling for air, but his mind was sipping an elegant wine and therefore he had closed himself off to Ira's sadism. It took a few attempts for Ira to realise Faust wasn't breakable, so then he tried to connect with Faust through conversation. Maybe something would slip. It never did. And now Ira sat opposite a man he didn't know how to read in order to get any intel to try and destabilise Rome.

Faust was intrigued by Ira. He had heard of a disgraced Centurion and rumours of Augustus covering it up, but nothing ever concrete. When he learned of Nero's bloodline and the fact that Boatman shared that bloodline, it opened a door of opportunity, but an opportunity to use that information never came to pass because he was imprisoned by the father of Boatman and grandfather of the current emperor. Faust had come to the end of his patience with Ira and the entire situation he had been placed in. He was, after all, the Grand Protector of Rome, and after all these months they hadn't broken him or garnered any information from him. And it seemed to him that, judging by Titus, he had been much stronger willed. "What is it you are trying to get from me?"

"You are a key player in Rome, just tell us what makes it vulnerable."

"I'm not your patsy. Move on. I can tell you how the Senate operates and I can tell you that Caesar never does an interview before midday. And I can tell you that to be a Centurion means lots of random patrols through pointless areas. But then I would guess you know that. Based on your history and, I assume, patrol areas."

"You can judge all you want."

"I will, thanks," said Faust.

"But at the end of the day, I'm the one in control here," said Ira.

"Yes, a very formidable situation," said Faust. "But your sway holds little over me."

"Maybe so, but I'm certain Bjorn may hold a little more *sway*."

Ira's back was to the kitchen door and he heard it swoosh open.

"Not now, soldier. Whatever it is, it can wait." He felt something cold against the back of his head.

"No. It can't," said Boatman and then he slammed Ira's head against the table. Ira fell to the floor and Boatman picked him up and bundled him away from the door. Boatman was holding a gun and pointed it at Ira. Ira had managed to get to his feet. He was holding his forehead, the initial pain from the blow causing a headache to wrap its fingers round his brain. He brushed away the pain and said, "How the hell did you get here?"

"I walked through the door," said Boatman. Ira shouted for the guards. "Unless your words reach Hades, they won't hear you," said Boatman.

"Are you that stupid to think you can defy Askå?" Ira said.

"I believe I am," said Boatman. "But boldness comes with stupidity, doesn't it?"

"Boldness is irrelevant when Askå tears out your lungs. And eats them."

"I'm not an expert in human physiology, but I do know it's difficult to eat when you have a broken neck."

Ira squinted and took a step towards Boatman. Boatman raised his gun a little higher and Ira stopped moving. "You're delusional. Askå is almost a god."

"It seems almost wasn't enough," said Boatman. "And if I'm not mistaken, you are nowhere near a god, so it will be even easier killing you."

Ira stepped back. "Wait, there's something you need to know."

"It's funny how vital information appears when death makes his final call."

"I'm your father," Ira spluttered, anticipating the gun firing.

Boatman's aim faltered. "What?"

"It's true," said Faust, observing the scenario from the other side of the room.

Boatman kept the gun aimed on Ira but looked at Faust. "And how the fuck would you know?"

"Aside from the records I have seen, I would think it obvious when you're both in the same room."

Boatman frowned at Faust and then looked back at Ira. Everything became an out-of-body experience where the dim glass of subconscious denial gave way to the bright and intrusive moment of reality. Boatman, for the first time, actually looked at Ira. He had seen him from a distance or heard his name mentioned, but he realised he had never been in close contact with Ira. He had never even exchanged words with him or been threatened by his presence for a moment. Now he was able to see the man and it was unnerving. Ira had exactly the same almond-shaped eyes, colour and a straight nose that Boatman had. Boatman held a close cut, dark beard, but if he had grown it a bit more and allowed grey to dominate, then he would have looked like the man standing before him. There were uncanny similarities and only age and the relentlessness of life made more than superficial differences between them. Boatman really looked at the man before him and felt a weirdness about seeing someone who looked like him. He'd always been used to living a life without anyone looking like him or him looking like them. But now there was someone before him who he *could* see something of himself in and it triggered something in him that longed to connect to that. He didn't realise something so simple and so primal would tug at his heart so powerfully. Instinct wanted the man before him to be his father because seeing someone who shares your genes is magnetic and intoxicating. He needed to know this man's history and therefore what could potentially be his history. It made him yearn to know about who he was. It was bizarre and it was paradoxical because then the rage and pain of what the man before him had done surged through his veins and he was on Ira before Ira even realised what was happening.

Boatman had kicked Ira's feet away and Ira was kneeling with a gun pressed down on the top of his head. "Tell me," said Boatman, "How did it feel, raping my mother?" Ira stayed silent. Boatman pressed the gun down harder. "You'll fucking answer me. Dad."

"I've made mistakes, I know it."

Boatman stepped back, put the gun on the table and then grabbed Ira by his hair and tore his head back so the men were looking at each other. "Mistake? Forgetting a friend's birthday is a mistake. Raping a woman is not a mistake, it's an abomination. You killed my mother. You discarded her like trash."

"I made terrible decisions when I was a young man."

"You chose to rape my mother and beat her skull in. Obviously you thought you'd done a good enough job, but you hadn't. She survived and here I am as the result, to bring vengeance for what you did to her."

Ira held his hands up. "Wait, wait. I know all you can see is killing me will solve whatever it is you're feeling, but who I am now is not the man I was then. I can help you get into Rome. I can help you achieve what you always wanted to do."

"You can help me with what I always wanted to do: to see the man who brutalised my mother be wiped off the face of this earth."

Faust felt it was time to step in. "Might I suggest something to ease the intensity of the situation?" Faust had stepped within a few feet of Boatman and the instinctive part of his brain said he was making a huge mistake, but he had been analysing Boatman for months, storing the information in his memory palace. He had been absorbing Boatman's nuances and untangling the man's trauma. And, by the gods, this man had a lot of trauma. But in this untangling and lying awake at night, walking through his memory palace, observing Boatman's words and actions, all he saw was a man who craved the intimacy of a father. It wasn't particularly complex, but it was easy to miss because who would look at Boatman with any real investigation without fear of his terrifying stare? Or worse? But Faust was willing to take a chance, because he knew all Boatman wanted was to find a connection to something of his past. He needed an identity. The mythical rebel leader who killed an emperor was a vacuous identity, and Faust could see that in Boatman. So he took a risk and said, "This man will be of use to us," Faust said. He stopped a beat and said, "And wouldn't you like to know something of who you are?"

Those words made Boatman release his grip on Ira's hair. He turned to look at Faust. "I know who I am."

"Judging by your face, I would say that's a lie," said Faust. "Why don't we at least find out before you bash his skull in? At least let's get enough information so we can get the hell out of here." Faust looked over at the door. "I mean, it seems pretty clear you've killed whoever crossed your path on the way here, but we will still need to find a way out of Aestii and I would think your father here is the best bet for that."

Boatman looked down at Ira and said, "Tell me. Tell why you did that to her." He pulled Ira to his feet and dumped him on a seat at the kitchen table and sat down opposite. Faust moved round the table to the fridge and pulled out three beers, opened them and placed them on the table. Ira guzzled his, adrenaline making him thirsty. Boatman necked his too. Faust went back to the fridge and pulled two more beers out. This time Boatman and Ira sipped them. Faust sat down and said, "So? I think honesty is the best policy, General Ira."

Ira nodded and started to speak. He spoke about his childhood. He spoke about his proclivities as a teenager and he spoke about the dark desires he had as a soldier and how he found it difficult to contain. And then when he became a higher profile soldier how it was almost encouraged to do things that weren't acceptable in general society. And then Ira shared a lot more of his story, and Boatman listened and Faust listened and Ira's words drifted further and further into the night. And then Ira started speaking about things that sounded similar to things Boatman felt, and Boatman then started speaking about things that Ira related to, and Faust watched on as there was no doubt they were father and son.

A few hours into Ira sharing his story to negotiate for his life, Boatman said, "I'm a product of your violence. You served Rome and I want to destroy it. You destroyed my mother and created me. I don't know what I feel about you. I hate you, I know that, but I can see an endgame with you in it. I hate you even more for that."

Faust moved the conversation away from the personal. "Tell me, General Ira. You were at Augustus's side for many years; are the rumours true about the tunnels?"

"Nero would have collapsed them, for certain."

"So they are true."

"Look, Augustus saw London's impressive network and also the benefits of such infrastructure and decided to do it himself. The thing was, he wanted it as a backup, in case he was betrayed. He saw a tunnel system as defence. And he was right. But he wanted anything like that done in secret and nothing on the scale of London. Of course, that wasn't possible if he wanted it done in secret. He wanted some basic tunnels which would get him out of his palace and to safety if there was an insurrection."

"Was he that afraid of such a thing?"

"Come on," Ira started, wiping some beer froth from his beard. "Paranoia was as much a part of being an emperor as believing you're a god or part-god."

"But how did he keep it a secret form the Senate?"

"Disposable workforce. And gold keeps eyes blind," said Ira. "By the gods, you're not that naive, are you? How the hell did you become Grand Protector?" Ira snorted. "If that's even a title."

"And clearly it wasn't a secret," said Boatman. "You heard rumours."

"I did, but no-one ever found anything."

"Or they didn't look very hard," said Ira. "The tunnels are there. But like I said, Nero would have collapsed them."

"What makes you so sure?" Faust wasn't convinced.

"Because Nero was more paranoid than ten of his fathers. He would have collapsed them because he would have assumed everyone knew about them and therefore would have used them to attack him."

Faust shook his head. "Nero never mentioned tunnels. Ever. It never came up in Senate meetings and it never came up even when Nero was in a drunken rage."

"He didn't know," said Boatman, as a thought out loud.

"No, I don't think he did," said Faust. "Which means your father has a rather privileged place right now because I assume, General Ira," Faust looked at Boatman's father, "You do know where the tunnels are."

Ira nodded the affirmative.

Boatman swigged his beer, not saying anything for a minute. "We could, of course, force the information about the tunnels' locations. We don't need you there."

Faust raised his hand. "As much as I understand your hatred for your father, Boatman, like I pointed out, we need a way out of Aestii and Ira is the best chance we have. Otherwise we're wandering around with no means of transport or funds."

Boatman growled; he knew Faust was right.

Faust had noticed Boatman hadn't comprehended something bigger in this situation: Boatman wasn't joining the dots that he was the half-brother of the now-deceased emperor Nero. And the ramifications of that were immense. Over the centuries, emperors had come and gone and although Rome liked to make believe each emperor was a direct, divinely chosen descendant of the last, the reality was much more muddled. Caesars became Caesars through deception and political manoeuvring. Generals committing treason took the throne violently. Bastard sons tore the power away from the fathers who tried to forget them. Rarely did power pass in romantic succession from a father to a son to a grandson. No, it was messy and usually power came drenched in blood. So, for Faust, he really found it wilfully blind of Boatman not to see where things could be heading. He needed Boatman to reach that conclusion naturally, though. He couldn't slap the rebel round the face with it. After all, Boatman was understandably struggling with the knowledge that General Ira was his father. Pointing out Boatman was technically the next in line to the throne of Rome, but also that he had executed his own brother, well, that wasn't going to be a smooth transition of information. And Faust needed to tread carefully with a man whose rage was likely to erupt at any moment. No, he had to tease Boatman to realisation like the gentle unpicking of stitches. Again, he found it strange Boatman wasn't realising his connection to Nero, but he wasn't going to press. Instead, he said, "I'm tired. As riveting as it has been listening to General Ira's confessions and desires for absolution, I need to rest. And it seems, if we are to rest, General Ira may need to ensure the house is secure from anyone finding something or someone they shouldn't?"

"I'm not an amateur," said Boatman. "Aská will be unfound for long enough that we'll be gone."

"Good," said Faust. "So that means we can rest, yes?" Faust looked at Ira. Ira nodded. "Although, I'm afraid, General Ira, I'd rather not sleep with one eye open, so you will need to be restrained whilst we rest." Ira said he understood.

Once Ira was restrained and Faust and Boatman went to their beds, Titus crept out from the shadows of the corner of the room. He sniffed the air and could smell his master's blood in the air. Boatman was telling the truth. Titus felt a tear run down his face. He was going to grieve the man who'd taken his tongue.

Chapter 33: Rejection

Maverick looked around the pteron-chariot, his head was fuzzy from whatever had been in the stun grenade that had knocked him out. He leant forward and put his head between his legs to ease the nausea bubbling in his belly. Waking up a few thousand miles high in the air, after having been knocked out by a blast, meant his head and body weren't in sync and the feeling of wanting to throw up all over the floor was becoming an extremely favourable option. He managed to compose himself enough to sit up and look around again without the blurriness that had dominated his vision a few moments before. Tobias was asleep or unconscious in a seat on the aisle opposite. He slowly turned his head to look behind and it appeared the whole gang were present. Olivia, Bella and Alypia were aboard and they were all awake and engrossed in conversation. "What the fuck is going on?" Maverick said, breaking the rhythm of the women's conversation.

"The RIA have decided you're all a liability," said a voice coming from the rear of the pteron-chariot. It was Newen.

"And what does that make you?" Maverick had stood up and his size made the chariot appear much smaller. And Newen felt much smaller, too. Newen was a deft assassin but he wasn't sure how he'd fare against an angry Beast in an enclosed space.

"A liability too."

"Or a useful spy," said Maverick. Maverick took another step toward Newen.

Newen held up his hands. "I'm not a spy. I assured them Olivia would do what we needed. But I was wrong. They concluded I was potentially wrong about many other key decisions. The 35 decided I needed to be relocated."

"To where?" Maverick was looking like The Beast was about to tear Newen's head off.

Newen still had his hands up but didn't back away. He knew better than that. He wasn't afraid, more pragmatic about his chances if The Beast did attack. "It seems you're being given what you want and will get to say hi to Bjorn Aska in a few hours."

"It's not what I wanted," said Olivia.

"No, but knowing how the 35 think, they believe you still are, in a way," said Newen.

"How?"

"You'll be reunited with Molly very soon. That's what you wanted isn't it?"

"Not like this."

"Think of the positives of seeing her," said Bella, who was sitting next to Olivia, and stroked her arm.

Olivia shook her head. She wasn't even convinced Molly was alive. Aska seemed to take delight in people's pain and Olivia had been deceived enough and hurt enough when it came to loved ones. Her father had been brutally murdered by two psychopaths employed by Faust to find Boatman. Her mother had been abducted by those working on Faust's orders and Olivia had no idea if she was still alive or had been left to die in some unknown cell. And now Molly's name had been uttered, giving Olivia hope, but there was no proof Molly was alive. It was like another cruel promise of hope wrapped in deception.

"Surely we're being dropped into Askå's lap like wrapped gifts?" Alypia said.

"The only gift I'll give Askå is a sword to the heart," said Maverick.

"You talking about other men behind my back?" Tobias had woken up.

"Only in that I will finally kill him,' said Maverick.

"You know, that's ironic. You'll kill Askå before you've got round to sorting a wedding date for us."

"You know what's also ironic? I might end up killing you before I kill Askå," grunted Maverick.

"I'm not sure you understand irony," said Tobias.

"I'm not sure you understand how close I am to opening the door of this chariot and throwing you out of it," said Maverick.

"If it means I land on a huge-ass wedding cake and am surrounded by people congratulating me on becoming Mr Beast, then go for it, my darling."

"You're a dick," said Maverick.

Newen looked to Olivia and said, "Are they both okay?"

Olivia waved her hand. "They're fine. That's how they flirt."

"What do they do when they fight?"

"They get a room," said Olivia. "Can we get back to the problem in hand?" Olivia pulled Mav and Tobias out of their strange banter.

"Which is?" Tobias had been passed out when Newen had explained how the pteron-chariot they were aboard was on its way to Aestii. Maverick filled him in. To which Tobias said, "Not wanting to be the pessimistic one in the room, but has anyone thought about how we might get shot down before we even land?"

"We're like a chariot of gifts to Bjorn Askå," said Newen. "The 35 have messaged Askå and said that this chariot is an offering to him, so ensure it lands safely."

"Like hell we are," said Bella. "The only gift Askå will get is an arrow from me between his eyes."

"I would like to point out that we are impressive in how much we can fuck things up," said Tobias. "In a very short space of time we have gone from being celebrated rebels, lauded by the 35, to being bundled on a pteron-chariot and given as a buy one rebel, get one rebel free gift. Are we that difficult to get on with?"

"Yes. You are," said Newen.

"Well, American boy, you've been bundled in with us, so I wouldn't get too judgy," said Tobias.

Newen conceded the point and slumped next to Olivia. Olivia put her hand on Newen's leg and no-one missed the significance of it. As if pointing out the elephant in the room, Alypia said, "What about Augustus and Boatman?" Olivia removed her hand from Newen's leg.

"What about them?" Bella asked.

"Are they alive? Are they part of whatever plan it is Askå has?" Alypia wasn't feeling as relaxed as Tobias.

Tobias wasn't going to let Alypia's anxiety ruin his mood. "We don't know, Alypia. And I assume it's at least a couple of hours until we do find out, so I don't know about anyone else, but I'm going to get a bit more shuteye before I have to think about fighting for my life or defending the honour of my husband. Oh, hang on, I don't have a husband."

"Go to sleep before I knock you out," said Maverick. Tobias

saluted his lover, settled back in his seat and was snoring in moments. Maverick shook his head and then said, "As much as I hate to admit it, I think Tobias has the right idea. It's best we all rest before we arrive in Aestii. We don't know what's waiting for us there. We need to have our wits about us."

Everyone agreed and within a few minutes the fatigue of recent days reared its head and the entire pteron-chariot was a cacophony of snoring.

Chapter 34: Flight to Nowhere

Newen went into the cockpit and the pilot had bad news. "We're not landing here."

Newen didn't need an explanation. He looked out of the cockpit window and saw the runway they were meant to be landing on, engulfed in fire. Newen wasn't sure how far away they were from the runway, he guessed five miles based on their height, but he could see the fires burning. It didn't take him long to also realise that if these fires were burning then they weren't going to be redirected to somewhere else because there had been no contact from Askå's team to say there was a problem. No, this problem was either caused by Askå to send a message or… And the 'or' made Newen think a bit. What if this was a problem not caused by Askå? What if it was a problem for Askå? And, for Newen, he wasn't sure what that meant. Newen looked at the pilot. "Have you been able to contact the tower?"

"No response, sir."

It didn't take Newen any time to think about it. "You need to change course and we need to redirect."

The pilot didn't hesitate. A burning runway in the distance was enough motivation to know he didn't need to be any closer and flying away was the best option. "Yes, sir." The pilot hesitated. "But where are we redirecting to?"

"That's a damn good question," said Newen. His mind went into frantic mode, trying to work out the play. He had no idea if Aska was trying to deceive and a missile would come out of nowhere. He had no idea if somehow Aska had been attacked and now Aestii was vulnerable. He had no idea what was going on, but as his mind worked he realised one thing: Rome was silent. It was understandable to know nothing about Aska's activities if Aska was going to make a move, but Rome had mentioned nothing. If they had made a move on Aska then they would have announced it as a show of power. They would have declared their interests. Rome enjoyed the power of propaganda and especially sharing their triumphs. This burning runway, with chariots decimated, if done by Rome, would have not only been announced but legions and legions would have been seen on the ground and giant war-chariots circling the air. No, Rome wasn't involved. And if Rome wasn't involved then that made Newen's next decision easy. "We're going to Rome."

"Sorry, sir? I didn't quite hear you."

"We're redirecting to Rome."

"Sir, we're an RIA pteron-chariot. Rome will shoot us down."

Newen shook his head. "They won't. We have precious cargo. Make the redirection. And let me know when we're a couple of hours away."

Newen exited the cockpit and knelt beside Alypia's seat. She was dozing. He gently touched her shoulder and it jumped her out of whatever she was dreaming about. He apologised for waking her and explained the situation. It didn't take Alypia any time to understand why Newen had approached her first. She found it ironic that somehow she had become the gatekeeper to the rebels' efforts. She had felt useless and inconsequential. She had felt like an invisible add-on to this core team. She had felt like an imposter watching, from a distance, the lives of Mav, Tobias, Olivia and Bella. Yes, she was in love with Bella. Yes, Bella made her feel more than she had ever felt. But. There was still a but. There was a but because it was like she was impeding on the lives of a special little group. She was always made to feel welcome and loved, but there was that niggling thing, in the back of her brain, that told her she still wasn't welcome and maybe she was just a pawn? Alypia couldn't help but think about when she first met Bella and thought that maybe Bella was the gateway to escape the awfulness of Rome and Faust's behaviour. Faust had never abused her but his obsession with not necessarily serving Rome, but ruling everyone and proving he was the not only the smartest man in the room but the smartest man in the world meant she was a footnote in his life. Alypia had thought Bella was an authentic route out of that nonsense but, alas, she was wrong and was being used for information to help the rebellion. And even though Bella had proved things had moved on since then, she couldn't help but believe maybe she was still part of that scheme. And maybe her worth was only because she was part of the establishment.

And then Newen made a point to wake her and say that the only way the chariot would be able to land would be because she had to contact her father and make sure safe passage was possible so that they weren't shot out of the sky. And she hated that. And she wanted to do the opposite and say to her father that he should shoot them out of the sky to put them all out of their misery but, of course, she wouldn't, because she wanted to see how things would play out and actually, maybe, just maybe, Rome might, ironically, provide a solace that she had never found anywhere else.

And with that thought of solace, Alypia took the phone from Newen. It rang for a beat and then it was answered. "Senator Frigus speaking."

"Daddy?"

The line was quiet. Alypia took the phone away from her ear to check it was still connected. The screen was lit up, numbers ticking, showing the call was active. She put the phone to her ear again and said, "Daddy? Are you there?"

There was a gulp at the end of the line. "Alypia?"

"Yes, it's me."

"I can't believe it's you. I thought you were missing. Or worse."

"No, I'm alive."

Frigus breathed out. A bit too dramatically, thought Alypia. "By the gods I am thankful that you're alive. Are you safe?"

"I'm safe. For now. Which is why I'm calling you. I need your help."

"Of course Alypia, whatever you need," said Frigus.

"I'm on a pteron-chariot which is flying in from the RIA and we need to be able to land safely near Rome," said Alypia.

"The RIA? Alypia, you're on a chariot associated with a nation not loyal to Caesar."

"But you have no Caesar, so what's the problem?" Frigus paused long enough for Alypia to know her father was mentally scrambling. "Why would you think we have no Caesar?"

"Because he's dead, father. And even if he was alive, I'm asking, as your daughter, for you to help me come home safely."

"I will make sure your journey is a safe one. Tell the pilots to stay in touch with me and I will ensure your flight arrives without any hindrance," said Frigus.

Whilst Frigus was navigating the surreality of talking with his daughter, who he had assumed was dead, his assistant came into his office. "Sir, you need to take this call."

"Commodus, I'm currently on a much more important call. Tell them I will phone them back."

"But, sir…"

"Commodus, you're trying my patience and my goodwill. I'm speaking with my daughter, whoever is on the other line can leave a message."

"But sir."

"Commodus!"

Commodus wouldn't relent. "Sir! You really need to see this. It's Grand Protector Faust."

Frigus looked at Commodus. "What do you mean?"

"Faust, my lord, he's calling from a pteron-chariot on its way to Rome."

"Hold on a moment," he said and spoke back into his phone, "Alypia, who's on that flight with you?" Alypia told him. Frigus took a moment to process the fact that some of Rome's most wanted were on the flight and that, if his daughter wasn't, he would order it to be shot down. But then he focused on how he could be a hero capturing The Beast and having him crucified in the Colosseum. And maybe put an end to the fantasy and mythology that surrounded men like Maverick. Frigus snapped back to the fact that Faust was apparently calling from a flight headed for Rome so asked his daughter again who was on the flight. "I told you. Why?"

"Is Faust with you?"

"Augustus? No? Why?"

"Are you sure?"

"I would know if my husband was here. I don't understand what you're getting at."

Frigus didn't know what to think. "Can you stay on the line, Alypia? I need to take another call and will get back to you to ensure you land safely." Frigus put the call on hold and left his office, following his assistant to the comms room. Inside the room were a dozen large screens, showing satellite imagery of various cities in parts of the Empire and places that weren't part of Rome's influence. The centre screen, though, that wasn't a bird's eye view of a city, but a live view of a video call. And the person in view was Augustus Faust.

"My lord?"

"Hello, Frigus," said Faust.

"I'm not going to lie, I'm shocked to see your face."

"Shock can wait; I need you to clear this chariot to land in Rome and approve an armed escort to Caesar's palace. And I need to speak with the emperor as soon as possible."

"My lord," Frigus began, "the emperor is dead."

Faust rarely let his face slip, but the shock was visible. "When?"

"I'm not sure that's the most important thing, my lord. The point it, you being alive is the most important thing. This call potentially saves the Empire from collapsing."

"We will be arriving in Rome in a couple of hours. I want you to meet me when the chariot lands and you need to debrief me on everything." Faust cut the call and Frigus went back to his office. He picked up his phone and Alypia was still on the line. "Alypia? Are you still there?"

"Yes, father. Is everything okay?"

"I'm not sure," Frigus said honestly. "Your husband is alive and on another pteron-chariot bound for Rome."

The line went silent and the Alypia said, "Does he know about me?"

"No. I didn't mention you," said Frigus. "But that will have to change."

Alypia didn't answer.

"I will protect you as much as I can, but I can't promise anything."

"I know," said Alypia and she cut the call.

Chapter 35: Maverick's Peace

Alypia woke the rebels up and explained her call to her father. Everyone had the same train of thought: they were potentially flying to their executions if Faust had managed to stay alive and make his way back to Rome. It also seemed inevitable, in Olivia's eyes, that the cause of Maximus's death would be revealed at some point in the near future, so optimism about either defeating Rome or, bizarrely, finding refuge there was fading fast. A solemn mood descended on the flight, apart from Maverick. Maverick seemed happy, which to normal people looked like a slight smirk instead of a grimace. Tobias picked up on the glee. "Why the happy face? Didn't you absorb what Alypia just shared?"

"I did," said Maverick.

"And that makes you the happiest I've seen you in months?"

"Of course," said Mav.

"You need to elaborate because us flying to certain death is a weird flex to get all happy about," said Tobias.

"Do you not know me by now?"

Tobias arched his eyebrow. "You really need to elaborate."

Maverick sighed. "It's the perfect opportunity. At last I can put a sword through everyone who took delight in my imprisonment. We can smash the Empire apart. It's not certain death, Tobias, it's our chance to tear the head off the beast and this beast can take the throne."

Tobias turned to look at his partner. "Sorry, what?"

"You heard me."

"You want to be the emperor?"

"Why not?"

"Well," Tobias started, "because that sounds absolutely insane. And, not being funny, you'd look weird wearing a crown."

"You need to focus on the right stuff," said Maverick. "We've been hounded and vilified our entire lives. And now there's an opportunity to make everyone realise we have always been the ones that keep this fucking Empire moving. How often are our fights replayed again and again? How often are our faces paraded and imitated on movie posters?"

"I mean, I'm flattered, Mav, but I think it's only your face that's paraded. I could walk into the middle of Rome's Square and not a single person would recognise me," said Tobias.

"You know what I mean," said Maverick.

"Honestly, Mav, I don't think I do. This is the first time I have no idea what you're talking about."

Maverick rarely looked desperate, he always appeared calm in the face of adversity and to make Maverick sweat was as difficult as getting close to him to land a punch, but Maverick looked desperate and it unnerved Tobias. "Mav," continued Tobias, "we're not politicians. We're not emperors. We're washed-up gladiators who have somehow managed to stay alive long enough to have the chance to marry each other. And that's all I want. I don't want to run the world. Hell, I can barely rule my own mind. My side still aches from being stabbed."

Maverick's face darkened. "Sorry."

"For what?"

"For not protecting you," said Maverick.

Tobias put his hand on Maverick's cheek. "You have nothing to be sorry for. I'm alive and I'm here with you. I just don't understand what this conversation is about. It's not you. I get the anger. I get the need for revenge. An angry and vengeful Maverick is what I recognise. I don't recognise a beast who wants to somehow play a game of thrones."

Maverick put his hand on Tobias's and then pulled it away from his cheek and kissed it. "I just think we deserve the chance to live life without fear."

"But I'm not afraid," said Tobias. "Fear is only what we make for ourselves. You know this. You were never afraid in the arena."

Maverick looked at his partner and said, quietly, "But I'm afraid now."

"Of what?"

"Of losing you."

"You're not going to lose me. And I don't get what that's got to do with wanting to be some sort of angry black emperor."

"If I rule the world, then no-one can harm you," said Maverick.

Tobias leant over and kissed Maverick. "That's weirdly the most romantic thing you have ever said, but also the stupidest thing you have ever said. I'm not going anywhere. Please, Mav, focus on how we can get out of whatever is going to happen. We don't need to rule anything. If we can slip out of this and mange to have a cute little house in the middle of nowhere and have no-one bother us, I will be happy. Okay?"

Maverick nodded. "Okay."

"So no more talk of becoming Caesar? You weirdo."

"Okay."

"Promise?"

"I promise," said Maverick. And then the couple got comfortable and fell asleep to the hum of the chariot and although they didn't know their fate, they were at peace because regardless of the potential pain, they had each other.

Chapter 36: Rome's Disarray

Faust had got off the call with Frigus and once the screen had gone dark, turned around and looked at his flight companions. "The emperor is dead."

"How?" Boatman asked.

"I don't know," said Faust, "But it appears Frigus is running the show."

"What does that mean?" Ira said.

"It means Rome is in disarray," said Faust.

"But isn't he the Grand Senator?" Boatman said.

"That means nothing," said Faust. "He thrived during Nero's reign because it meant the Senate never had to do anything. The Senate were there for show during Nero's tenure. Those frauds would have gone white with any real responsibility. They enjoyed debating how flawed the emperor's decisions were without having any real responsibility."

"But the Senate helped craft certain laws and regulations necessary for the general population," said Ira. "I remember Augustus bemoaning how he had to keep the Senate happy and abide by certain decisions they made."

Faust shook his head. "I'm sure you did, but when Nero came into power, fear was the driving factor in everything. You remember Jonas, right?"

"Of course. He was Augustus's best friend. A good man."

"And you remember how he died?"

"I saw his funeral when it was streamed. Natural causes was the official line," said Ira.

"Nero murdered him. In front of a lot of witnesses," said Faust. "Jonas disagreed with Nero's approach to something and, apparently, Nero murdered Jonas in front of a room full of people. It was brushed aside, but it put the fear of the gods into the Senate and they became a group of men who agreed with the emperor on everything. Any decision they made was focused on how it would make Caesar appear in the polls and press. And then Maximus came along and it was ramped up to another level. I don't think Frigus even knows how to think beyond propaganda."

"You sound paranoid," said Boatman.

"Good," said Faust. "It means I won't be taken advantage of. The question I have though, is that if the emperor is dead and I am reinstalled as the leader of Rome, what does that mean for you, Boatman King?"

"I could bring this chariot down and the Empire implodes," said Boatman.

"You could, but I don't think you need a history lesson before deciding to do that. I wonder, the closer you get to Rome means the closer you get to wanting a slice of that power?"

And that was the rub, for Boatman. He had spent his life determined to break the back of Rome, to destroy its legacy and see people freed from the crucifixions and soldiers patrolling the streets. But all that had happened is that he had enabled more bloodshed and Rome stayed stubbornly in place like an unstoppable force striking an immovable object, causing chaos but changing nothing. Now he was almost in Rome, almost invited in some weird paradox, and the closer he got to setting foot in the place he vowed to destroy the more he wondered if the way to find victory was to become part of the beast. To merge himself with it and grow within its belly. Maybe the solution was always about becoming what he despised. Maybe his transformation was the way to transform an Empire which always believed was ordained by the gods. Maybe the gods had ordained him to be the change the Empire needed to see it survive for another millennia. The antiquated rule of Caesars was now at a close, with Maximus dead and no children in line to rule. Faust was sitting on the throne as a self-made Grand Protector. Frigus was pretending to be a man caretaking the establishment but a grand event at the Colosseum to distract the masses was a blunt tool with no longevity. Boatman saw an opportunity to be the man to cement certainty in Rome. The only question he had was how would he do that?

The biggest thorn in his brain was that his wife had betrayed him. If there were gods moving their pieces, then Olivia's actions said that maybe he wasn't the man meant to break Rome. Maybe this was all moving as as sign for him to be the man to make Rome what it was always meant to be.

Chapter 37: Welcome to Rome

Faust's flight landed and after exiting the chariot, he and his two guests were greeted by Frigus and a large portion of Rome's army. Faust was pleased. It would mean Boatman and Ira would think twice about trying to do anything untoward.

"Welcome to Rome, Grand Protector," said Frigus. He looked past Faust and his eyes widened at the sight of Boatman King standing there.

"Thank you, Senator. Let me introduce you to General Ira, former bodyguard of Augustus II, and I don't think my other guest needs any introductions."

"I – I don't understand, my lord," said Frigus.

Faust smiled. "No, neither do I, in all honesty," said Faust. "Please give them a Roman welcome and take them to my palace. I assume it is still my palace?"

"Yes, my lord. Nothing has changed."

"Good. And once they're settled I would like them to meet the Senate and to be filled in on recent events since I have been away."

"My lord? That's sensitive material."

"I know, Frigus. I don't need reminding. A lot has changed.

Rome needs allies and these gentlemen are allies we can't afford to lose." Frigus nodded and instructed his assistant, Commodus, to escort Boatman and Ira back to the city centre and give them the tour. Commodus nodded in obedience and off they went.

Once they were alone, Faust said to Frigus, "So, Senator, what do I need to know?"

"I'm not sure where to start, but the one thing you should know immediately is that another pteron-chariot is due to land in the next hour and on board it is Alypia."

"My wife is coming here?"

"Yes. I spoke with her a couple of hours ago."

"Who is on the flight with her?"

"I don't know," said Frigus.

"You had a phone call with the wife of the Grand Protector, who has been missing or presumed dead and all of a sudden is flying to Rome and you failed to ask her who it was flying her here and who else might be with her?

Frigus went red. "I was so shocked to hear my daughter's voice that all questions left me."

"And that is why the Senate has become obsolete," said Faust. "Find us a room nearby and brief me on everything, Senator. And I mean everything. And then we will welcome my wife when she lands. And I would think we will also be welcoming the Empire's most wanted. I would hope, for your sake, Senator, she has her new friends in tow, because that could be your saving grace."

Faust had spent a lot of time in his memory palace, wandering its vast corridors and locking away emotions connected to his relationship with Alypia. He had conceded that she was no longer in love with him and no longer committed to their relationship. With this acceptance, he had decided to emotionally detach himself from his wife so that if a time came he would have to decide whether she was a help or a hindrance to the Empire, his emotions wouldn't cloud that judgement. And now it seemed that time was upon him in much more a surprising way than even he could have anticipated. It appeared everything was merging in Rome and there was a finality approaching. Faust could feel it and even though he knew he was in control and had the might of an army behind him, he couldn't shake the feeling that he was missing something. And that feeling lingered even when surrounded by a legion of soldiers willing to lay down their lives for the Grand Protector.

Chapter 38: A Warm Welcome

The pteron-chariot carrying Alypia and the rebels landed in Rome and as the doors opened the passengers were greeted by the sight of dozens of soldiers. Alypia, Bella, Olivia, Newen, Maverick and Tobias descended the stairs, all eyes on them. "I've a feeling this isn't going to be a warm welcome," said Tobias.

"Thanks for pointing the obvious out," said Maverick. "It's sunny, too, did you want to share your thoughts on how bright and warm it is?"

"Flying makes you grouchy."

"Flying with you makes me grouchy," said Maverick.

Frigus and Faust were waiting at the bottom of the stairs. "Welcome to Rome, everyone. I'm not quite sure how to greet such esteemed guests. You're pretty famous," said Faust. "I mean, Alypia, you're famous for very different reasons, but it seems I can lump you all together as the daughter of the Grand Senator has changed allegiance."

"Fuck you, Augustus. What you see is the consequence of your own actions," said Alypia.

"Ah yes, I distinctly remember throwing you into another

woman's arms."

"You might as well have," said Alypia, "And now, Grand Protector, you stand here looking at me like a stranger."

"Because, *Alypia Faust*, you are a stranger to me." He walked over to his wife and looked her up and down. "My memory palace keeps safe the woman I married and built happiness with. The woman before me is just an echo."

"An echo maybe. But a happy one," said Alypia.

"We'll see," said Faust and then he looked at the rest of the party. "Rome welcomes you and thanks you for giving yourselves up so peacefully. I promise you, your executions will be swift and merciful."

"I think you need to brush up on your hospitality skills," said Tobias. "And your negotiation skills."

Faust laughed. "Without having to point out the obvious, this clearly isn't a negotiation. You have nothing to negotiate."

"I beg to differ," said Maverick.

"Beg to differ? When did you start speaking like that?" Tobias said.

"You know, your brain doesn't need to vomit every thought that comes into it."

"Sorry to interrupt you love birds, but Maverick here seems to think he has something to negotiate."

"Of course we do." Maverick looked at Newen and back at Faust. "We've just flown from the RIA and spent time with the leadership there. And we have a member of the inner circle of the leadership standing here with us. I would say we have a lot of information to negotiate, wouldn't you?"

"You son of a bitch," said Newen and tried to get round Olivia to Maverick. Olivia put her hand on Newen's chest and shook her head. Newen stopped, taking in the seriousness of Olivia's look.

She mouthed that it was not the time.

Faust squinted and frowned at the interaction between Olivia and Newen. "Okay, I'm listening."

Maverick looked back at Faust and said, "You can kill us all or you can realise that we're gatekeepers to Rome finally finding a way to invade the RIA. And imagine what would happen if the Empire had the RIA in its grasp. You would be considered the greatest leader of Rome to have ever lived."

Faust knew Maverick was blowing smoke up his arse, but he couldn't help but be intrigued by the offer. He wanted to kill Maverick simply because Maverick had sucker-punched him a couple of years ago, but his pragmatism reminded him that absolute power meant swallowing pride at times and he would surely have another opportunity to make Maverick feel pain. If he was instrumental in conquering the RIA, well, Maverick would be irrelevant and he would be able to make The Beast a gladiator again. Faust smiled. Yes, killing Maverick was too easy. He could put Maverick back in the arena and have his first bout against Tobias. That would bring much more pain and suffering. Yes, Faust enjoyed that idea. Mercy for now. Suffering later. "Okay, I'll bite. We'll talk more about what you all know tomorrow. For now you can all be escorted off to the city."

Faust called over a couple of dozen soldiers and warned them not to be complacent or dismissive. The people they were guarding were the most dangerous people on the entire planet. The soldiers looked at Maverick particularly and gulped. They had grown up watching re-runs of The Beast as a gladiator and also heard about what happened on London Bridge a couple of years ago so knew what Maverick was capable of. As the group were escorted away, Faust stopped them and said, "Oh, by the way, I forgot to mention:

Olivia, it seems fate and circumstance has brought you here at a very interesting time."

"What are you talking about?" Olivia had never enjoyed vague statements. She liked directness instead of men trying to be clever with their words.

"Earlier today, your husband was escorted to Rome's city centre."

Olivia couldn't hide her surprise. "He's a prisoner here?"

"By the gods, no, he's not a prisoner. He's my guest."

"I don't understand, said Olivia.

"No, join the club," Faust said, quietly. "It's quite simple, really, he's decided working with Rome makes more sense."

"You're lying," said Olivia.

"Am I? Tell me, Mrs King," Faust glanced at Newen, "what did your husband always put first? His marriage? His friends? The mission?" Olivia glanced down but then defiantly stared at Faust. "Exactly," he said, "Boatman always is thinking about the mission. Which, evidently, you're not," he said and looked at Newen again. "Oh, and before you go, have a little think about the fact that I took a flight with your husband and his father. But you know who wasn't on that flight? Molly. Guards, take them away."

The soldiers escorted Olivia and the rebels away whilst Olivia cried out about Molly and where she was, but to no avail. Faust realised that without drawing any blood he had managed to torment his prisoners in the space of a few minutes. He was impressed because, really, all the torment came from Boatman's actions. He admired how utterly selfish Boatman King was and thought that it could well be possible to have a very lucrative allegiance with the man.

Chapter 39: The Comms Room

Commodus led Boatman and Ira into the main Senate building in the centre of Rome. An ostentatious setting, with statues of the current Senators guarding the courtyard like deities watching over the plebs. "This is not only the main Senate building, it's also a hub of activity for communications, administration, logistics and other services vital to Rome," explained Commodus. "Lord Faust told me I need to show you around so you get a flavour of the operations here as you might be helping us as the Empire continues to grow."

"Indeed," said Boatman. "Tell me, I've always been fascinated by how quickly communications travel across the Empire. We were always good, but nowhere near as slick as you guys."

Commodus beamed. "I can happily show you some of how that works. I'm quite passionate about our comms and have some ideas I hope Lord Faust will be interested in, so if you can put a word in, I would be grateful." Commodus immediately blushed as he felt he had shared too much about himself.

Boatman grinned. "We'll see what we can do," he said and put Commodus at ease.

"Well, in that case, let me show you one of the comms rooms where we make and air some of our breaking news segments. We have a good team who work in shift patterns so that when a major incident occurs there is always a strong team ready to announce the news."

"Sounds great," said Boatman.

Commodus looked at Ira and said, "You don't seem as interested, so apologies."

Ira managed a tight smile. "I'm a bit old for this stuff. I prefer telling people my news face to face."

"Don't worry about him. My father has been out of the loop for a while," said Boatman. "Please, lead the way, Commodus."

Commodus obliged with a bit of a bounce in his step and guided them to the Communications department. Boatman was impressed by the scale of the operation. He wasn't surprised, as it was the Empire after all, but the calm efficiency which seemed to be present was a different world to what he had experienced leading the rebellion underground. He had a great team working propaganda, but there was always an air of desperation because there was never any certainty their message would make it to the people. Here, it was clear there was confidence in the message and confidence in the message making it around the world.

Commodus showed his guests where breaking news announcements were made and sitting at a news desk was one of their anchors practising a script for a bulletin due to be aired later in the day. "Commodus, can I ask you a question?" Boatman asked, looking around the room at the screens and microphones and cameras.

"Of course. What do you want to know?"

"When you have breaking news, how quickly are you able to get it out there?"

Commodus seemed to revel at the question. "Oh, that's easy and also amazing. We can get a news announcement broadcast within minutes of finding out what it is."

"Really?"

"Oh yes! You see Flavia over there, sitting at the news desk? She's a pro. She can be given any piece of news and manage to announce it in a professional and calm way even as she's learning it herself. She never gets ruffled."

"Never?"

"Goodness, no," said Commodus. "Do you, Flavia?"

Flavia had been keeping one ear on the conversation as she was intrigued by the new faces in her newsroom. "Oh, Commodus is being too kind. I have certainly been ruffled in the past, like when Nero was murdered."

"I apologise for that," said Boatman.

Flavia laughed. "Why would you need to apologise for that? You didn't kill the emperor." Boatman didn't say anything, and then Flavia stopped laughing as she realised who was standing in the room. Context is a powerful thing, and she had never expected to see the leader of the rebellion, who killed an emperor, in her newsroom, but then the coin dropped and she went a little pale.

"Don't worry, Flavia, I'm here on the Grand Protector's invite. We're going to be working together from now on. And Commodus?" Boatman looked at the young guide. "I think there's some breaking news your team can announce in a moment."

Commodus looked confused and glanced over at Flavia, who shook her head, unaware of any breaking news. "Sorry, Mr King, I haven't been made aware of any breaking news."

Commodus looked back at Boatman and Boatman said, "Sorry, Commodus." Boatman stepped towards Commodus and as quick as a flash grabbed Commodus's head with both hands and violently twisted. Commodus's neck was snapped in an instant and he collapsed on the floor. Dead. If Flavia wasn't pale before, she was definitely pale now. Ira stepped over to the body of Commodus and removed his gun from his belt and pointed it Flavia. Boatman stood in front of the half a dozen staff who worked the monitors and cameras and said, "If any of you try to raise an alarm you will receive the same fate as Commodus, you understand?" Everyone nodded. "Okay," continued Boatman, "I need you to make a breaking news announcement and it needs to be now. Understand?" Everyone nodded. "You think you can do it without being ruffled, Flavia?" Flavia nodded. "I need some words, Flavia. After all, that's your job." Flavia managed to croak out an affirmative and then asked for a glass of water. "Good," said Boatman. "Now let's get to it."

Chapter 40: Breaking News

Faust and Frigus were sitting in a makeshift office when the breaking news announcement hit everyone's televisions and phones. Faust asked what breaking news Frigus had arranged, and Frigus had assumed it was Faust who had organised the news flash. Frigus turned on the television in the office where they were sequestered, and it was the popular Flavia reading a statement. Faust knew something was wrong instantly because Flavia was reading from a sheet of paper and she was white as a ghost. He got on his phone and called security. The soldier on the other end of the line was confused why he was being contacted as he was watching the breaking news and assumed it was sanctioned by Frigus. Before Faust could try to get the soldier to understand something majorly wrong was happening in the centre of Rome, the newsreader Flavia got to the heart of her announcement:

Emperor Maximus is dead. The leadership of Rome are deceiving you. Maximus was murdered by the leader of the Kingdom of Askå, Bjorn Askå. And even though Maximus had no children, there is an heir to the throne that Grand Senator Frigus and Grand Protector Faust tried to hide from you. In complete opposite to what you have been told and what you think you have seen,

Faust stared at the screen in disbelief. He knew Boatman was clever but hadn't ever seen such a move. He got on the phone again, calling the Centurion in charge of the city's central army. "Centurion, there is an insurrection happening live on television, why are you not storming the Senate building?"

"My lord, we can't."

"What do you mean you can't?"

"Because we would be committing treason, my lord. The Senate building is protected from military influence," said the Centurion.

"Forget that, this is an emergency and my authority supersedes any antiquated law," said Faust, spittle forming in the corners of his lips.

"My lord, I will have to end this call because you are trying to incite me to treason and insurrection." The Centurion cut the call and Faust stared at the phone, confused and completely off guard. "What the fuck is he talking about?"

Frigus cleared his throat and said, "The Senate building was created to preserve democracy for the people. And to preserve democracy it is hallowed ground that no soldier can enter with aggressive intentions. You know this."

Before Faust could pick apart what Frigus had said, the television screen was filled with the image of Boatman. He spoke briefly.

People of Rome. I understand the confusion this broadcast must be causing, but I am here to reassure you that as the gods have ordained, I am your true leader and here to lead you to a new level of glory and prosperity in Rome and beyond. I speak to all the peoples of the Empire: I am not here to bring fear but hope. I am not here to bring death, but prosperity. I understand that whilst I am in this building, the legions of Rome cannot approach me so now I speak to the military leaders of Rome and say this: I am your true leader and on the screen now is evidence of my heritage.

On the screen, an image of Boatman's DNA results appeared, which showed that it was more than 99% probable he was the brother of Nero.

My blood is Roman and the gods have brought me here to fulfil my destiny. I say to all the military leaders this: give me your allegiance and bring about a smooth transition of power or face not only the wrath of the gods but also my wrath for your treason. On the screen now is a phone number. I would like all Centurions posted in Rome to call it and swear allegiance to me in the next thirty minutes. I have a list of who you all are. If any of you do not call, you will need to leave the city and find refuge somewhere far away because I will find you. Show me respect and I will honour your act of good will.

And to the citizens of Rome, I invite you to convene on the streets and show your allegiance to this new era of Rome's glory.

The broadcast ended, and Faust and Frigus sat in silence. Finally Faust spoke. "The clever bastard. How did I not see that coming? Although he's very naive; there's no way the Centurions of the city will do as he says." Faust redialled the city central Centurion to instruct him to escort him and Frigus from the airport, as they would need protection.

"My lord, I am honouring you by taking this call because of the enormity of your service to Rome over the years, but I have received orders to arrest and detain you and Senator Frigus. I'm giving you fair warning out of respect." The soldier cut the call.

Faust got up and opened the door to the office. Before he could call the guards posted outside the door, he was faced with the guns of the four guards pointing at him. "Futuo," said Faust and he raised his hands. One of the guards had the decency to apologise before leading the Grand Protector and Grand Senator away.

Chapter 41: Supreme Leader

Boatman and Ira strode across the Senate building away from the communications department to the main wing of the building where the Senate convened. They opened the giant oak doors which were the grand entrance to the debating hall and inside were all the Senators of Rome. There were twelve of them present. The Grand Senator would have made thirteen. "Good evening, Senators," said Boatman. "I assumed you would all be here, most likely panicking about what is currently happening."

A Senator spoke up, "This is highly dubious, Mr King."

"Lord King," corrected Boatman.

The Senator was not swayed. "As far as I'm concerned, you're Mr King in this room. And a piece of paper showing your connection to the bastard Nero doesn't make you a lord or chosen by the gods"

Boatman laughed, but there was no humour, and the Senator who bravely spoke wasn't feeling so brave because the fire in Boatman's eyes stirred a primal fear that things like snakes and spiders do at the back of the brain. And then he felt like he'd made a mistake. Boatman looked at the Senator and said, "I lived underground for years, being chased by Rome like a ghost. I spent years like a myth in the narrative of Rome. And now I'm here in the Senate building with no-one able to touch me. And no-one able to even remove me, arrest me or stop me. I would think the gods have been smiling very kindly on me, Senator. And I would like to point something out."

"Which is?" The senator's voice faltered.

"The gods aren't going to protect you like they protect me."

If the Senator had heard about Boatman's almost supernatural speed, he was now privy to it in real life. The Senator was roughly the same height as Boatman but in seconds he was higher because Boatman had him round the throat and was picking him up. The Senator choked for air and Boatman said, "I've avoided assassination and I've avoided betrayal. I have found myself here like the gods gave me an open door. I would think very carefully about how you want this to play out, Senator, because I will be your leader whether you like it or not." Boatman threw the man to the ground, leaving the Senator coughing and gasping for air.

Another Senator felt enraged enough to speak up and said, "The military has no power here, and acts of aggression are treason. Your act is treason and, by law, means you've lost your power before you even gained it."

Boatman didn't hesitate. "I'm not military."

"Caesar is head of the military."

"I'm not Caesar," said Boatman. "The military will be ruled by my father, General Ira, who has remained passive the entire time he has been in this building. I am accountable only to the gods, so will be the Supreme Leader of Rome. I will not pass orders, only convey my will to those around me. And those around me will interpret my will and make decisions accordingly. Rule of law and talk of treason are irrelevant to who I am and what the gods have decreed for me."

"You're insane," said a Senator.

"No," said Boatman, "I'm the future. This Senate has existed for two millennia and what does it achieve? You haven't made a decision for the glory of Rome and its citizens for years. Cowards hiding in this building passing self-righteous judgement on those of us who want to see this world thrive. I don't need your toxic ramblings and snide remarks clouding what will be a new era."

"You can't get rid of us," said another Senator. "You don't know about the complexities of law and legislation. Rome coped without a Caesar, it wouldn't cope without a Senate."

"We'll let the gods decide that, shall we? After all, the gods stopped my death happening on many occasions. If they believe you are all meant to be part of the future of Rome, then they will stop your deaths, too," said Boatman.

"We don't believe in that superstition," said a Senator.

"Maybe you should," said Boatman. "Father, I think it's best you step outside. For reasons of integrity."

"Of course," said Ira who slightly bowed to his son and left the room.

"So," said Boatman. "Shall we see what the gods think?"

Ira stood outside the debating hall and from the screams he heard, he concluded the gods had chosen not to favour the Senators on this day.

Chapter 42: The Deal

Maverick, Tobias, Olivia, Bella, Alypia and Newen sat together in a comfortable room which had fridges full of drinks, and had sofas and two televisions. Maverick was lounging on a sofa, eyes closed. "I must say, Mav, you're very relaxed, considering what we've just seen on the television," said Tobias.

"He's hoodwinked an entire Empire," said Maverick. "Of course I'm relaxed. There's no way Boatman has installed himself as Caesar. It's all a ploy. And he'll be down here soon enough to get the team back together and finish the job we started all those years ago. So, yes, Tobias, I am very relaxed."

Olivia wasn't convinced. She knew her husband. She knew it when he was speaking the truth. When the fire is his eyes was so strong that all she could see was blind determination to win and destroy anyone in his path who would dare to attempt to stop him. The announcement she just saw made her think of when he killed Nero. There was no remorse or reflection on taking a life, it was pure fire and his eyes didn't change for a long time. That look was back and so she sensed her husband believed the words he had been saying. And that raised a huge question for her: what had happened in Aestii to make him believe joining the Empire was a necessity? Olivia had been pacing around the room. Newen went over to the fridges and grabbed a couple of beers. At least Roman hospitality was good, he thought. He wasn't sure what it meant for them now it appeared Boatman had somehow seized control, but Maverick's relaxed nature gave him enough confidence to get a drink and try to decompress until someone came to see them. He passed a drink to Olivia who took it and then she stopped pacing and smiled at Newen, thanking him.

"Maybe you need to come and sit down. The pacing doesn't relax anyone."

"Sorry, you're right," she said and she and Newen took a seat on one of the sofas. "Thanks," she said.

"For what?"

"Just the little things."

"I only got you a beer out the fridge," said Newen.

"I know. But to me that means a lot," said Olivia. She'd been thinking a lot about where life had taken her. She had been thinking about how she had almost accepted Boatman had died and then struggled with knowing he was alive. It had confused her and angered her. She wanted to love the man she married and find a way back to him. But seeing him on the screen, with the eyes intent on death and focused solely on achieving his end goal, it brought back resentment in her heart. She had realised as she watched him on screen that she no longer loved him. She could see all love he felt had disappeared too. His only love was having dominion over everything and everyone. Power was his marriage, and she felt relief that her involvement in his life no longer complicated or clouded that for Boatman. She didn't know how things would play out when she eventually saw him, but she felt peace in that she finally knew how she felt. And with that feeling of peace, she put her beer down, placed her hand on Newen's leg, which made him look at her, and she kissed him. And he kissed her back and in that moment everything felt shiny and new and she loved it.

"What the fuck is going on?"

And then everything went rusty and old.

Olivia turned away from Newen to see Boatman standing in the doorway. She stood up and said, "Boatman?"

"What are you doing?"

"We need to go somewhere to talk," said Olivia.

"No, we don't. You need to explain why you're kissing another man."

"Actually, I don't."

"We're married."

"On paper, Boatman. But surely that's all that's left of our relationship," said Olivia. Her anger triggered.

"It's over when I say it's over," said Boatman.

"Fuck you, Boatman. I'm not some slave of yours. Power always went to your head."

"Shut your mouth."

"Hey," said Newen, "Show some respect."

Newen had stepped round Olivia and before she could warn him off, Boatman was on Newen in a flash. Newen had a lot of experience doing dirty work for the 35 and just about saw Boatman coming, so went to nullify him by hitting him on the bridge of his nose. Boatman was too fast, though, much too fast and avoided the blow. Newen's whole stance was open at that point and Boatman punched Newen in the throat. The crunching sound seemed to echo through the room and Newen collapsed on the floor. Dead. Olivia screamed and knelt beside the now-still figure of Newen. Maverick and Tobias ran over, putting a barrier between Olivia and Boatman.

"What the hell, Boatman?" Tobias said. "Have you lost your mind?" Boatman looked at Tobias like he was a stranger and Maverick stepped in front of his partner, making a barrier.

"Boatman," said Maverick, "That was beyond unnecessary. We're all here to help you."

Boatman remained unfazed. "He was kissing my wife. There's consequences to that. And, Maverick, I don't need your help."

"You can't destroy Rome on your own."

"Destroy Rome?" Boatman looked genuinely confused. "I don't want to destroy Rome. I want to expand it."

Olivia was crying and screaming that she hated Boatman. Boatman ignored her, and that's when Maverick saw his old friend and boss had been lost to something so sinister their presence was now one of danger. Maverick felt fear prickle the back of his neck.

"I know what you're thinking, Maverick. I haven't forgotten our history. I haven't forgotten your loyalty. Which is why I want you to join me. Be my second-in-command again and I will even give you the opportunity to showcase your old skills again."

"As in, become a gladiator again?"

"No, of course not. Just the odd exhibition bout to keep the masses placated. Spending time with Askå made me realise how lucrative a business it is, and think of the gold you could generate. It seems like we spent so long underground, feeding on the scraps, we now have the opportunity to reverse that."

Maverick looked over his shoulder at Olivia who was weeping over the body of Newen. Bella was hugging her, the sobs now heaving and quiet. Maverick looked back at Boatman, who seemed unaware of the distress. He'd known Boatman to be brutal and terrifying, but this coldness was different. It disturbed him and he wondered how close he was to death. So he trod carefully, "I appreciate the offer, but I can't go back to that life, Boatman. You know that. And I'm struggling to understand why you're choosing this path? I thought you wanted to see Rome destroyed and freedom merge from it."

Boatman's face changed for a moment, like he'd been stung by a bee and then he composed himself and said, "And that's the point you're missing. Maverick, I respect you and therefore I'll give you a day to get yourself out of Rome and find somewhere far away for you and Tobias to settle. I won't come after you, I promise. As long as you don't try to come after me. Understand?" Boatman looked to the rest of the room. "And that applies to all of you. I appreciate the journey we shared up to now, but if none of you can see the potential of this next stage and how this is what we always aimed for, then I need you to leave and never look back. I don't want to make any of you my enemies."

"Go to Hades," Olivia said. "You are my enemy. I hate you." She was heaving tears and struggled to get the words out, but they were clear and her hatred burnt through the room like a raging fire.

Boatman glanced at Olivia and then looked away like he hadn't even heard her and said, "You will have the full disposal of any transport you need and you won't be followed or tracked. It's my thank you for the years of your service. There will be no record of where you have gone, and I will not spend any time or energy trying to know your whereabouts. If you take a flight, the pilots will be on very strict confidentially agreements that if they ever told me where you went they would be executed. I promise. Like I have already said, you can stay here and enjoy a life of freedom that we never experienced whilst in London, or you can leave and I give you my blessing. My team outside this room will deal with whatever requests you make in either way."

And with that, Boatman turned and left. No goodbyes. No sense of sentiment. It was like the man who ferociously loved the cause of bringing freedom had died and Maverick felt his heart ache at it. He had believed, when he met Boatman, that there was a potential for hope. He had believed Boatman was the man to prove an Empire could be crushed with the passion and ideology of a small group of people. Instead, Boatman was now the epitome of the Empire. A man who seemed drunk on power. And what of Aská? Had his encounter with Aská in recent months corrupted his soul? He knew of many men who left Aská's presence shadows of themselves. He knew that, because after he had been trained by Aská he had struggled to maintain his humanity. And, at times, the darkness of Aská loomed over him and caused him to do things he felt no remorse for. It was only Tobias who kept him human. It was only Tobias who kept his heart alive and his empathy intact. Yes, he killed with ferocity, but it was sometimes like he allowed Aská to take over in those moments. He knew he was making excuses, and he still believed every kill he made was necessary, but he genuinely mused at night if the terror he went through with Aská meant the giant's spirit hovered over him at times. And that made him wonder if Boatman was influenced by the same spirit. Maverick didn't believe in the Roman gods and didn't worship the God-Carpenter, Jesus, like Tobias did, but he did think that humanity was so entwined that even when someone wasn't close by, their otherness could still influence. And some people had a powerful otherness, like Aská. So maybe Boatman had been consumed by the otherness of Aská because the change in him was so stark, it was horrific to think of any other reason.

Maverick turned to face the room and said, "We need to get out of here. No good will come from staying." Tobias nodded and went over to Olivia. He knelt in front of her and whispered something for a couple of minutes. Olivia began to calm down and nodded at whatever Tobias said. Eventually, she kissed Newen's forehead and then stood up, letting Bella hold her close still. Maverick looked at Alypia, 'What about you? You could stay and maybe negotiate your husband's life?"

"Augustus has always been good at negotiating his own life. He'll slip his way out of this one. He'll always find a way," said Alypia. "And besides, I have so much more to live for now." She held Bella's hand and gave it a squeeze.

"Okay, let's get the fuck out of here," said Maverick and the women walked out of the room. Before Maverick and Tobias walked out of the room, Maverick said, "What did you say to Olivia? I've never known you to calm someone down like that before."

"I'm still full of surprises," smiled Tobias. "It doesn't matter what I said. It's just important that she knows we're here for her through every step of now until forever."

Maverick kissed Tobias and said, "And I'm here with you every step of now until forever."

The former gladiators left the room and the rebels were escorted away to begin their journey away from Rome and the reaches of Supreme Leader King.

Chapter 43: Reunion

Bella, Alypia and Olivia opened the door and gasped. They weren't sure what they would see but what they did see blew all expectations out of the water. Olivia couldn't contain herself and ran over. Molly's joy couldn't be contained, either, and she ran over to Olivia and they hugged and cried and hugged some more and cried some more. "I thought you were dead," said Olivia.

"I thought the same," said Molly. "I was told you were dead." Molly buried her head into Olivia and hugged and cried and hugged some more.

Whilst Molly and Olivia reunited, Bella walked over to the corner of the room and knelt down. "It's okay," she said. "It's okay." She repeated the words softly until Titus felt able to come out of the shadows. Titus looked at Bella and saw safety, not pain. The way Molly had shown him safety and humanity, and he allowed Bella to hug him.

When Boatman, Faust and Ira left Aestii, they left behind them chaos and pain. Boatman had found Molly and said that he wouldn't be taking her with him because it was important for her to find her own path. Molly hadn't truly understood the implications of that and discovered, after Boatman had abandoned her, that Aska's mansion had become deserted. The soldiers that had survived after Boatman tore through Aska's grounds had run away, finding joy in freedom from Aska's regime. It had ended up being a couple of servants who made sure Molly was fed each week, and she had the mansion and grounds to herself. It had been a few days before she had even thought about entering the outbuilding that contained Titus. When Molly went into the building, Titus was on the floor, barely moving. He'd become so used to being given food and drink like an animal he had forgotten how to feed himself. Molly wasn't horrified by him, though. She saw a man in pain and, being an orphan, she saw something of an orphan in him and wanted to protect him. So Molly spent her time and energy on making sure Titus got back to health and although he couldn't speak, he eventually was able to show her how appreciative he was.

So when Bella hugged him, he nestled into her with such joy, because at last he was experiencing unconditional love and, at last, he was understanding what it was to be human again. Titus had forgotten the man who was once Commander of Britannia and was now learning what it meant to be a man again, and he thanked the wonderful women in his presence that he was alive and that he was loved.

The women knew this place wasn't safe from Boatman's reach, no matter what he said about not coming after them, but just for today, in this moment, it didn't matter. In this moment, there was reunion and love. In this moment, there was hope and there was humanity. In this moment, there was happiness and Boatman couldn't ruin that.

Chapter 44: Faust's Reckoning

"I'm surprised," said Boatman.

"About what?"

"You're not begging."

"Why does that surprise you?"

"Because I might change my mind if you begged."

"That's complete nonsense," said Faust.

"True. But I would still like to hear you beg."

"I don't think you would. It wouldn't be appropriate," said Faust.

"I guess not," said Boatman.

"Shall we get this over with?"

"Of course," said Boatman. Boatman raised his sword above his head and said, "I told you I was coming for you."

"And I enjoyed it," said Faust.

Boatman smiled and then drove the sword into Faust's chest. And the crowd cheered.

Chapter 45: An Itch

After Boatman executed Faust, he took his place on his throne. The crowd continued to cheer inside the Colosseum, chanting his name. Boatman looked around, enjoying the spectacle. His father took his seat beside the Supreme Leader and nodded at his son. Boatman leant forward, indicating Ira to listen to what he had to say, "I have an itch."

"And what would that be?" Ira asked.

"Faust didn't get away. But others did. I was too kind."

"Well, let's go hunting," said Ira.

Boatman smiled. "Yes. Let's."

"And we have a hook to lure in the prey," said Ira.

"Which is?"

"Didn't you hear? Your mother-in-law was never crucified. She's being very well looked after. She's comfy in a unit on the outskirts of the city. I would think that she would be rather enticing to come and retrieve."

Boatman shook his head. "I don't want Olivia coming back here. But Liv's mum being alive will be like a red rag to a bull for Maverick. He will be compelled to come and save her." Boatman shook his father's hand and said, "And that I am looking forward to."

Epilogue

"Do you, Maverick, promise to love honour and cherish Tobias, through the rough winds and serene summer days?"

"I do."

"And do you, Tobias, promise to honour and cherish Maverick, through the rough winds and serene summer days?"

"I do," said Tobias.

"Who has the rings?"

"I do."

The celebrant smiled and said, "Please bring them to the front and place them on my book." Damba walked to the front and did as he was instructed. He looked at Maverick, and Maverick hugged his brother. Damba hugged him back and then went and sat back down with the rest of the congregation. Although, to call it a congregation was a stretch of the imagination. It was Bella, Olivia, Alypia, Damba and Molly. Sitting at Olivia's feet was a dog, happily gnawing on a treat. The dog was called Newie, and Olivia scratched his ear. Newie's tail thumped the sand floor in appreciation.

The women had stayed at Aska's mansion for a few days, gathering their thoughts and then decided the darkness of the place was too much. Life wasn't possible here, so they fled. They phoned Maverick and he assured them there was a better place to go. And much warmer. He said it would be a bit of a trek because they would have to stay outside of Boatman's radar. Although Boatman promised he wouldn't follow, Maverick knew different. So the women took Maverick's advice and went by his instructions. Maverick also assured them that they would be able to afford it, because The Beast had built substantial wealth from being a gladiator and now was the time to use that wealth.

So the women sat on a beach on an undisclosed island, in a random part of the world and enjoyed seeing their two favourite men get married.

"You may now kiss your husband," said the celebrant.

"You took your time," said Tobias.

"You ground me down," said Maverick.

The former gladiators kissed, and Tobias felt his heart flutter because he had seen hell and been in close conversation with death, but now, here he was, married to the man of his dreams and nothing could replace that. Love had found a way.

After the ceremony, Maverick had one thing to do: he went to a local tattooist and had six dots added to the 307 already on his left arm. Each dot was a representation of the people he had saved over the years from Roman oppression. The newest dots signified the six closest people in his life, and although he didn't believe he had personally saved any of them, he wanted a permanent reminder that through all the chaos, they had been saved.

His arm still had a lot of space, and he knew that space would need to be filled. Fate willed it. In this moment, he was content with life, but he a sensed a force of rage was coming, and he had to be prepared.